Karaoke Killer
Another exciting novel in the John Bodie Detective/ Polygraph series

John Lawrence Ketchum

ISBN: 1-4751-7513-2
ISBN-13: 9781475175134

Dedication

This book is dedicated to my wife Donnie Finley-Ketchum whose sacrifices throughout the years have allowed me to take the time to complete these novels.

She is a good woman.

A special thanks to Tom McKee, and all the members of my Ventana Scribblers for their editing assistance. God bless you all.

Special contributors making this novel posible are Donnie Finley-Ketchum, Sharon Stephens and Pauline Mounsey. Thank you for the hours you gave for this book.

Other books in the John Bodie series

Innocent Liar
Laser Liar
Telepathic Liar*
Lie to me*
Liar, Liar House on Fire*
Vengeance in Vallejo*

* Also on Kindle

.

To Jeannie,

I hope you enjoy.

Thank you!

John Lawrence Fletcher

chapter

ONE

Martha Hires stood in the glow from the lighted lobby of the I and J Fountain Restaurant in Surprise, Arizona. She listened as the sliding glass doors closed behind her. The music was nice, but the karaoke singer sounded like someone choking a moose. She smiled at the image that it presented. The smile disappeared as fast as it had appeared. Concern with the serious events of earlier in the day had returned. Hires sang two songs and could have sung two more. However, her heart wasn't in it. It was only eight o'clock but that didn't matter. She needed to leave.

The matronly, heavyset woman fished in her purse and found her cigarettes, lit one, took a deep satisfying breath and started for her car. She left the lighted entryway and turned the corner into the darkness of the overcast night. Her concentration was so focused on the possible threat to national security that she didn't hear the approaching footsteps behind her. Hires stared down at the dusty gray sidewalk ahead of her.

Her eyes became wide with panic as she felt a hand pulling her chin upward. It clamped her jaws together, preventing her from crying out. She wrinkled her forehead in confusion and pain as an arm came around, and the knife blade penetrated her breast and embedded itself in her heart. Hires' body shuddered then became still. The assailant let her slip to the dirty sidewalk. A shadowy figure leaned over and wiped the blood from the knife on the blouse of the still form on the sidewalk, then walked casually into the night.

———

Thirteen hours earlier the secretary to the director of Homeland Security called Harry Holiday into her office. "Harry, I know you're the person in our organization who is the most familiar with the RAW Laboratory."

"RAW?"

"Come on, Harry. Research for Advanced Weaponry down in Avondale, Arizona. You and your team recovered the stolen classified weapon from there a few years back. Well, I have a new situation that might interest you."

"For crying out loud, Francis, Arizona is getting hot this time of year," replied the leader of the Terrorist Activity Control Team (TACT).

"Listen for a minute, will you? A Martha Hires called and said that someone has been in her top secret files. She said if that information should get into the wrong hands the United States could be in real trouble."

"How does she know someone has been in her files?"

"She suspected someone had been in them so she placed a tiny piece of paper in the corner of the closed file drawer. This morning, that piece of paper was on the floor when she came to work. She's pretty sure she knows who it was."

"But why me, woman?"

"Since this laboratory is known only to the President, the National Security Advisor and our Director, no one else can go down there," answered Francis.

"I'll leave my team here and check it out. Who's the big man on campus down there now?"

"My records show it's under the administrative control of a Colonel Basset. The operational 'big daddy' is a Dr. Richard David. Oops, it's pronounced 'Da Veed'. I think he is from Israel." Francis closed the file and picked up her coffee cup.

"Does the Military Police still secure the facility?" Holiday sat on the corner of Francis' desk.

"I guess. I don't know."

"Call Andrews AFB and see about a flight for me. Oh yeah, get in touch with Luke AFB and line up a GSA car for me. I'll let the team know to stand by."

"You got it. Have fun." The secretary turned and picked up her phone. Holiday headed for the door.

Harry Holiday, a 63 year old retired Navy Seal, stood 6'4" and weighed 210-pounds. He was nobody to fool with. His muscular body and firm jaw were evidence of that. The team he commanded consisted of four of the toughest men selected from Army, Air Force and Navy. TACT, like the RAW Laboratory, was top secret and its existence was known only to the President, National Security Advisor and the Director of Homeland Security. As far as anyone else knew, he was just another Homeland Security bureaucrat. His cover is that of a problem solver.

Holiday drove to his Georgetown apartment. After packing for a week's stay, he drove out to Andrews Air Force Base. The air base had his transportation warmed up and standing by.

It was ten o'clock that night when he arrived at Luke AFB. He picked up his car, found a motel by the Phoenix University Sports Dome in Glendale and settled in. Due to the hour, he decided to contact Hires in the morning.

Holiday arose with the sun, shined, shaved, showered and checked out of the motel. He drove across Glendale Avenue to his favorite restaurant, The Cracker Barrel. The big man ordered his big 'Uncle Hershel's' breakfast. There was no way he could get biscuits and gravy like that in D.C.

After eating, he drove to US 101, down to I-10 then west to Avondale Boulevard and the RAW facility. He parked in front of the chain link fence, and sat there for a few minutes recalling his last visit to the facility. It had been a major undertaking. It involved the theft of the top secret Laser Guided Electromagnetic Pulse (LGEP).

The RAW facility was located in a large warehouse in Maricopa County just south of the Avondale, Arizona, city limits. Actually, the warehouse contained hundreds of empty boxes and crates in the hundred-foot by forty-five-foot building. There was a single front entry door on the west side of the building. A loading dock the length of the building was located on the south side. The four overhead roll-up doors were always closed...except on the few special occasions when shipping or receiving large crates containing secret devices. There were no windows or other entrances in the building.

A ten-by-ten foot building connected to the corner of the warehouse hosted the guard. It provided observation and a place to cool off from the desert heat after making his rounds. It was equipped with windows allowing a view east along the loading dock, south to the fence and beyond. A large window gave a north view of the fence and across the front of the building, to include the building entrance. The entry door to the "guard shack," as it was called, had a glass window that provided a view westward toward Avondale Boulevard and the sliding vehicle gate. That gate was the only entrance through a high chain link fence, topped with a concertina barbed wire overhang.

The inside of the building consisted of neat rows of what appeared to be full, but actually were empty, crates and containers. One of these was a large Conex container located in the southeast corner of the building. This was a large metal box used to store and ship military equipment and supplies. It measured approximately eight feet tall eight feet wide and twelve feet long. A pair of metal doors was on one end. The floor of the container had been removed. The sergeant in charge, the military policeman on the upper landing and the one in the basement were armed and had remote control devices that unlocked the Conex container's doors.

Once having entered the container, you began a descent on a ramp to the basement. There was a desk and chair placed beside a closed door at the bottom of the ramp. An armed military policeman staffed the desk. His mission was to check identification, observe the personnel as they placed their eye to the Iris Identification System, and otherwise secure the entrance.

The warehouse had a wooden set of stairs that led up to one end and a ramp that led to the other end of the two, ten-by-twenty foot office structures on the inside of the north wall. There were windows from about waist high to the ceiling surrounding the office. This would normally be the warehouse supervisor's office; however, in this case, one was the facility administrator's office and the other, the security director's office.

An armed military policeman was constantly on duty in the office, overseeing the warehouse area. The security director joined him during the day. One of the armed military policemen impersonated a warehouse worker and provided security on the ground level main floor of the warehouse as well as the outside. None of the security personnel were in uniform. Nobody on the outside of the fence would ever know of his or her true purpose.

Due to the immensely classified nature of the work being carried out in the laboratory, security was a strict requirement. This facility remained non-existent to all government agencies except for the President, National Security Advisor and the Secretary of Homeland Security. The research carried out in this facility could definitely affect the security of the United States.

Holiday pulled out a notepad from his shirt pocket and reminded himself of the name he was going to ask for. He slid out of the car and approached the guard at the gate. He noticed the man's shirt was not tucked in and it appeared there was a slight bulge over the right hip.

"Excuse me, partner. I hate to bother you. I'm here to see a Martha Hires."

At first the gate attendant looked surprised, then suspicious. "Mind if I ask your name, Sir?"

"Harry Holliday."

"Wait here." The attendant trotted back to the guard shack and picked up the phone, punched in a couple of numbers and waited for a few seconds. "Steel, there's a guy out here asking to see Hires."

"Is that right? What's his name?"

"Harry Holliday."

"You've got to be kidding. Hell, send him on back. I'll meet him at the door." Sergeant First Class Steel hurried out the door and down the ramp from his elevated office to the warehouse floor.

The plainclothes MP was surprised at his sergeant's response on the phone. He hurried back and quickly opened the gate. "Sir, my supervisor will meet you at the door."

"Thank you, Son." Holiday proceeded to the entrance on the opposite corner of the building with the MP watching his every step.

"Wow, Mr. Holiday. How did you get here so quick?" questioned the sergeant as he stuck out his hand and gave a sincere shake.

Confused, Holiday asked, "What do you mean, 'so quick'?"

"We just got the word less than an hour ago ourselves", continued Steel.

"What are you talking about?" Holiday couldn't help his confusion and puzzled expression.

"Aren't you here about the Hires murder?"

Holliday felt like someone had thrown cold water on him. His shock was evident. He let out a deep sigh and said, "I guess I am now."

———————

The silent serenity of the Eastern Washington State woods was suddenly interrupted. The earsplitting sound of the all terrain vehicles vibrated off the trees as the two riders passed. The exhaust belching machines gave warning to the woodland critters to take cover.

Ted Swanson, the owner of the local Vallejo Texaco station, had traded his old machine for a new quad. It was an ATA-300Ai. The 2010 model was the color of Army camo and sported a 250cc engine. He'd never beaten John Bodie with his old machine, but he was grinning from ear to ear now as he pulled out in front of John's big Kawasaki.

They had picked what had probably been a trail many years ago. Neither of them had ever been in this section of the woods before. John was nervous in the unfamiliar terrain and began to slow down. The overhanging limbs were striking his helmet and hitting him on the shoulders and arms.

He had no sooner slowed his machine, than he saw Ted's quad go airborne. Ted and the ATV went their separate ways about five-feet above the ground. John locked up his brakes and skidded on the leaves and twigs to stop just before a two-foot dip in the ground.

At first glance, he thought he saw a gray stick. He dismounted his quad and picked it up. Then he realized he was holding a thighbone. John dropped it where he found it and hurried over to Ted.

"Hey, Guy, are you all right?"

"Don't worry about me. Worry about my machine." Ted winced when he tried to raise himself up.

"Your machine is not showing pain. You are. Let me get you to the hospital and have you checked out."

"John, I'm Okay. It's my arm. It really hurts."

"You may have busted it. Let's get you out of here."

"What did it look like when I hit that hole?"

John helped Ted to his feet as he answered, "Your machine did a total flip, landed on its wheels and bounced over on its side. You dropped straight down. It was a sight to see."

"Wow! We need to set it up and I'll ride it out of here," said Ted as he limped over to the vehicle.

"You're in no condition to help. That thing weighs more than 600-pounds. I'll take you in and get one of the officers to come back out and help. We need to look at those bones anyway."

"Bones?"

"Yep. It seems as though you hit a shallow grave."

"Grave? I'm ready to go now. Let's get out of here." Ted walked around the indentation in the ground, looked down and moved rapidly to John's quad.

John called in to the station and talked to Barbara, the chief's administrative assistant. "I need an officer to meet me at the hospital. Also, I need Chief Ortega to wait for me in the office."

John Bodie had moved to Vallejo, Washington, from the Seattle area a little over five years ago. His private detective and polygraph company was sold to one of his employees when he retired. This was his second retirement. The man also had retired from the Army as a Lieutenant Colonel. He had been a man of many trades, such as a child actor, then a drummer with Shirley and the Dukes. His résumé included work as an electrician in Dalton, Georgia, an architectural draftsman in Chicago, and a plant engineer in Miami, Florida.

During the Korean Conflict, he was kicked out of the Army at age sixteen for being underage. John returned home and joined the National Guard and was in and out of the reserves and Guard throughout the years. He became a police officer in the Miami area for six-years. After serving two-years as a police undercover agent in the Miami/Dade location, he needed something less stressful. John volunteered for Viet Nam and accumulated a couple Bronze Stars, five-Army Commendation Medals for valor and a Purple Heart while serving with the First Infantry Division. He returned stateside and served the next eleven years as an Army Advisor. The Army released him from active duty and he returned to the Reserves to finish out his career.

John founded the third largest private investigative agency in the state of Washington. He conducted or supervised over 3000-investigations and performed more than 6000-polygraphs, most of which were court ordered. He was heavily involved in the sex offender treatment program conducting plethysmographs as well.

As a private investigator, he became involved in several criminal cases in Vallejo. Chief Ortega convinced the city council to appoint him as a criminal investigator for his police department. This was done primarily to give the chief more control over John and to make use of his polygraph skills.

Mary Mastrovoni met John in the emergency room. The newly appointed police officer quickly took over. She told him she would see that Ted was cared for and then taken home.

John rushed back to his Kawasaki and drove to the Vallejo Police Department. He jumped off the quad and ran up the steps. Barbara stood up from behind her desk, pointed and waved him on to the chief's office. He continued his trot into the office.

"Whoa, Nellie. What's the matter with you? Is your butt on fire?" asked Ortega, looking over his glasses. He threw his pen down on the desk and sat back in his wooden swivel desk chair.

Frederick Raul Sortis-Ortega had been the Chief of Police of Vallejo, Washington for over twenty years. He was a jovial person who enjoyed being grumpy to get a rise out of people. He had a department of eight sworn officers and one administrative assistant. He was well respected in the community and could normally be found either at the police station or at the café across the street.

The donuts in the station and the food across the street were causing his belt notches to increase each year. His only nemesis, for lack of a better word, was John Bodie. They usually ate together at the café. The waitresses and the other patrons enjoyed their constant bantering back and forth.

"Fred, did we account for all those guys from that *Asesinos* gang?" John asked as he sat in the old wooden chair in front of the desk.

"Of course we accounted for them. We counted them; the sheriff's department counted them and coroner's office counted them. However, I guess I'll never know which one shot me. Why do you ask?"

"If we did, then we have a new case."

"Crap, John. What have you done now?" Ortega sat back, picked up his ball point pen and threw it on the desk again. John removed his pen from his pocket and threw it on the desk as well.

"Ted Swanson and I just found a skeleton in the woods."

chapter

TWO

Holiday followed the sergeant to his office. Steel moved over to his desk and retrieved his notes. "Miss Hires left I and J Fountain Restaurant about eight o'clock according to witnesses. She was discovered just before nine on the sidewalk at the east side of the building."

"Who discovered her?" asked Holiday.

"A Jennifer Jones. She was one of the singers. They have karaoke there on Mondays and Tuesdays."

"Do you have the info on her?"

"Not yet. Just the basics. We haven't gotten the police report yet. They said it's under investigation. I'm not sure how cooperative they're going to be."

"Okay, sorry to interrupt. Go ahead."

"She had a stab wound in her chest. The M.E. has the body now. Wait…if you didn't come here for this situation, why are you here?" asked Steel, as he placed his notes back on the desk.

"Can I trust you, Sergeant?"

"Can you trust me? You know you can trust me. Mister Bodie found out my sergeant and the security director were in cahoots with the terrorists that killed three of my buddies. The ones that stole that secret laser weapon five years ago. I stuck by Mister Bodie when he killed those two after they tried to kill him. I think I proved my loyalty to my country then and nothing has changed."

"That's what I wanted to hear. Thanks for reminding me about Bodie. I might use him again. Someone has been getting into Hires' secret files. She sent a request for help from my agency. The lady was sure that she knew who the person was. She wasn't sure who she could trust here."

"Man, that's heavy. None of my crew, me included, knows exactly what's brewing in the lab. I do know that all the brains down there are excited about it. They're really keeping it hush-hush." Sergeant Steel sat in his chair behind the desk.

"I don't want to tip off the person who's doing it. The murder will give me a perfect opportunity to snoop around the facility. How about your colonel? Do you have a gut feeling about him?"

The sergeant wrinkled his brow, "Maybe, a little. I've never seen him go down to the lab. He appears to be interested only in the maintenance of the building and grounds, paying utilities, making the payroll and reminding my soldiers that he is the colonel. I think he's harmless."

"Do you have much contact with the scientists and other workers in the lab?" Holiday sat on the wooden chair in front of the desk.

"Not much more than 'Hello'. 'Have a nice day'. 'Good bye.' 'Have a nice weekend'." The sergeant shook his head and continued, "I'm not on their level...just an underling. Some smile when they come and go. Others are curt and sometimes rude. I guess they don't appreciate the fact that we're here to protect their asses."

"Well, you can enjoy the fact that they're about to meet someone who is going to put them in their place. I'll be especially on the lookout for the curt-and-rude for you." Holiday smiled.

"Thank you, Sir. If you need anything you can depend on me. I trust my MP's, but I'll keep a close eye on them anyway."

Holiday stood and said, "What do you say we start with a look at Hires' office?"

"First, I think we should let the colonel know you're here, Sir." Steel rose and started for the door.

"Good idea." Holiday followed him out onto the elevated walkway next door to the facility commander's office.

The colonel was cordial and appeared to enjoy the break Holiday gave him from his mundane workday. He presented the appearance of receiving this assignment to the facility as punishment. The officer, in his fifties and somewhat overweight, was going to retire soon. He didn't let much bother him.

The pair walked down the stairs to the warehouse floor and over to the large metal Conex container. The sergeant pushed the button on his remote and Holiday heard a loud click. Steel opened one of the double doors and they entered the ramp. After the door was closed, they descended to a well-lit twelve-foot by twelve-foot room. The military policeman dressed in civilian clothes and seated behind the typical military gray metal desk greeted them with concern.

Who is this guy with my boss? No one is supposed to be down here. Is he forcing the sergeant to bring him down here? He was reaching under his shirt for his weapon when Steel stopped him.

"It's Okay, Tim. He's one of us."

Holiday showed his credentials to the young MP. He also thanked him for being alert and doing his job. The MP smiled and shook Holiday's hand.

Steel placed his eye on the Iris Identification System (IIS). Again, Holiday heard the click as the door unlocked. He followed the sergeant in.

They no sooner entered, than Doctor Hardwood rushed over to them shouting, "Get out! You don't belong here! Steel, you know better than to bring anyone down here. What the hell is the matter with you?"

"Just cool it, Mister," responded Holiday calmly.

"It's Doctor! And who the hell are you?" snapped Hardwood, as he gave Holiday his meanest look.

"I'm the man who can have this MP put you in cuffs and march you the hell out of here if you don't calm down." Holiday's six-foot four-inch frame stood two-inches taller than the doctor. Their faces weren't more than six-inches apart.

"Wh—what do you mean?" asked Hardwood, with eyes wide as he backed away.

"I'm from Homeland Security, here to investigate the murder of one of your employees. I'm sure you want it investigated. Right?"

"Uh, yes of course. But, do you have high enough clearance to be down in our laboratory?"

"I have clearance enough to sleep with the President of the United States. There is no clearance higher than mine. This isn't the first time I've worked a case in this facility."

"Excuse me. What's going on over here?" questioned Doctor David as he approached the trio.

"Sir, I'm Harry Holiday. I'm an agent with Homeland Security sent here to investigate the Hires' murder. Sergeant Steel has checked my clearance. I would appreciate your cooperation."

"You certainly have it. I'm Doctor Richard David. I have operational control over the laboratory. I assure you that you have the cooperation of everyone here. Where would you like to start?"

"If you don't mind, I'd like to start with Ms. Hires' office."

"That's no problem. The sergeant will stay with you in case you need anything. I'll make sure Doctor Hardwood is available if you need him as well." David shook hands with Holiday. Hardwood gave David a dirty look and walked away.

Holiday forgot how large the lab was. He was still amazed at the number of instruments and machines located in the room. The man counted three women and five men, all wearing lab coats. Some were scurrying around from instrument to instrument. Others were bent over theirs staring into monitors and microscopes. He knew, sooner or later, his curiosity would get the better of him and he would have to find out what the big secret operation was all about.

Steel broke his concentration by asking, "Sir, have you heard from Mister Bodie lately?"

"As a matter of fact, Sergeant, we have worked a couple big cases together. But, now that you mention it, I haven't seen him in three or four-years. Haven't had any need of his lie detector skills. I think it's about time I correct that. What better way to catch a killer than with a polygraph. Let's take a quick look in Hires' office."

A forty-five year old retired Navy petty officer rushed out of Hires' office and right into Holiday.

"Excuse one of us," said Holiday.

"I'm so sorry. My mind was preoccupied. I was in a hurry," apologized the tall thin brunette.

"So it seems. Let me introduce myself. I'm Harry Holiday. I'm here to investigate Miss Hires' murder. Who might you be?"

"Rachael Holmes. In addition to my job, they have piled this one on me." She waved her thumb in a hitchhiking motion toward Hires' office.

"And your job is…?"

"Logistics and Maintenance. Now it's also Security and Files."

"Are you experienced with security?" asked Holiday with a smile.

"I will be by this time next week." She returned his smile.

"Good answer, Miss…or is it Mrs.? What were you doing in there just now, if you don't mind my asking?"

She smiled, "It's Miss. I was looking for the key to the security files. We have an overbearing scientist who is busting my chops to get him his lab notes."

Steel interrupted, "Miss Holmes, you have to get the key from the MP at the foot of the ramp. Miss Hires leaves it with him every night." Homes started for the door. "Wait, Ma'am, he won't give it to you without me Okaying it. You say that's going to be your job now?"

"I'm afraid so. At least until they find a replacement. You know I have the clearance or I wouldn't be down here."

"Right. I'll go over the security requirements for the key with you and we'll talk to the MP." Then the sergeant turned to Holiday. "Sir, this should only take a few minutes. Do you mind?"

"Absolutely not. It's good to see you helping a damsel in distress."

"Oh my God. I not only get more work piled on me, now I'm called a damsel." She giggled and followed Steel back to the ramp.

She's not a raving beauty, but she ain't bad. I might enjoy this investigation. Holiday grinned as he entered the office. Finding the desk drawer locked, he reached in the scabbard on his belt and pulled out his automatic tactical knife. The spring-assisted blade flew into position. He quickly placed it between the upper part of the drawer and the frame. A slight twist, a little pull and the drawer opened. The top drawer was very organized. He noticed a post-it note in the middle of the drawer with numbers, as though she was adding something up. The numbers looked familiar:

202
555
4001
4758

He realized that it was the secretary at Homeland Security, Francis', number at…(202) 555-4001. Turning it over, he saw the letters 'keynoforce'. *She's saying that a key was used. It wasn't forced.* The search of the remaining drawers met with negative results. There were a few personal items, unclassified three-ring binders and files, plus office supplies.

"Wow! You opened the desk. Hell, I couldn't find that key, either." Rachael continued on to the filing cabinet, struggled with the lock and finally opened the drawer. "Damn, there are four files in here with his stupid name on them. How am I supposed to know which one he wants?"

Holmes slammed the drawer shut, locked it and took the key as she rushed out of the office. Holiday watched as she headed for Hardwood. He observed her give him some animated conversation. Then the scientist followed her back to the office. She returned to the filing cabinet, opened it and stepped back. "Have at it, Doctor. Pick your file."

"I never had to do this before. Martha always delivered the files to me," he said indignantly, as he removed his file. "I never had to come and get it."

"One, I'm not Martha. Two, I'm not psychic and can't read your mind. Three, I don't know what the hell I'm doing yet. Four, if you ever want to see another file, adjust your attitude."

"Humph," uttered Hardwood, as he glared at her for three seconds. He spun around and hurried out the door. She watched him as he mumbled to himself all the way back to his work area.

"I didn't have to put up with this crap in the Navy. I'm not used to cowering down to a bunch of prima donna brain bums."

"Navy, huh? I guess we have that in common. I'm a retired Seal," Holiday said, proudly.

"Cool. I'm a retired CPO Quartermaster."

"Chief Petty Officer, very impressive. We'll have to grab a beer and swap war stories sometime." Holiday stood and smiled.

Rachael looked him over and was impressed with his size. She stood nearly six-feet and weighed 144-pounds. But she still had to look up to this guy. *Whoa, this could get interesting. Screw playing hard to get. He's probably not going to be here that long. Strike while the guy's hot or whatever that saying is.*

She walked over to the desk and picked up a pen, then pulled the drawer open and took out a note pad. After she quickly scribbled on it, she tore off the sheet and handed it to him. "Squid, whenever you're ready, here's my number. I may not be the best company for a while. I just lost my best friend."

"Would that be Ms. Hires?"

"Yeah. We always did karaoke together. Last night I didn't go and look what happened. I'm feeling responsible. If I had gone, would she still be alive?"

"Or would you be dead?"

"Who knows? I love karaoke, but I don't know if I can ever do it again. Hell, I don't know if I can ever see my friends at I and J's again."

He squeezed her shoulder and gave it a pat. "I'm going to be busy tonight and possibly tomorrow night. I promise we're going to talk about this later. We'll quench our thirst the first chance we get."

"Whenever. I'm thirsty already." She gave him a sad smile. "Not that I'm a heavy drinker."

Holiday grinned, turned, and left the office. He was entertaining some very pleasant visions involving the drinks to come when he approached Sergeant Steel. It had been a long dry spell for him. He made a quick mental adjustment and asked, "How many employees down here?"

Steel looked up at about a forty-degree angle, thought for a second or two, then said, "With Miss Hires gone, that leaves nine. Eight of them are scientists and one, who you just met, is administrative."

"So there appears to be more people working upstairs than there is down here. How many MPs do you have?"

"My detachment consists of four-sergeants who are shift commanders, eight-specialists and me."

"Okay, if you throw in the colonel that'll should total out to be twenty-two bodies. Is that right?"

"No, Sir. I believe its twenty-three…the nine-personnel down here and then the fourteen upstairs."

"Damn. You're right. Let's go up to your office. I need some privacy to make a phone call."

"You bet. I don't have a problem turning my office over to you while you're here, if you want."

"I don't want to run you out of your office. I'll use it as little as possible." As they turned to the door, Holiday saw Hardwood watching them closely and remarked, "There's something about that I guy I just don't like."

Sergeant Steel looked at Hardwood then over to Holiday and said, "You're a good judge of character, Sir." The sergeant led Holiday up to his office. "He is a real loner. I don't think his colleagues much care for him either."

As they left, Hardwood turned his attention to Rachael. He watched her whenever she spent time in Hires' office. On several occasions she noticed him watching her. She would stop what she was doing and stare back until he turned away. She enjoyed going out of her way to irritate him. It was a daily activity with her.

chapter

THREE

John gave the medical examiner a ride on his Kawasaki quad to the remains. Officer Tomlinson walked with the medical examiner's assistant through the woods a half mile to the ancient grave site. Tomlinson led the way with the assistant on the other end of the rolled up stretcher, complaining about trying to keep up with Tomlinson's long legs.

"What are you looking for, Doc?" asked John.

The M.E., sweeping the leaves and twigs away and without looking up replied, "I basically start off looking for four things... age, sex, race and stature."

"How do you determine that from bones?"

"We can get an idea of the age by the length of the bones. Also, the caps on the end of the long bones fuse with the bone around age twenty. The epiphysis of the sterna end of the clavicle fuses about age thirty. The sterna end of the fourth-rib begins pitting and judging the depth of that we can determine within two-years the age of the victim."

"That's something. Without the body parts how do you determine sex?"

"That part is easy. Gender is a dead giveaway by looking at the pelvis. If it's elongated to allow for childbirth, it's female. Plus about ninety-percent of the time the size of the skull tells you. It's true; men have bigger heads. Females are smaller."

"I guess that proves men's brains are bigger. No wonder men are smarter."

"The M.E.'s head jerked up and he looked at John. "Don't ever let my wife hear you say that."

"Or any other woman for that matter," advised John.

The M.E. stepped out of the indentation and stood next to John. "Looking at this femur, I'd say you have a cold case, John. You might have a hard time solving it."

"Why is that?"

"I'm going to send these bones to a forensic anthropologist. For now, I'd say they are over a hundred years old."

"Well, that's good news…I think." John turned to see the arriving officer and M.E. assistant.

Tomlinson stared at the bones for a few seconds then said, "Can't we just tag it and bag it?"

"I'm afraid not, Officer. We need to lay them out. We don't want to miss anything. I'm sure you understand," replied the M.E.

Tomlinson nodded and helped the assistant prepare the stretcher. Then he began photographing the bones and indentation. He stepped over by John and watched as the other two transferred the bones to the stretcher. He whispered to John, "It's going to be fun carrying those out of here."

Overhearing him, the M.E. said, "That's all right. My assistant and I would rather carry the remains out. It's a delicate undertaking. We're used to it. If you want, you can go ahead and leave. There is nothing for you to do here now."

"I appreciate that. Because if you don't mind, I'd like to get started on my report," returned John.

"Certainly, John. Take your officer with you. I'm sure he has more important things to do."

John gave Tomlinson a ride back to his car that was parked at the edge of the woods by the medical examiner's van. Tomlinson drove to the station to print out the pictures. John rode his quad to the Towne Café to have lunch. When he entered he was surprised to see the police chief was not in his normal booth at the rear of the row of booths along the wall on John's right. He continued on back and sat down in the booth.

"Your place or mine tonight, lover?" Dede asked as she placed his glass of iced tea on the table in front of him.

"You know what, how about we have dinner here tonight and decide then?" requested John.

"You know what..." asked Dede sweetly. "Are you nuts?" she hollered at him with her hands on her hips. "I work here. I'm a waitress. I see this food all day."

"Sorry about that. How about the cantina, then?"

"You've got to be kidding. Rosa wants you for herself. She doesn't like me. God only knows what she does to my food."

John gave out a deep sigh. "All right. Go home and change. I'll pick you up at seven; we'll ride into Pasco and do it right."

"Now you're talking. By the way, are we in a committed relationship?" asked the five-foot two-inch, blue-eyed blonde-haired southern beauty.

"I thought we were friends with benefits."

"John Bodie, you can kiss my grits." She spun around and stomped off to the kitchen with her pigtail swinging in the breeze.

John watched both, the swing of the pigtail and sway of the hips. She was good at both. He knew if he could ever love anyone again it would probably be Dede. When his fiancé was shot in Arkansas and died in his arms, something inside him shut down. He didn't want to give up Dede. But he wasn't ready to commit.

Chief Fred Ortega entered the café, waved to a couple in a booth, stopped at a table and laughed with the male occupant. He continued to another table and shook hands with the couple there. Stopping at his booth, he looked down at John. "Aren't you supposed to be out investigating bones?"

"Fred, I know Russ told you the bones were over a hundred years old. Hell, those bones were probably there before you were on the department."

"You know, the last thing I want to do is hurt you. But it's still on my list." Ortega sat down opposite John, facing the front door.

"Fred, seriously, what should we do about these bones?" John put the artificial sugar in his tea and began stirring.

"I'm not doing anything about it. The medical examiner and the forensic anthropologist will have a field day."

"Shouldn't we go look around the area? There may be more."

"The guy probably starved to death waiting for service in this restaurant. He just went into the woods and died." Ortega gave a dirty look toward the kitchen.

"I heard that, Fred," Dede scowled. "If you don't like my service when I'm happy, you sure as hell ain't gonna like it when you tick me off. Now, you've got two choices. You either apologize, or... go on a diet."

"Whew, you're a little touchy today. Panties too tight?" Ortega turned to her and slid further into the booth.

"No. John already upset me. What do you want today?" She gave Ortega a no-nonsense expression.

"I'll just a have the double burger and fries with a Pepsi."

"Fine. Your order's coming out, John." She informed him coldly, and then hurried up to the register to cash out a customer.

"Fred, those remains may turn out to be very valuable. It...." John's cell phone interrupted him. He looked at the caller information on the screen. "Sorry, Fred, I have to take this."

John leaned back in the booth and flipped the phone open and answered, "Well, if it isn't Mister Top Secret himself. Harry, how have you been?"

"I've been great. But the team misses you. They would like to see you again. It's been a long time," said Holiday.

"Sounds good to me. When are you guys going to be here? I'm sure Barb would also like to know."

"Boy, I would love to be there for a visit. However, I thought you would like to traipse out here and visit me and get paid for it."

"Harry, every time I see you some damn fool tries to kill me and almost succeeds. I've been beat up, shot at, and damn near drowned. So, I think I'll just wait until you wander out here to see me." John looked over at Ortega who was shaking his head.

"Hurry on down to sunny Arizona. You remember the lab down here where you first met the team?"

"Oh yeah, it's a wonderful place...of which I have fond memories. That's where two guys tried to kill me."

"Hey, Buddy, now think about it. We came to help you last time. I really need your help this time. All you have to do is come down and do some polygraphs and that's all. Quick and easy." Holiday tried to talk with a smile in his voice.

"That's exactly what I was told last time. A couple of weeks later I was almost beaten to death and wound up in the hospital. Not to mention my ex-employee and friend Karen being shot."

"Yeah, those were fun times all right. So, what d' ya say? I can be in Vallejo this evening to pick you up."

"Yeah, and I can be in hiding by this afternoon, too." John couldn't help but laugh.

"Think about it. You can make some good money. All expenses paid. You'll get to see old friends. But most of all, you'll be doing your country a great service. Uncle Sam needs you, John Bodie."

"How long?"

"You do four polygraphs a day if I remember correctly. So... five-days plus a couple of days for travel. Figure on a week."

John paused for thirty-seconds then said, "Okay. But it's not done out of patriotism. Don't get me wrong. I love my country. But I fear my government."

"It's eleven here, so with daylight savings time it should be eleven there, right? I should be out of Luke AFB within the hour, arrive at Fairchild AFB and chopper out of there by two-thirty. I'll pick you up around three-thirty. Can you be ready?"

"Sure. I'll get moving. There's a change since you were last here. We have a shopping center that isn't in use. You can put the chopper down in the parking lot. I'll be waiting for you there."

"Got it, Partner. I owe you one." With that Holiday hung up and immediately called flight operations at Luke AFB.

"Sounds like you're going off on one of your stupid adventures." Ortega sat up straight and stretched.

"Fred, my adventures, as you call them, are not stupid. I'm protecting my country. You should be proud of me."

"John, every single time you go to help these guys you end up in the hospital. I don't know about you, but I'd call that stupid. Besides, I didn't tell you that you could go."

"What are you...my mother?"

"No. I'm your boss. I'm the Police Chief and you're my detective."

"Excuse me, uh, part-time detective. This part ain't the time." John leaned forward on the table.

"How long are you going to be gone, or do you even know?" asked Ortega also leaning forward in the booth.

"Gone? What gone? When? Where?" Dede set the BLT down in front of John and stared wide-eyed at him.

"Now see what you've done, Fred."

"Answer my questions. Are you leaving me again?" Dede stood with her hands on her hips.

"I'm sorry, sugar. I haven't had time to tell you. I just got the call. My country needs me." John reached for her.

She pushed his hand away. "This country has a million military people, FBI, CIA, ATF and lots of other initials and I'm supposed to believe they need some weird, old, retired private investigator."

"Watch it with that 'old' crap. I just need to do a few polygraphs and I'll be back. That's all."

"Just where and when are you going?" Dede stepped back as John reached for her again.

"Arizona. This afternoon." John winced as he said it.

"What happened to our night out in Pasco?"

"We'll have to postpone it."

"Well, get this straight. You ain't the only dog barkin' up this tree, Buster. I'm sure I can still get a night out in Pasco." The petite southern belle spun around and returned to the kitchen.

"Huh, I think that went well," mumbled John reaching for his sandwich.

"I take it back, John. It's not your adventures that are stupid... it's you." Ortega looked at John and shook his head.

———

"José, I'm nervous," said Isabel, rubbing her hands together. She paced back and forth in front of him.

"Slow down, *amante*. Why? How come you're so nervous?"

"What do you mean 'why'? It should be obvious. We had a customer murdered right outside our restaurant. The police detective said it wasn't robbery. They don't know why she was killed."

"Maybe somebody didn't like her singing." José laughed.

"It's not funny, you Spanish sad sack."

"I thought it was, you Polish pickle-puss."

"Get serious. Martha and her friend Rachael have been coming here for over a year. They were good customers. Rachael may stop coming now. In fact, it could scare a lot of our customers away."

"We'll see if she comes tonight. You may be worrying about nothing. This was probably a fluke thing."

Isabel, the 'I' part of I and J Fountain Restaurant, is a beautiful woman. Her beauty is not only in face and body but in personality as well. Her blonde hair, brown eyes, slender cheeks and full lips would make her a standout in any crowd.

She has the remarkable ability to take and serve the orders of a hundred customers single-handedly. This, no doubt, accounts for her slim figure. Her friendly treatment of the customers is a major contributing factor to the large number of returning regulars.

Isabel emigrated from Poland. She studied hard in the few hours she had between raising a family, keeping up a house and working long hours at the restaurant six-days a week. It paid off on 4th of July. She became a citizen of the United States.

José, the 'J' part of the partnership, emigrated from Mexico. His dark skin and black hair is quite a contrast to Isabel. He would be considered handsome by any standard. His five-foot eight-inch frame consists of wide shoulder, muscular chest and back. His arms give the appearance of being a weightlifter at one time. He's not someone you ever would want to cross.

His extraordinary talent in the kitchen not only manifests itself in delicious meals but in the speed with which he produces them. Most nights he is the only one in the kitchen. Like his partner, he has a great personality. This, and the food he provides for his customers, is the other major contributing factor for the returning regulars.

Today is Tuesday and tonight is a karaoke night. Isabel can't shake a feeling of foreboding. In this case her apprehension is justified.

chapter

FOUR

Detective Rodriguez, of the City of Surprise, placed his hands on his hips and looked perturbed at Holiday, "Do you mind if I ask you why the Feds are interested in the Hires' murder?"

"I'm afraid I do mind," returned Holiday. "It's a subject I'm not at liberty to talk about. I'm sorry."

"If you're not willing to give me information, why should I give you any? If we're into this case together, we should share."

"Maybe you should take another look at my credentials, sonny."

"Okay, Okay, if you're going to play the 'I'm bigger than you card' I guess I have no choice. But, I'm telling you now, I don't like it."

"I understand. I'm sorry you feel that way. May I see the file, please?" Holiday read the police report. He noted the lack of evidence. The crime scene photographs revealed no useful information. The City of Surprise detective answered his questions the best he could. He didn't actually volunteer anything that helped.

After leaving the station, Holiday stopped by the I and J Fountain Restaurant. He was surprised at the size of the place. It looked small from the outside, but it had a dance floor, band stand, karaoke area, and seating for what appeared to be for more than a hundred-customers.

He introduced himself to Isabel and José and did a quick interview with them. They were friendly and very cooperative. Promising to return, he hurried out and drove to Luke Air Force Base.

———————

"Sir, I don't know who you are but you must be somebody important," said the highly impressed Airman. He escorted Holiday out onto the tarmac and walked Him to the plane.

"Why would you say that, young man?" asked Holiday.

"Because the Air Force only has eleven of these C-37 Gulfstream Vs. This one was just flown in from Travis for this mission. They're only used for VIPs. You know, like for the Vice President, Congressmen, Speaker of the House, Secretary of Defense and other service secretaries."

"That's interesting. Now you can tell all your friends that it was used for someone else. How about that?"

"Like who?"

"Son, if I told you, I'd have to kill you."

"Man, oh man, that's a major wow! Sir, the bird's warmed up and ready. The crew's on board."

"Thank you, Airman. By the way, I was never here." Holiday gave the young man a wink and walked up the steps to the plane.

"Yes, Sir." The airman was still staring at the plane as it lifted off. He couldn't wait to tell his buddies about the man who wasn't there.

Holiday settled back in the luxurious interior of the modified Gulfstream aircraft as it cruised at 580-mph. He figured he'd be on the ground at Fairchild Air Force Base in three-hours. His estimate was right on the money. He told the flight crew to take about a three-hour break.

A UH-1 Iroquois modified Bell helicopter began turning its blades as the Gulfstream landed. Holiday rushed over to the helicopter pad, hurriedly entered the chopper and was still fastening his seat belt as it lifted off. He gave the flight crew his destination. Cruising at 138-mph, the crew estimated a little over an hour flight time southwest of Spokane, Washington.

When they were thirty-minutes out of Vallejo, Holiday called John and told him to be in the parking lot. He didn't want any down time. John called Officer Mastrovoni and had her drive him to the rendezvous.

"I take it our favorite chief's not too happy with you leaving town," ventured Mary as she pulled into the lot.

"Why do you say that?" asked John.

"Because he didn't drive you."

"You're right. I don't know who is the angriest over my departure, Dede or him. Actually neither is speaking to me."

"Then why are you going?"

"A very good friend of mine needs my help. Nobody here really needs me at this time. My friend is a federal agent who is involved in a case that involves national security. Wouldn't you go?"

"I suppose so. You've always been good at helping friends in need." Mary sat with John until the helicopter arrived. She briefly met Holiday and waved goodbye as the chopper lifted off.

After the greetings were over and the pair had settled down, John hollered over the whine of the engine. "Okay, Harry, talk to me. What are you getting me into this time?"

Holiday did his best to communicate over the noise. By the time they arrived at Fairchild AFB, John knew what was expected of him. He actually looked forward to helping out his friend. Once on the ground at Luke, they loaded the polygraph and John's luggage into Holiday's car.

"Harry, you rushed me around today and it just dawned on me, I haven't eaten since breakfast."

"You're right. Hell, I haven't had anything to eat since this morning either. Let's stop by the food court in the Base Exchange. It's the closest food around and it's already after eight o' clock."

"Sounds good to me."

After consuming their Philly Cheese Steaks and fries they drove to the motel. John checked in. After some brief small talk, both headed for their rooms. Both were tired and the lights were out before ten o' clock.

At the same time John and Holiday drove to the motel, I and J restaurant was entertaining seventeen singers and three times that in listeners. It was a typical Tuesday night. Everyone was talking while the singers tried to sing. Sylvia and Tyler had their family there. The King and Queen of karaoke, Fred and Scooter, were seated at the 'A' table. Ira, a good country/western singer, was giving the karaoke comic, Jasiu, a hard time. However, the Karaoke Jockey (KJ), Arnie and his wife, Sandie, were expertly making organization out of otherwise chaos.

Gwen had a great singing voice. However, a lot of her entertainment came from clowning around while she sang. She danced around with exaggerated movements. The woman had a super sense of humor and was liked by all the other karaoke participants. After finishing her song she handed the microphone over to Scooter, the cute little eighty-six-year-old petite singer, and rushed off to the restroom.

The fiftyish, five-foot eight-inch woman hummed to herself as she entered the restroom. Gwen was startled as she opened the stall door. The person standing in front of her was smiling as the knife plunged deep into Gwen's heart. The blade was given a sharp twist and quickly removed.

The surprised expression turned to one of pain. She released her grip on the door, grabbed for the killer and fell to the floor. The assailant wiped the blood from the knife on Gwen's shirt jacket and walked out of the restroom to the sound of Scooter singing, 'Forever on Your Mind'.

Jerome did an excellent job with the 'Ballad of the Green Beret'. He followed Scooter's husband, Fred. Jerome's attractive wife, DeAnne, and Rachael Holmes excused themselves and headed for the restroom. DeAnne entered first and saw Gwen's bloody body on the floor. She froze and started to scream, but Rachael quickly placed her hand over DeAnne's mouth. While still holding on to quivering DeAnne, the retired Navy CPO turned to look at Gwen's lifeless body.

Then turning back to DeAnne she said, "Wow! You're white as a sheet. It's a good thing you didn't scream. It would have panicked everyone in the restaurant," said Rachael.

"Yeah, I know," replied the attractive DeAnne. "I thought of that in time. What should we do?" She stood there wringing her hands.

"I don't know. Maybe we should go tell Isabel. It's her restaurant. She'll know what to do." Rachael could no longer look at the body on the floor. Instead she had her hand on DeAnne's shoulder and was looking at her.

"Wow, let me think about this. It's a quarter-to-nine now. Karaoke is over in fifteen-minutes. Maybe she can put an out-of-order sign on the door and call the police," offered DeAnne.

"Okay. That's an excellent idea girl. You stay here and watch the door," suggested Rachael. "I'll go get Isabel and let her know what's happened." Rachael rushed back through the lobby and into the restaurant.

During breakfast, at the Cracker Barrel across the street from the motel, Holiday decided to have John test only on the killing of Hires. He figured whoever killed her was the one who broke into the classified filing cabinet. Since security was so important, he told John to start with the military police unit. That would take three or four days to do all thirteen of the men.

When they arrived at the secret facility they were met by an excited Sergeant Steel. "Wow, Guys, did you hear the latest?"

"What's the latest?" asked Holiday.

"There has been another murder at that karaoke place in Surprise. It was another woman. She was stabbed right through the heart, just like Miss Hires. It's probably the same killer."

John and Holiday looked at each other then back to the sergeant. "Maybe the Hires killing didn't have anything to do with the lab," said Holiday. "There could be some nut out there killing karaoke singers."

"Either that or someone is trying to make us think that," mused John. "Somebody probably knows he made a mistake killing Hires and your presence here is making that person nervous. The guy may be killing others to get the heat off him. I bet he didn't expect a federal investigation."

"Why don't we go down to the station and look over the report and the crime scene pictures. We need to talk to Detective Rodriguez."

"Sounds like a plan to me. Is that guy being cooperative with you?" questioned John.

"Reluctantly. So far the guy has given me whatever I've asked for. However, he hasn't volunteered anything. The poor guy's not sure why I'm nosing around in their investigation and I can't really tell him."

The visit with the Surprise Police Department didn't add anything of value to the Hires' murder. Holiday drove away from the police station, "I'm surprised that Rachael Holmes was the one to find this last victim."

"Who is Rachael Holmes?"

"Holmes is an employee at the laboratory. The woman was also a friend of Hires and sings over at the place in Surprise. She's sort of a cute, lanky brunette who happens to be retired Navy."

"How do you know her?"

"Like I said, she works at the facility. I'll introduce you. You'll have to find your own. This one is mine."

"Damn, Sam, I've never heard you say that before. Are you in heat? That's so out of character for you."

"It's been a long dry spell, John."

"Remember, Buddy...professionalism, ethics and a clear head," advised John. "If all that fails, I'll hold her for you."

"You're a true friend."

John had a strange feeling as they entered the facility. He looked up at the offices and recalled how his friend, with the help of a military police sergeant, tried to kill him. His friend shot at John but hit the sergeant that John had pulled in front of him. Then John and his friend fought. John threw him over the railing of the office. He died from the fall. The memory both saddened and angered him.

Sergeant Steel enjoyed seeing John again. He was quick to escort him to the sergeant's office and set up a place for him to do his polygraphs, after which, Steel brought Holmes up to his office for Holiday.

"I suppose you heard what happened last night?" were the first words spoken when Rachael saw Holiday.

"It must have been traumatic for you," returned Holiday.

"It was the first time I ever saw a person who died by violence. I have to admit, it was a shock."

"We just left the police department. I read the detective's report. Do you think there's a nut-case out there targeting karaoke singers or is someone trying to put the restaurant out of business?"

"It's rather strange. There're lots of karaoke places. Only I and J's seems to be having this problem." Rachael kept glancing over at John.

"I'm sorry. I wasn't thinking. Rachael, this gentleman is John Bodie. He's here to polygraph everyone. John, this fine lady is Rachael Holmes. She's retired Navy and presently in charge of logistics, maintenance, and security of the lab."

"It's a pleasure to meet you, Ma'am."

"Don't call me 'ma'am'. I was enlisted."

"Okay, lady," said John with a grin.

"That's sort of questionable, too," Rachael shot back. "Can you just call me Rachael? Okay?"

"Sure. You got it," answered John.

"Well...that was a bit awkward. I'm glad it's over," offered Holiday. "It's probably typical when Army meets Navy."

"Oh, a grunt, huh?" asked Rachael. "I should have known he was a ground pounding grunt."
"
That's 'ground pounding grunt, Sir' to you squid...I was an officer," responded John, smiling. Everyone laughed.

"I think we should leave and let John get down to business. He's behind already. Why don't you and I go on downstairs?" Holiday took Rachael gently by the arm and the two left the room.

"Mr. Bodie, you can set up on my desk. Is there anything I can do to help?" asked Sergeant Steel.

"You bet. Find me someone to polygraph. This instrument works a lot better when I have somebody attached to it."

"You polygraphed me before. Why don't I start?"

"That's fine with me."

"That way I'll set the example for my troops."

"Spoken like a true leader. I'm proud of you, Sergeant. Have a seat there beside the desk." While setting up his instrument, John continued with a reminder on the polygraph testing procedure. Having experienced one of John's polygraphs five years before, the sergeant breezed through this one with no deception indicated (NDI).

John continued on until shortly after 8:00 p.m. He finished with the remaining sergeants, all of whom finished with NDI. None of these men had murdered Hires nor knew who did. A very tired polygraph examiner grabbed a bucket of chicken and headed for his room at the motel. A more energetic TACT Commander decided to interview Rachael Holmes over dinner…a meal most satisfying for both.

———————

"José, these karaoke singers are not only our customers, they're our family. We have a lot of steady non-singing patrons who are our family as well. They show their loyalty to us by coming here week after week. What kind of loyalty do we show them? We let them get killed outside and inside our restaurant."

"Isabel, *novia*, what do you want me to do? The police are investigating these killings. They're doing their best."

"Great. While they're investigating, our friends and customers are getting killed," stated an exasperated Isabel Kozlowski.

"How about if we get hold of that federal agent guy, the one who stopped in yesterday, and see if he can give us any help?"

"That's a great idea. People will be afraid to come here, especially the karaoke singers, if we don't do something. This could put us out of business. I'll try to find him tomorrow. Thank God we're closed on Wednesday. I couldn't take three in a row." Isabel turned out the light and they did their best to fall asleep.

———————

John was awakened by an irritating sound. It was the ringing of the telephone on his nightstand. He rolled over with eyes half open and finally pulled the receiver out of the cradle. "Uhlo. Is it time already?" he mumbled.

"You bet, ole buddy. Shine, shave and shower, friend. I'm going to change clothes and I'll be over to your room to get you. So hustle up."

"Huh? Why would you have to change clothes this hour of the morning? Have you not even been to bed?"

"Oh, hell, yeah...I was in bed early. I just didn't get back to my room until now. You know how it goes. The old battleship was in the harbor last night."

"Interesting. Sounds like a busy harbor." John threw his legs over the side of the bed with a grunt.

"It sure was last night. Hurry up. I'll be right down."

"Damn…Navy one and Army zero. Well the fried chicken was good, anyway. Not only that, I could roll over and go to sleep when I was through. I win."

John answered the staccato beat on the motel room door. "We've got a hell of workday ahead of us. And you're standing there grinning like a revenuer looking at a still. Your car keys are on top of the television. Thanks for the loan."

"Nooo problem, Jonathan, old boy, anytime. Now, tuck your shirt in and let's get out of here."

"Man, what is your hurry this morning?"

"We're going to meet Rachael at Denny's on Dysart or Litch-field by the freeway." I forget which street it's on. Holiday walked over by the window and peered out.

John hooked his belt and pulled it through the last loop. "Tell me again, Harry, why I have to go?"

"Because I don't want to drive all the way back here and get you when we're finished. Besides, you need to get to know her. She has friends."

"I'm still taking it slow. I'm not looking for a relationship yet."

"Who the hell said anything about a relationship? I'm talking about taking a safe harbor tour. I'm not talking about docking the damn boat."

"Knock off the Navy babble. I'm ready. Let's go."

Holiday exited Interstate 10 onto Dysart Ave only to find that Denny's wasn't there. He drove up to Thomas and west to Litchfield and located the restaurant. They entered to find Rachael already seated in a booth. Holiday slid in beside her and John sat across from them. He was uncomfortable with his back to the door. He had a real issue with that but managed to stick it out.

Holiday's cell phone rang. "Holiday here."

"Mr. Holiday, this is Isabel Kozlowski. I met you at my restaurant, I and J's, last Tuesday."

"I remember you. What can I do for you, Miss Kozlowski?"

"José and I would like to meet with you again."

"Is it pertaining to the unfortunate problem we discussed at our last meeting?"

"Most definitely."

"I could come over this morning."

"We won't be available this morning. If you come over later this afternoon, say four o'clock, I'd appreciate it."

Holiday looked over at John, "Can you be through by four o'clock?"

"If I work through lunch I can," answered John.

"How's four-thirty sound, Miss?"

"Fine. You can be our guest for dinner. Thank you so much."

With breakfast finished and the small-talk completed, they headed out to work, Rachael and Holiday down to the lab and John up to the sergeant's office. The military policemen were previously polygraphed to qualify for this facility. John had no problem speeding four of them through the process again. However, he was careful not to sacrifice accuracy for speed.

chapter

FIVE

Jasiu turned sideways and put his feet up on the couch and spoke into the receiver, "Look Ira, I'll make a deal with you, buddy. If you'll sing the song 'Padre', I'll do 'Old Rivers' for you."

"Dummy it doesn't matter which one you do. You'll probably screw up that one too," replied Ira.

"It's beginning to feel more and more like you're family. Ira, you remind me of my cousin."

"Is that so?"

"Yeah, I hate that sucker."

"You ain't exactly no bundle of pleasure yourself. I only hang around with you because it makes me feel better when I leave. Another thing, what's with the Polish name, Jasiu? Why don't you have an American name? You are an American, right?"

"Don't talk about names. There ain't been anybody named Ira in the last eighty years. Another thing, you can't even pronounce my name correctly. It's pronounced 'yawshu'. I ain't going to I and J's so's I can hear you sing next Monday. I'm only going there to see who's going to be killed next."

"That is a rotten thing to say. You're an insensitive dumb-ass. However, I'll put two dollars on Julie."

"Little Julie? Why Julie? She's so cute and perky. I can't think of anyone who would want to hurt her," questioned Jasiu.

"You just answered your own question. She's little. I doubt she'd be able to defend herself."

"I don't think size has anything to do with it. Hell, there wasn't a little bone in Gwen's body and they got her."

"If Gwen was here now she'd kick your butt over the table. I'd bet money. No, I'd pay money to see it," said Ira.

"I rest my case. She already threatened to kill me once."

"Hell, I don't blame her. I can understand that. I've considered it more than once myself."

"You've stepped in it now, buddy. This conversation is recorded and if anything happens to me...you're going down," threatened Jasiu.

"Ain't nothin' going to happen to you. Only the good die young and it's way too late for you."

"You don't know me very well, idiot. I might just murder myself just to get you blamed for it."

"Jasiu, you really are dumber than a box of rocks, a big box at that. I'm tired of talkin' to you. Goodbye."

"There ain't no way you're as tired of talking to me as I am of listening to you. Goodbye."

———————

John drove Holiday's car and followed him and Rachael over to I and J Fountain Restaurant. He parked in the lot alongside the building while they parked in front, and trailed behind them as they entered the gated entryway. Holiday opened the door and John held it for them to enter. Isabel met them by the bar.

"It's good to see you again, Mister Holiday."

"Please call me Harry. It's good to see you again, Miss Kozlowski. I believe you know Miss Holmes."

"I sure do. How are you, Rachael?"

"I'm just fine."

"And who is this handsome man?" asked the pretty restaurant owner. Isabel moved over in front of John.

"This is John Bodie. He's the investigator I told you about."

"I'm glad to meet you, Mister Bodie." Isabel offered her hand.

Holding her firm handshake, John said, "I'm even more than glad to meet you." He smiled and quickly looked her over.

"John, be careful. José can break you in two. Wait till you see him. Plus, he has a lot of experience with a cleaver," said Holiday, with a grin.

"In that case forget 'more than glad', and I'll only be 'just glad' to meet you. Sorry." replied John.

Isabel blushed and led them to a table in front of the band-stand near the dance floor. The owner handed them menus. She left and returned with water for all. Then sat down across from Holiday, John to her right and Rachael to her left.

"José is very busy this time of night preparing for the dinner hour rush. Our music starts in less than an hour and the guests well be arriving shortly. So, I'll make this quick. Mister Bodie, your Mister Holiday says you're the best. Are you?"

"I do have a lot of experience. I try hard to be the best. However, he's probably prejudiced."

"I'm not happy with the investigation the local police are doing and I'd like to have more help than I'm getting. Do you think you can help me? Please keep in mind; I don't have a lot of money."

"I'm working with Harry now and I don't know how much time I'd have to help you." John looked over at Holiday.

"I think we can work out something, John. Her investigation could tie in with ours. We can reduce the number of polygraphs per day which would give you some time to help her." Holiday smiled at Isabel.

"I'm all for it. I know you have to go now. I see people coming in. I'll make out a list of things that may help you. I'll start right away, while we eat." John asked for a note pad and pencil.

Isabel returned with the paper and a pen. She took their orders and disappeared into the kitchen. They watched her seat more than twenty people, take their orders, and serve most of them in the next thirty minutes.

John and Holiday were impressed with the flat iron steak dinners Rachael recommended. They all were too full to have dessert. Holiday told John that he and Rachael were going to stay and dance. They enjoyed the country/western and fifties music that Arnie's trio created. For only three-people they put out a lot of music.

"You know the old saying, 'three's a crowd'. I can take your car, Harry, and head back to the motel." After wiping his mouth, John quickly folded his napkin leaving it next to his plate and slid back in his chair.

"Nonsense. You sit right where you are." Rachael jumped up from her chair and rushed over to the bar. She returned accompanied by an attractive middle aged lady with gorgeous red hair.

"John, I would like to introduce you to Polly. She's a regular here that includes Monday and Tuesday nights. She's also a fine dancer."

"Rachael, you are not only good…you're fast." John stuck out his hand, "Miss Polly, it's nice to meet you."

"I have a distinct feeling it's going to be a pleasure to meet you as well," returned Polly. Displaying a friendly smile, she took John's hand in hers, lightly shaking it. Then she continued to hold on to his hand even as she sat down.

Holiday noticed this friendly encounter and smiled as John said, "I feel a dance coming on."

"That's because I haven't turned you loose," Polly interjected. "I intend to drag you out on the dance floor. Are you ready?"

"Yeah, and for a dance, too." They all laughed.

John noticed the faint smell of perfume and sweet aroma of her glistening red hair. She held him close as they danced. He could feel the heat of her body.

Between dances Polly asked John what he had been writing. John told her about his conversation with Isabel. He mentioned that he was just jotting down some of his ideas for her.

"Let's hear them," Rachael requested.

"Yeah, share them with us John," ordered Holiday.

"Okay. First, this kook seems to prey on lone females. Therefore, all females should be escorted to their cars when they leave. No female should go to the ladies' room alone. If they have cell phones, they should call I and J's when they arrive and a male will come out and escort them into the restaurant."

"I agree with all that, John. However, that's not going to catch whoever is doing this," Rachael excitedly answered back.

"You're right, but the first priority is prevention. We don't want anyone else killed," clarified John.

"That makes sense," said Polly.

"Secondly, I want Isabel to do her best to list every customer present during the time of the Monday night killing. I want Rachael and Isabel to give me a list of everyone they can recall seeing here on Tuesday night."

"John, I'm sure the police have those lists," offered Holiday.

"I'm sure they do. I'll compare the new lists I get to the ones that they gave to the police and any other lists they have. We may find someone new. Trust me. There is a method to my madness."

"That's true. There usually is." Holiday nodded and took Rachael back onto the dance floor.

When Holiday returned to the table, John asked him to accompany him to the men's room. The ladies couldn't help but giggle. "Down girls, we need to plan our strategy," said John, with a smile.

"Yeah, well maybe we'll plan a counter-strategy of our own," said Polly with her sexiest voice.

As the men maneuvered between the tables toward the door John asked, "Why do women always think it's about them?"

"Well, who the hell is it about?"

John cocked his head to the left. "One o'clock in the booth. See the two dudes?"

Holiday gave a quick glance, "Huh, yeah." He continued to follow John out into the lobby and on into the restroom.

John looked in the stall and felt relieved to find it unoccupied. "Harry, it's either you or Rachael. They watch the two of you everywhere you go. I thought it might be Polly or me. I really believe it's you."

"Let's just go in and I'll sit on the outside of one and you sit on the outside of the other. We'll just ask them why they're eyeballing us." Holiday said grimly as he decided to head for the urinal.

"We don't want to turn over tables and duke it out in the restaurant on our first night here. If they leave, we'll follow them out. If they don't, you leave first and I'll see what happens. If they follow you, I'll follow them."

"I only see one problem with that plan," advised Holiday.

"Harry, my plans don't have problems!"

"What if they don't follow me when I leave? Then they follow you?"

"Oh, yeah. Well, don't drive away. Wait outside and we'll be behind you within minutes. How's that?"

"Now, that sounds better. In the meantime, what about you and your girl?" inquired Holiday.

"Girl? Harry, she was a girl back when I was a boy…which isn't bad now that I think of it."

"Are you interested?"

"What part of 'me Tarzan and her Jane' do you not understand?" John looked at him quizzically.

"Ah, good. I feel better leaving you then." Holiday slapped John on the shoulder in his response.

"Not as good as I feel or at least expect to feel."

"It's good to see that Dede hasn't ruined you, John."

"Harry, she as good as told me that she was going to play while I'm gone. She was angry that I left."

"With luck, we will kick butt as well as chase it." Both men were laughing when they returned to the table. Their laughter came to an abrupt stop.

"John, where are the girls?"

Looking over to the booth, John's response was, "Where are the dudes?"

They walked as rapidly as they could without startling any of the customers. As soon as they were out of the restaurant door, they ran through the lobby and the open sliding doors to the sidewalk outside.

The two men were just stepping off the curb on each side of a black Toyota Camry. One opened the passenger door and was half in when John arrived. He was a head taller than John. However, John equalized that by slamming the door on him. He fell to the street, groaning. John placed his foot on the man's throat.

"If you even reach for my leg, I'll stomp your Adam's Apple into the blacktop. What's your name?"

"John Smith, asshole."

"Well, Mister John Smith Asshole, I'm Pocahontas and I want to know why you were watching us."

Holiday, the same size as the driver, spun him around, and then shoved him back against the car. "Please do me a favor and be aggressive. I have a lot of pent up emotion I need to get rid of."

"Man, what is your problem?" asked the wide-eyed guy. "Are you some kind of psycho nut?"

"You're my problem. Why were you watching me all night? Are you an idiot or do you just find yourself attracted to me?" asked Holiday.

"You're crazy, old man. I ain't got no interest in you. I was just watching them people dance." The stranger stared hard at Holiday.

"Show me some identification."

"You a cop?" The young man sneered belligerently at Holiday.

"No, I'm not a cop. Show me some identification," demanded Holiday

"I ain't showing you a damn thing."

"Fine. You can show it to the doctor." Holiday's move was faster than the young man anticipated and he caught him on the side of the head with a right cross. As he slid down the side of the car, Holiday quickly reached into the man's back pocket, and removed his wallet. He read the exposed Tennessee driver's license out loud, "Cleduus Tolman, age twenty-eight." He made a quick mental note and rushed to the other side of the car to help John with the man on the ground.

John moved his foot from the man's throat and Holiday snatched him up from the ground and pushed him back against the car. "Show me some identification."

"Screw you. I heard. You ain't no cotton pickin' cop." He shot a go-to-hell look at Holiday.

"Do you want me to look at your ID over your unconscious body or not. You can go sleepy-bye just like your buddy. What's it gonna be, pal?"

"All right, damn it! Here." He handed his wallet to John while Holiday kept his grip on him.

"Albert l. Hobbs. What's the I for...Ivan, or some other stupid name?" questioned John.

"It's Idell."

"My, my, you're a long way from Georgia. What's a twenty-four year old doing out here?"

"On vacation, man. Me and my buddy decided to visit the southwest. We want to see where the old gunslingers roamed."

John handed him back his wallet and asked Holiday, "Are you going to put him to sleep, now?"

"No, he needs to help his buddy get the hell out of here." Holiday turned him loose and patted his cheek. Hobbs quickly got his buddy in the car and they wasted no time leaving the area.

The two men watched the car drive away. Holiday returned to the restaurant with John in tow. They hurried back to the table to find the ladies sitting there.

"We thought you ran out on us," said Polly.

"That is so sweet. Did you hear that Harry?" John asked with a proud smile. "They hated to see us leave?"

"That's not it. We didn't want to get stuck with the tab," Polly politely informed the guys as they sat down.

John's smile turned to a frown and he said, "Figures." Everyone laughed. The men had decided not to tell the ladies of their outside activities. The rest of the night John was bothered by the number eighteen (18) that he had seen tattooed on the young man named Hobbs' wrist. He remembered it from someplace but couldn't recall it.

———————

He was in that twilight zone of delta brainwaves and almost asleep when he sat up in bed and said, "I've got it."

"Man, that's good news, because I want it." Polly reached over and pulled him down to her.

"What? Oh yeah, well I've got that, too. I know what eighteen means."

"What are you talking about?" She rolled over on her elbow and looked at him curiously.

"One eight (18), the first and eighth letter of the alphabet."

chapter

SIX

John looked for Holiday the next morning when he arrived at the facility but didn't locate him. John jumped in with the polygraphs, skipped lunch and finished the four Military Police personnel and the Colonel by 6:30 p.m. If Holiday could get five of the scientists to come in on Saturday, he would work late and do the final four on Sunday. This would free him up. He could finish his paperwork and be out of there by noon on Monday if there were no complications.

Holiday spent the day in Rachael's office watching the procedure involving the handling of classified documents. He interviewed five of the scientists. After reviewing his interviews and finishing his copious notes he sat back, looked across the room, and asked Rachael to go dancing.

"My goodness sailor, I thought I whipped you last night. You must have been at sea a long time." Rachael strolled over and put her hand on his chest and smiled at him. He leaned back in his chair and his hand fell to her leg.

"You're not dealing with an ordinary squid. You've tangled with a tried and proven SEAL."

"I have to admit it. I tried and you've proven. How about I meet you at I and J's about 2000 hours?"

"That would be a good time, because I need to go over some stuff with John." Holiday rose, gave her shoulder a squeeze then followed some of the personnel up the stairs. He continued across the facility and climbed the stairs to the sergeant's office. Looking through the window, he saw John conducting a post-test interview. The colonel's office was locked so he sat on the steps.

He watched as Rachael came out of the Conex container talking on her cell phone. She was walking with one of the male employees. The last employee out was the Israeli, Dr. David.

The final MP to be tested came out from the polygraph examination with a wide smile. Holiday stood as the soldier approached him. The soldier looked at Holiday, gave him 'thumbs up' and said, "Piece a cake."

John was just hanging the finger probes on the cover of his polygraph when Holiday entered. John turned and said, "Where have you been, Harry? I've needed to talk to you all day."

"What's so important? Did you find our killer?" The SEAL's expression was more shock than anything else.

"No. It's not that exciting. Nevertheless, it is damn interesting," answered John with a frown.

"Interesting. Like how?"

"Those two guys we had that little discussion with last night, well at least one of them, had a tattoo on his wrist."

"What kind of tat?"

"The guy I had down on the ground had the number '18' on the inside of his wrist." John smiled proudly.

"What do you mean inside his wrist? If it was inside how'd you see it?" Holiday cocked his head a little to the left.

"Come on Harry. You know what I mean. I'm talking about the part of the wrist that you can't see if he was standing at attention." John snapped to attention and demonstrated how that part of the wrist wouldn't be seen.

Holiday laughed and shook his head. "I know what you mean. Why is '18' so significant?"

"Didn't you go to the FLETC? How can you possibly not know what that means? That's basic law enforcement information."

"Well, John, I guess I was sick that day. Do you want to play twenty questions or do you feel like telling me?" asked Holiday impatiently.

"That number means those guys are skin-heads. They are bona fide members of the Aryan Nation. Those numbers stand for letters of the alphabet. The number one is 'A' and the number eight is 'H'."

"Hell, that's probably the guy's initials. His name was Albert something that started with an H. I've got it written down."

John put his hands on his hips, looked disgusted at Holiday and said, "It means Adolph Hitler."

"Come on now, Polly, what's with the hesitation?" questioned Rachael over the cell phone.

"John's really a nice guy and all. I mean...I really like him. There is one little thing though."

"Like what? I mean what's little?"

"No, no, not that, silly. Like he's a first for me."

"Polly, what in the hell are you talking about? You were married for years. And I'm sure you practiced years before that."

"Yeah, all that may be true. But there is one difference. My husband didn't have an implant!"

"A what?"

"You heard me."

"Don't it ever go down?" Rachel was so enthralled with the conversation she drifted into the next lane and was shocked by the horn blowing beside her.

"No. Never."

"Eureka." Rachael's heart was pounding from the near collision with the vehicle next to her.

"Eureka, hell. Like, I can't touch my ka-what's-it with a powder puff. I mean my legs didn't stop quivering until almost noon." Polly poured herself a glass of White Zinfandel and returned to the couch.

"My God, girl, you're complaining about that? I haven't had that problem since I got so drunk in Singapore."

"I guess I shouldn't, huh?"

"Hell no. I know it's been a while for you. Right now you need to get back up on that horse and ride. That stable could be empty any day. Grab those reins and enjoy the journey while you can. Count your blessings while you're at it."

"Rachael."

"Yeah."

"Can we change the subject? I think this conversation is gross and getting worse by the minute."

"I forget you weren't in the Navy. Sorry if I've offended your sense of propriety. Sometimes I think the service warped my head. Nevertheless, a good lay is a good lay in any language."

"Okay, fine. You made your stupid point. What time are you going over to I and J's tonight?"

"The guys have to work late so we're supposed to meet them at eight o'clock. Can you make it?"

"I have to admit, I do want to go. The man is fun, a little weird, but fun. What are you wearing?" Polly took a sip from her wine glass.

"Hell, I hadn't thought about it, probably as little as possible. Do you have any suggestions?"

Polly placed her wine glass on the end table. "I wore jeans last night. I think I'll go a little more feminine tonight. I'm going to wear a skirt and blouse."

"I will, too. I got to go. I'm getting into that Interstate 10 rush hour traffic. I'll see you tonight…lucky girl."

———————

Holiday drove around the parking lot and he and John checked it carefully before locating a parking spot. Friday and Saturday night is pretty much 'reservation only'. It doesn't matter if the winter visitors are here or not. Once inside it was obvious why reservations were needed. The dance floor was packed and those who weren't dancing were consuming delicious food and great drinks.

John walked to the far side of the dance floor looking for the skinheads while Holiday searched the nearside. José's daughter, the young and attractive Natalie, informed Holiday they were fully booked. He and John stood by the bar figuring out their next move. Rachael came in and Natalie informed her that her table was ready.

Isabel spotted them and led them over to Rachael's table, which was in a booth close to the entrance. "I'm so glad you made it back. Elizabeth and I have done our best to recall the customers who were here last Monday and Tuesday. I'll get you the lists when you're ready."

John, sliding into the booth next to Rachael, looked up at Isabel, smiled at her and said, "I'm ready now."

"So I've heard," mumbled Rachael. She had trouble holding back a laugh and couldn't help the snicker. Holiday looked at her strangely and thankfully, John didn't understand what she said.

Isabel left and quickly returned with four lists…two from Elizabeth, who actually is Isabel's assistant, and two from Isabel. Polly approached John, blushing and smiling at the same time.

Her short sleeve white cotton blouse and long pleated blue skirt enhanced the beauty that was already there. He slid out of the semicircular booth and let her move in next to Rachael.

After standing and looking at her for a second, he followed her into the booth and asked, "How are you doing tonight?"

She leaned her head on his shoulder and replied, "I'm looking forward to some slow dancing with you."

Rachael snickered at the word 'slow'. Neither John nor Holiday had any idea why. They just shrugged it off. John thought she meant she was looking forward to some hugging set to music. It turned out to be a great night for both couples.

chapter

SEVEN

John arrived at the laboratory early Saturday morning. He set up his polygraph, and after doing his calibration, relaxed and waited for his first examinee.

"Top of the morning, Rachael. What did you do with Harry? Isn't he with you?" asked John.

Rachael entered the sergeant's office wiping the crusty rheum from the corner of her right eye with her fingers. "The hard core Navy SEAL is still sleeping. He said that he probably shouldn't be here when you polygraph me. I think it was an excuse to roll over and go back to sleep."

"Well, it is kind of iffy. I mean…I can't polygraph friends. I damn sure can't polygraph Polly."

"Wow, so are we friends?" Rachael asked in a sexy, raspy voice. "Man, I didn't know that. Do you have any special deals for friends?"

"Stop that. I can't look at you as though you're a friend. As far as I'm concerned you're someone suspected of murder. I need to find out if you did it."

"Oh, come on! John. After what we've been through together?" She batted her eyes at him.

"If you don't quit, I'll have to have you tested by the county. I mean it." John backed away and walked over to his polygraph.

"Gee, John, I was just kidding. I want to prove I didn't kill anybody. Do what you have to do."

"That's better."

"I must warn you. I don't do polygraphs very well. I had to have three before I passed, to get this job. The idiot couldn't decide if I was telling the truth or not on the first two. I'm the nervous type, John."

"Well let's hope I'm better than he was. In fact I'm not going to take any shortcuts with you. I'm going to give you the exam as though you never have heard of a polygraph. Maybe that will help."

"That's going to be hard to do since I've had three before. How are you going to do that? Where do we start?" Rachael gave a nervous look at the polygraph.

John indicated the wooden armchair beside the sergeant's desk. He and Rachael sat down face-to-face in front of the desk. Their knees were just a few feet apart. John sat back in the armless old wooden chair with his legs crossed. He placed the clipboard on his lap. Rachael sat in the sergeant's old, typical military padded metal desk chair with her knees together and hands folded in her lap. She was wearing a freshly-ironed light-blue blouse, with one too many buttons undone, and a navy-blue cotton skirt.

John wondered how someone this lady-like could kill anyone. However, he had to shake off any thoughts along those lines. He could not prejudice himself before the test. She was just an examinee. He had to know the truth and the results of the test had to be based solely on his interpretation of the polygraph charts. The man had extensive experience in separating his prejudices from his examinations. It was second nature to him. He trusted only his instrument for his conclusions.

It's impossible, as the old cliché says, to tell a book by its cover, John thought. *I found deceitful people in all walks of life: doctors, dentists, nurses, policemen, school teachers. They even were discovered in daycare workers, priests, pastors and other professions in which we put our trust. I also found honesty is not guaranteed with gender, race, age, educational level or type of occupation. Honesty never can be taken for granted.*

"Rachael, before we start the test, I'd like to learn a little more about you. You know, psychology plays a big part in the polygraph just as much as the central nervous system does. For me to do the job, I need to know who you really are. We're just going to sit here and talk a little about your history, such as family life, education, health, jobs you have held, hobbies, and a few other things. This will help me to determine some of the questions I'm going to ask on the examination."

John watched closely for physical indications that were associated with deceptive people. He watched for signs of her closing herself off by crossing her legs and/or arms, avoiding eye contact, picking lint from her clothing, and a number of other patterns indicative of deceptive behavior. It pleased him to see they were non-existent. He listened carefully during their conversation for any verbal indications of deception. Again, none were obvious. He felt good about the test.

During the thirty-minute pretest interview, they laughed at some of their similar experiences and interests. John gathered sufficient information to help him formulate the questions he would ask during the examination. After making his notes, he placed his pen down and looked at her for a couple of seconds.

"Rachael, I want you to know how the polygraph instrument works. I think it's important for you to know. The unknown is scary."

"John, I've had three, remember? I know about that. But I'm curious to hear your version. Plus, there is one thing I'd also like to know. Do you go into everyone's personal background like this before you polygraph them, or do you just have a special interest in me? If you do, that's fine."

"I go into everyone's background this way. You're no exception. Every examiner is required to learn about his examinee before he tests the person. It would be unethical to test without that. I might've found out something in the pretest interview that would have prevented me from testing you."

"Like what?"

"Certain medical problems, such as respiratory ailments, heart conditions, as well as neurological problems, pregnancy, ingestion of certain narcotics or drugs. Even some psychological afflictions, among other things, could stop me from testing you. At least they would require that I adjust the type of test I did on you. This way, you and I both know it's safe to test you and that we'll come up with accurate results."

"Are you saying you can't test me if I am pregnant?"

"Are you pregnant?"

"Absolutely not, John. That ship sailed years ago."

"You never know."

"John, I'm forty-five-years-old. Get serious."

"Sorry. I had to ask. I'm not picking on you, Rachael. I have to ask all females these questions."

"Is the machine dangerous to the baby?"

"Positively not. The reason I don't test anyone who is pregnant is due to the liability aspect of it. There's no known occasion in which a polygraph has caused a problem for an expectant mother. However, there is a lot of stress during one of these examinations. If she were to have a miscarriage after the test, you can bet they would try to blame it on the stress of the polygraph examination procedure."

"That makes me feel better. I was starting to get a little uncomfortable with all those personal questions. You're kind of learning more about me than I want Harry to know. Are you going to tell him this stuff?"

"You're safe. This interview is confidential information. There is no need or requirement for Harry to know what we talked about. The only information he gets from me is whether or not you lied about the killing of Hires."

"That's good to know. I feel a whole bunch better. Now tell me how this machine works."

"First of all, it is not a machine. You, being in the scientific field, know as well as I do, a device designed to measure something is an instrument. The polygraph is designed to measure your psychological and physiological responses to the questions you're asked. Now, have you ever heard of the 'Fight or Flight Syndrome'?"

"Of course I have, John. I had all that crap in the last test, but go ahead and refresh me."

"Did you ever start doing something and were so involved in it you were totally oblivious to anything going on around you? And someone spoke to you causing you to jump? Or maybe on a dark night you were taking a short cut home. You heard a noise behind you and it startled you. In each of these cases you took in a quick breath, your heart sped up, you felt it pound in your chest, plus you felt a tingling all over."

"Yeah, a few days ago I was driving on I-10. I was talking on the stupid phone. I drifted into the adjoining lane. There was this loud horn. I thought I'd jump out of the car. I'm a good subject for fight or flight."

"That's nature's way of preparing your body to either fight what startled you or to run from it. The little intake of breath you experienced sent extra oxygen to your brain. Your heart sped up and that sent extra blood to your muscles, and the tingling you felt all over was nothing more than the pores in the skin popping open. This was because they knew; whether you run or fight, your body is going to heat up, and the pores all popping open at the same time, allow the body to cool down. All that happened in the blink of an eye. You couldn't have controlled it even if you had wanted to."

Rachael looked at John with surprise. "Get serious, John. You don't go through all that funny breathing, heart pounding and pores opening when you lie. Not that I ever lied…that much. I've told a few little lies over the years and never felt anything like that."

John continued. "Yes you do. In fact, that's what makes the polygraph work. When you lie, you do go through a minute amount of that 'fight or flight syndrome'. Of course, it's not to the extent you experienced the day you veered into the adjoining lane. If it were the same, for sure, we wouldn't need an instrument to measure it. It'd be noticeable without the instrument.

"The polygraph instrument is so sensitive that it can measure the minutest amount of response. It operates by using devices to measure changes in your breathing, blood pressure and heart rate, and the opening of the pores in the skin. There're no sticky needles and I promise nothing hurts. You won't have to wear these devices more than fifteen or twenty minutes."

"Wait a minute." Rachael held up her hand. "Only fifteen or twenty-minutes? How come the test takes a couple of hours?"

"We've spent almost an hour in here already. As you can see, we have more to talk about than the questions that are going to be asked in the instrumentation part of the exam. For instance, now that we have gone through the pretest interview, and I've explained to you how the instrument works. We can start to work on the exact questions to be asked on the test."

"I'm going to know the questions you are going to ask me even before the test begins? Is that right?" Rachael had a 'hard to believe' expression.

"You bet. I promise there won't be any surprises during the testing portion. I will mix them up and ask them more than once, but the questions we make up now will be the only questions asked on the exam. Another reason the test will take as long as it does is after we do the test I have to interpret what the charts say. I know you don't want me to rush through that part. I'll go over them thoroughly. When I'm finished I'll sit down and go over the results with you.

"Some incompetent examiners will not take the time to do that. They'll tell you, they're going to pass the results on to your attorney, therapist, probation or parole officer, or some other interested party. This is not the way a good examiner works and it is against the American Polygraph Association rules. You deserve a chance to offer a rebuttal or explanation of the results." John looked at her with a smile.

"I'm starting to feel better about this. I have one big question, though. I don't think I ever would kill anyone. I certainly didn't kill Martha…but maybe I really, really wanted to and even entertained the thought in my mind. Now I have guilty feeling about those thoughts. So do I still have anything to worry about? That emotion could be very strong. I may have wanted her dead. The guilt would be awful."

"Don't you worry about that. If what went on in our minds was against the law, not many people would be walking the streets today. I know I wouldn't be around. The polygraph does not read intent. It reads only fear, the fear of being caught in a lie. Being caught in a lie damn sure creates fear."

John pointed at her, "Look at how nervous you are right this minute, thinking about your past fantasies of killing someone. Now imagine how nervous you would be if you actually did it. So you see you can relax with the knowledge you didn't do it. You have nothing to worry about. Are you ready to start making up some questions now?"

"Yes. I'm still nervous, but I'm also excited, knowing people will know the truth. I'm innocent." Rachael nodded and smiled.

John took up his clipboard and pen. "The test is going to consist of a total of ten-questions."

"Wow, how come so many questions? Are they all necessary? Can't you just ask me if I did it?"

"The other examiner didn't do that, did he?"

"No. He asked me a bunch of questions."

He leaned forward in his chair, "If I only asked you if you did it, I would certainly get a reaction out of you. Without something to measure that reaction against, it wouldn't tell me anything. I have to have what we call comparison questions. Those are questions I use to judge the response of your relevant questions. In addition, there are a few questions thrown in just to get a normal reading. This is standard procedure on all polygraph examinations. Now let's start with something we know is the truth."

"Wait." Rachael held up her hand. "What is a relevant question again?"

"Those are the ones that question you about the issue. In this case the issue is the killing of Martha Hires. Okay. Now let's start with the first question:

"Are you presently forty-five years old?"

Rachael frowned and responded with, "Yes."

"Is there something else you are afraid I will ask you, even though I told you I would not?"

"Rachael looked puzzled and said, "John, I'm sorry. I don't quite understand that question."

"Remember, I told you I wouldn't ask you any questions on the test we haven't fully reviewed before the test. In other words, I'm not going to ask you any questions we aren't covering right now. I promise you there will be no surprises. Think about it. If I asked you, 'Did you ever cheat on your boyfriend?' What do you think would happen if I asked you, 'Did you ever steal anything from the Navy.' If I asked questions like those in the middle of the test, do you think you'd respond?"

"I'd probably pee my pants."

John laughed and repeated, "No surprises. That means only the questions we have talked about."

"Okay, I guess I can say yes to that." Rachael shifted in her chair and looked seriously at John.

"Good. It's important you trust me on the test. It's so much easier for you if you do. Okay. Next question:

"Is your last name Holmes?"

Rachael smiled again, paused for a few seconds and finally said softly, "Yes."

"Regarding the killing of Martha Hires, do you intend to answer truthfully each question about that?"

"Yes I do."

"Come on, Rachael; concentrate now. Remember you must use only one syllable answers. And by that I mean either 'Yes' or 'No'. And try to answer them all in the same tone of voice."

"Sorry about that. Yes."

John took his time and continued formulating the questions, which, among others included:

"Did you kill Martha Hires?"

"Did you kill Martha Hires with a knife?"

Rachael answered "No" to those questions and to the remainder of the questions as well.

John propped his clipboard up on the sergeant's desk, moved Rachael's chair closer to the side of it and had her sit back down. He stepped to the side and picked up a pneumograph convoluted tube and had her raise her arms and then he placed the tube around her chest and back, over her blouse. Then he placed an identical tube around her stomach and back.

"This will measure the changes in the rate and depth of your breathing. Women are basically chest breathers and men are usually belly breathers. That's the reason we use two tubes."

Then he took the blood pressure cuff from the desk and placed it around the biceps on her left arm. "This will measure any changes in your heart rate and blood pressure. I'm sorry; I keep forgetting you're a scientist type. I have to tell you anyway. It won't measure blood pressure, just the changes."

Finally, he placed a small metal plate against the tip of the index finger of her right hand and then another on the tip of the ring finger of the same hand. He attached them with Velcro. He said to her, "I know you're familiar with 'galvanic skin response' and that's what this measures. As the pores open, more moisture is available, and moisture does transmit electricity. When the pores close, it creates a resistance to the electricity. This records the change in that resistance."

John adjusted the polygraph instrument and told the retired Navy quartermaster to close her eyes, relax, and concentrate only on each question being asked at the time. "Don't dwell on a question that's been asked or anticipate one that hasn't been asked. Remember to use only the one syllable answers…either the words 'yes or no', and try to answer them in the same tone of voice."

John stopped and looked at her. "You know what, Rachael; let's make sure the instrument is working. We'll do a little test with numbers first." John wrote seven numbers on a piece of paper. All the numbers were consecutive. He told her to pick one, write it down, and put it under her hand. Then he pumped up the blood pressure cuff, massaged the bubbles out of it, and turned on the instrument. After he adjusted the pens, he told her to look at and concentrate on the numbers. Then, starting with the first number, he asked her if it was the number she had picked, repeating the process for each number. Then he turned off the instrument, let the air out of the cuff and told her to give him the number six… the number she had written down.

"That's really cool. I'm impressed. I guess this thing really does work. Now I do feel better about taking the test," she said. "I feel better about you, too. I'm confident you know what you're do-ing."

He grinned and responded with, "I told you." The question-ing on the first chart began and she answered each question the same as during the formulation period. John asked the last ques-tion and waited the required fifteen seconds for the response as he had after each question before. He turned off the instrument, released the sixty pounds of pressure in the blood pressure cuff and massaged the air out of it. "Now, young lady, that wasn't so bad, was it?"

She rubbed her arm and complained, "That cuff was really tight on my arm. How much pressure did you put in it?"

John grinned again, "It is not nearly as much as the nurses use when they test your blood pressure."

"Yeah, you may be right, but they don't keep it pumped up as long. I was about to lose the feeling in my hand." Rachael flexed her fingers.

"I guess you are right. Nevertheless, it was only sixty-pounds of pressure. That's the standard amount. That's why, between each series of questions, I shut the instrument down and release the pressure and let the blood start circulating again. Besides, it's the way I get back at all the medical types for the many times they pumped up the pressure on my tender arms."

"How many more times do we have to do this?" asked Rachael, failing to see John's attempt at humor.

"An examiner worth his salt will always do at least three-charts or series of questions. Any amount less than that pretty much means the examiner is lazy or in a hurry and is taking a chance on getting a false reading. I would be willing to bet that you want me to be accurate. Right?"

"That's for sure. There isn't any question about that. John, I believe in you and I'm putting my freedom in your hands."

"I respect your trust, Rachael. I appreciate your belief in me. You're going to get an accurate test. Now that you have had a breather and the blood is flowing, let's do this again. Are you ready?"

After she acknowledged that she was, John pumped up the blood pressure cuff, turned the pens back to their calibrated positions, and asked the same questions previously asked on the test. He received the same answers. John wasn't sure on the first test, but he noticed on this one the responses were extremely close together. He couldn't mention it to her because it would, most definitely, cause a response on the next chart if he did. These responses surprised him.

After a break between charts again, John started the last set of questions. The questions were the same as the first two-times except that he swapped the order of the number five-relevant question with the number seven-relevant question. When the examination was completed he turned off the instrument and removed the polygraph paraphernalia from Rachael.

He asked, "Was that fun or what?"

She rubbed her arm and smiled up at John. "Yeah, right. It was probably real fun for the Army, maybe, but not the Navy. Thank God, that's over. I think a polygraph examination is an extremely traumatic experience for a person."

"If you think it is traumatic for the truthful person, what do you think the deceptive person thinks of it?"

She laughed, "Truthfully, John, I wouldn't know."

"Good answer," he said, as he laughed with her. "Sounds like the answer of a truthful person."

John left Rachael in the room while he did a little chart interpretation downstairs. He asked if there was anything she wanted, trying to make her comfortable until he finished grading the charts.

"A martini would be just fine about now. In fact, make it a double. Screw the olives. They just take up room."

"Don't we wish?" He left the room, sat down with the roll of polygraph paper, and began to concentrate on the outcome. Several questions were inconclusive. It was interesting to find questions that were inconclusive; not unheard of, but unusual. It didn't make sense to John, unless….

He returned to the sergeant's office and sat down with Rachael. He just sat and looked at her for a minute without speaking. Then he began his interrogation with, "Rachael, I'm surprised. You and I both know there's a problem with this test."

She laughed and said, "That's not funny, John. This is serious shit, man. I'm the most honest sailor you ever met. I couldn't have this job if I weren't."

"Talk to me. Tell me what's bothering you." His knees were just inches from her knees. John called this maneuver 'space invasion'. It was a psychological move. There was no humor in his expression.

"Oh, my God! You're serious. Oh, man! I told you I had problems on that damn lie box. Now I've proven it to you."

John put his hands in front of him with the palms down and did an up and down motion as though he was slowing someone down. "Just try to relax and think of what could cause you to have a problem. It's more than likely something very simple in your past. Have you and Miss Hires had any falling outs lately?"

"Absolutely not, John. We were the best of friends. We worked together, shopped together, and did karaoke together. We even loaned money to each other when it was necessary."

"I'm not going to be able to pass you. We need to resolve this." John laid the clipboard on the desk.

Rachael rose from the chair. John motioned for her to sit down. She shrugged her shoulders and sat back in the chair.

"I swear to God, John, I'm not lying." She leaned forward and put her hands on John's knees.

John leaned forward and gently grasped her wrists and moved her upright in her chair. He smiled and slightly shook his head. He leaned back in his chair and looked at her for a full minute before speaking.

"I'll tell you what we're going to do. You are too emotionally charged now to re-test. I'll give you a few days to get your thoughts together. I'll schedule you to be my last test on Monday. When you finish work, just come on up here and we'll see what we can do. We won't need to take as long next time."

"That sounds good to me. I don't care what the test is. I always seem to freeze up. I don't know what's wrong with me. I've got to overcome this." This time when Rachael stood John didn't stop her.

"Don't worry. We'll figure it out. In the meantime, you'd better get to work. I'm sure they need their files by now."

"There're only a couple people working today. But I guess you're right. Well, thanks for trying today. Will I see you tonight?" She started for the door.

"I think Polly is planning on it." John began putting a new roll of polygraph paper in the instrument.

"Good."

He spun around to face Rachael. "Oh, I almost forgot. Would you send Doctor David up, please?"

Doctor David entered, smiling. "Ah, another of those instruments that everyone says doesn't work. As a scientist, I'm obliged to say it as well. However, from my experience with them, I have to admit I've never seen one that didn't work."

"It's unusual for me to receive a satisfied customer. You're absolutely correct about the instrument working. It's the examiner you have to worry about."

"From what I heard from our young sergeant-in-charge, I don't have to worry about that either." The scientist stuck out his hand for John.

John shook David's hand and asked, "I take it you're familiar with the polygraph instrument?"

"You bet. You can't work for the government as long as I have and not had a few of them."

John motioned for him to sit in the chair by the desk. "I'll make it as quick and painless as possible. I'm sure you're going to hear some of the same information that you have heard time and time again."

"I'm sure. Let's get on with it."

In just under two hours David, with his 'no deception indicated' (NDI) polygraph, was preparing to return to the laboratory. John asked him to send Paul Hardwood up next. The laboratory director stopped inside the doorway and said, "I'm sorry. Doctor Hardwood went home ill this morning."

"That's interesting, Doctor. He didn't, by any chance, happen to tell you what was wrong?"

"No, not really. He didn't specify anything in particular. He just said that he wasn't feeling well. The man asked to be excused. What could I say? I told him to go home and get better."

"Doctor, do you think he will be back tomorrow? He doesn't have to work. He can just come in for the poly."

"You don't think he did this to get out of the polygraph do you? I don't think he would do that."

"Stranger things have happened." John subconsciously nodded his head.

"I'll check with him in the morning and see how he's doing."

"I'd appreciate that."

"Oh, that's no problem at all. I'm sure he'll be all right." David started for the door, stopped and turned back to John. "Give me another name and I'll send that person up."

John gave him the next name in line. The scientist was friendly and cooperative and the test went well. He continued conducting his examinations through the remainder of the day with no other problems. The other three personnel were found to be truthful. He looked forward to the polygraphs with Doctor Hardwood and Rachael the next morning. Today was easy. But he had a feeling tomorrow would be a little more challenging.

chapter

EIGHT

"Hey, guys. What are you doing here?" queried John, putting his polygraph probes away.

"We came by to see if you want to go out tonight. Are you up for a little dining and dancing?" asked Holiday as he danced into the room with Rachael following him. "I don't know how much longer we're going to be in this harbor. We want to make the most of it before the ship sails."

"I'm not quite sure what you just said. I don't know about tonight. I don't want to wear out my welcome with Polly."

"Hell, man, it ain't your welcome you're wearing out with Polly," mumbled Rachael, giggling.

"I'm sorry, Rachael, I didn't hear what you said," stated John as he closed up the instrument.

"I said you ain't wearing out your welcome with Polly." In fact, I think she might even be smitten with you." Rachael was proud of herself for her fast thinking.

"Now, there's a word you don't hear every day. Where did you hear 'smitten' and did she really say anything like that?" asked Holiday.

"It means she's taken a liking to old John, there. I can't put my finger on it, but there's something about him she likes." Rachael did her best to keep from laughing at her own double-entendre.

John rubbed his chin and stared at Holiday for a second. He started to say something, and then stopped. He looked down at the floor. His brow was wrinkled and he kept his hand on his chin.

"What's the matter with you, John? You're definitely preoccupied. Is something bothering you?" Holiday walked over to him.

"Yeah. Something is bothering me."

"Is it Rachael's poly?" Holiday gave him a troubled looked.

"No, that's not it."

"What is it?"

"Harry, I'm concerned about Doctor Hardwood."

"Why? Didn't he pass his poly? Did he lie? Is he our killer?"

"No. He went home sick just before the poly. I think that's pretty suspicious behavior for an examinee." John leaned back against the desk.

"Is that so? Well, I feel the same way." Holiday turned to Rachael, "Do you have access to his personnel file?"

"Of course I do. I have access to all the files. They stuck me with that job when we lost Martha. Why do you ask?"

"Would you mind getting the file for me?"

"Hey, big fella, I haven't said no to you since I met you. You wait here and I'll be right back." Rachael hurried out the door.

"Wow, Harry, she sure is an accommodating lady," said John, looking at the empty doorway.

"You don't know the half of it, buddy. I can tell you stuff that will have you drooling. Things that…. "

"Don't start, Harry. What's gotten into you? I don't remember you ever being anything but business on a case."

"You never worked with me without my team being present. I have to set the example when they're around."

Rachael returned with the requested file. She laid it on the sergeant's desk. Holiday quickly thumbed through it. He stopped, traced his finger over part of it and looked over at John.

"Why don't we stop by the good doctor's place of abode and see if there is anything we can do for him? The man being sick and all. We do want to make sure he is healthy by tomorrow."

"If that's what you want to do. Let's do it," responded John. "I'm all for helping the sick and lame."

"Rachel, do you want to wait here or go home?"

"Like hell, I'll do either one. Harry, I'm going with you guys. I wouldn't miss this for the world."

Holiday jabbed his finger at her. "You can't go in with us. He can't even see you. You'll have to wait in the car. We don't want to create any hard feelings here."

"The bastard already hates me. This won't change anything. I'll wait in the car, but you're not leaving me here."

John took the file and read the address out loud as he followed Rachel and Holiday out of the facility. He discussed the location of the address with Rachael. She knew that the man lived in the Garden Lakes vicinity of Avondale. His house was only a few miles from the laboratory.

They arrived at Hardwood's house a little after 6 p.m. There was still plenty of daylight. Rachael waited in the car as Holiday and John approached the house. John motioned that he was going around back and Holiday nodded in agreement as he knocked on the door. John hurried through the wooden gate in the cinderblock wall and ran across the pebbled desert-landscaped yard.

He was impressed with the pool and hot tub combination. John walked up onto the patio and peered in. After finding the sliding glass door locked, and seeing no movement inside, he started back around the house. John stopped at a wooden door on the side of the house and tried the knob. Much to his surprise it opened. He looked into a two car garage that was empty of any vehicles. Holiday came through the gate, saw John, the open door, and smiled. He motioned for John to go on in. Once inside, Holiday closed the door and the garage was in total darkness.

"Well, that didn't work," muttered Holiday as he reopened the door. "I guess we need the light."

John turned the knob on the door to the interior of the house and found it unlocked. He waved Holiday over and whispered, "You're the one with the license to kill. How about you go in first?"

Holiday didn't draw his weapon but he did rest his hand on the butt of his automatic as he entered. The house was silent. Entering the kitchen, only the ticking of the wall clock could be heard. The room was spotless. There were no dirty dishes. Food was not in sight. Everything seemed to be in its place.

Holiday called out, "Hello. Anyone home? Federal Agents here. If anyone is here, please speak up now. To surprise us could be fatal." The two-men looked at each other and Holiday shrugged.

They checked each room for anyone hiding. They also checked for any suspicious items. John and Holiday entered the master bedroom at the same time. Each took a different part of the room. John discovered clothing missing from the closet and Holiday found clothes missing from dresser drawers. Toiletries were gone from the bathroom.

"It looks like our man won't be there for his polygraph tomorrow, John." Holiday opened the medicine cabinet. He examined the handful of medicine bottles.

"What the hell are you doing, Harry? I think you have been watching too much television." John rose up from looking under the bed and saw Holiday looking at the medicine bottles.

"Maybe so, but it works on NCIS and Castle."

"Yeah, well this is Holiday and Bodie."

"Okay then, Bodie, Holiday won't tell you what the bottles say."

"All right, you win. What do they say?"

"Hell, I don't know, because I can't read them. The words are too long."

"Lot of help you are." John laughed.

John looked over at a scratch pad by the phone in the bedroom. He walked over and began rubbing the side of the pencil lead over the indentation that remained on the pad from the last note written. The previous writing began to appear.

"Talk about ME watching too much TV. What are you doing?"

"I saw this on the Mentalist. It worked for him."

"That only works on TV," said Holiday

"Is that so? All right; I won't tell you what the pad says."

"You're going to play my game on me, are you? What does it say?"

"Hell, I don't know. I can't read it," responded John.

"It appears as though you may close this case faster than you thought. At least it's going to let Rachael off the hook," advised Holiday.

"Who knows?"

"I still want her polygraphed. She may be fine, but I want to know for sure. How do we know she wasn't working with him?"

"You got it. I'll test her first thing in the morning."

"I need to get back to the lab. I've got some calls to make and some faxes to send. You ready to go?"

"Lead the way, partner."

Once they returned to the car, Rachael had a number of questions for them. She couldn't hold back her excitement. "I knew there was some reason that I didn't like him. I'm a damn good judge of character."

Holiday no sooner entered the laboratory than he was on the phone to the Homeland Security Investigative Duty Officer. "I want Tom Turner and Charles Avery prepared to travel. I'm faxing personnel records for a person of interest. I want a full history on this man and I want him found ASAP. Is there any question to my orders? Fine, I will start the fax immediately."

He had Rachael fax the documents and picture of Hardwood. Then he had her get Doctor David's phone number and informed him of the situation. He also had the military policeman on duty notify the colonel. After faxing the necessary information, photo and a 'Hold for Homeland Security' to the Maricopa County Sheriff's Office, State Patrol and the Airport Police, he sat back and rested.

"Now what?" questioned Rachael.

"We wait."

Rachael stood in front of Holiday looking down at him. "For what?"

"We wait for Avery or Turner to catch his name showing up on a credit card use," Holiday motioned for her to sit on his lap.

"You don't have his credit card numbers. How is that going to work?"

"Rachael, we don't need them. The credit bureaus will notify us when his name pops up. It's simple."

"Isn't that against the Privacy Act?" Rachael sat sideways in Holiday's lap and gave him a confused look.

"Hell, no. Nothing is against the stupid Privacy Act when it is a matter of national security."

"What else?" asked Rachael.

"It's possible Avery and Turner can pull up something as they dig into his background. Plus the cops might get him."

"Can we wait at I and J's? Arnie and the guys are playing tonight and sometimes on Saturdays Arnie's wife, Sandie, comes… and she is a good singer. I still feel like dancing. Come on, Harry, let's go."

"How about it, John? You up for it?" Holiday looked back over his shoulder at John, who was staring out the window.

"I'll pass. I want to be on top of my game tomorrow when Rachael comes in for her polygraph. I think I'll call this a health night and hit the sack early."

"What do I tell Polly?" asked Rachael.

"I bet she'll be glad to have a health night as well."

John was rudely awakened from a deep slumber with the incessant ringing of the motel phone by his bed. Lying face down on the bed he stretched his hand over and retrieved the receiver. "What?" he mumbled into the phone.

"John, you gotta get on your horse and ride, cowboy. We've got work to do," Holiday advised.

John rolled over and leaned on his elbow, squinting at the clock on the nightstand beside the phone. "I don't do work at two o'clock in the morning. It's a violation of the polygraph examiner's union bylaws."

"Number one, you don't have a damn union. Number two, the Arizona State Police picked up Hardwood someplace around Flagstaff. They just dropped him off at the sheriff's office."

"I can't polygraph anyone at two o'clock in the morning," John said sarcastically. "I got in trouble for that about twenty years ago. I'm not going to do it."

"Well, at least you can meet me at the lab. If nothing else we can talk to him there. Okay?"

"All right, Harry. I want you to know that I'm not too happy about this. I'll be there as soon as I can."

———————

John was still grumbling while setting up his polygraph instrument when Holiday arrived. He was preceded by a pale, very nervous, Doctor Paul Hardwood. John motioned for the six-foot two-inch, green-eyed man to sit next to the polygraph.

"I...uh...I'm not taking a lie detector test. Those things have been proven scientifically untrustworthy. I know the law. You cannot require me to take the test, nor can you fire me if I don't."

"Yeah, well I can break your face if you don't." Holiday made a menacing movement toward Hardwood.

"Hold on, Harry." John put his hand to Holiday's chest and stopped him. "The man is correct on both counts. You don't want to force him or intimidate him into taking a polygraph exam."

"Okay. That's fine. I'll lock him up for the murder of Hires." Again John had to hold him back.

"Lots of luck on that, buddy. You don't have any evidence for that charge," hollered Hardwood.

"I'll lock your ass up until I do. Now, you stupid brainiac, how much luck do you think I need to do that?"

"Come on, Harry. You know better than that," advised John. "We can't lock him up on just suspicion."

Holiday stared at Hardwood for a few seconds, and then said, "We're dealing with national security. I can detain him under suspicion of espionage. Hell, we might even send him to Guantanamo."

"Wha—What are you saying? Are you accu-sing me...of spying?" stammered Hardwood.

"Congratulations, your doctorate taught you the definition of espionage." Holiday raised both arms up and out to shoulder level to emphasize his sarcasm. "Now, all we have to do is figure to which terrorist group you're giving the classified information."

"Why are you doing this to me? I'm no killer and I'm certainly not a spy. What is the matter with you?"

"Then why in the hell did you run?" yelled a frustrated Holiday. "Innocent men don't run."

"That's none of your business. It was for personal reasons. It had nothing to do with your damn classified information."

"Look, gentlemen, although I'm using that word loosely at this point. Why don't you both calm down. Harry, you got me out of bed. I'm half asleep. Would you please drive over to the Waffle House and bring back a large cup of tea for me?" requested John as he moved a chair in front of Hardwood.

"I guess I could use some air. You're right. I do need to calm down. The more I look at this guy the madder I get."

"How about a coffee, Doctor?" asked John.

"I see what's going on. You're using the old 'good cop-bad cop' routine on me," announced Hardwood. "Well it isn't going to work on me. As far as I'm concerned, you're both morons."

"Hey, jerk, the man's trying to be nice. Do you want the damn coffee or not?" Holiday glared at him.

"I'd like a coffee, black. Don't think your tricks are going to work on me. I'm on to what you're pulling."

"Please, Doctor, I think you watch far too much television. No one is trying to trick you in any way. I think you have to agree. Though your running does cause suspicion. We do need to have a talk," offered John.

Hardwood didn't answer. He shrugged his shoulders in silent response. He sat down in front of John, leaned back in his chair and crossed his arms and legs while looking suspiciously at John.

"Do I need to cuff you to the chair?" asked Holiday. "I want to make sure you're here when I return."

"No, I'm not running. How could you possibly think I would pass up free coffee?" replied Hardwood sarcastically.

"John, if he even rises up out of that chair…shoot him. We'll make up a cover story when I get back." Holiday turned and left the room.

"Mister; who the hell are you anyway? What the hell agency do you work for?" demanded Hardwood.

"You seem to have our little meeting backward. You see, I'm supposed to be the person asking the questions. But, I can understand your concern. My name is John Bodie. I'm a criminal investigator and polygraphist. I'm presently working for the Department of Homeland Security. At this time, I'm investigating the murder of Martha Hires, an employee of our federal government."

"What's this spy crap you're trying to accuse me of? Is someone in our group stealing classified information?"

"Agent Holiday will talk to you about that. Right now, I'm only interested in your possible involvement with the murder of Miss Hires."

"This is just insane. I happened to like Martha Hires. I didn't kill anybody and I didn't do any spying."

"Doctor, if all that you say is true, if you are as innocent as you say you are, why not take the test?"

"I told you they are not accurate. I'm a scientist. I know all about the body and how it responds to stimuli."

"The rumors you've heard are just that. If I can prove to you that they are accurate beyond a doubt; would you be interested?"

"Why would I be interested?" Hardwood looked hard at John.

"Doctor, you said you're an educated man. However, you aren't showing me that your education has made you smart."

"What do you mean by that insult?" Hardwood leaned forward in his chair and glared at John.

"You need to think logically. A 'no deception' polygraph will remove you from suspicion. Holiday will owe you an apology. Everyone will know that you are one of the good guys. Can't you understand that?"

Hardwood sat back and stared down at the floor for a full minute. John waited silently. Then he looked up at John and asked, "How do you expect to convince me that the instrument is infallible?"

"I won't ask you anything about Hires or spying." John noticed an array of colored pens in a rack behind the sergeant's desk. "I'll have you pick a color and let's see if the polygraph can identify it."

Again Hardwood stared for a minute, but this time it was at the polygraph. "If you say one word about Hires or spying, I'm yanking that shit off. I know a little bit about polygraph. I've had a couple and I've read about them, so no tricks."

"You got it. If you recall from the previous examinations, we have a lot to do in the pretest interview. I need to know more about you, personally. We also need to formulate the questions."

"No way in hell are we going to discuss anything about me until you prove that damn thing works. There's absolutely no sense in wasting either your time or mine if that instrument doesn't work."

"You win." John rolled his chair around behind the desk and began to color little squares. He used the colors: red, blue, green, yellow, purple, brown and black. When finished, he rolled the chair back in front of Hardwood. The paper with the colors was placed on his chair, and the finger probes, blood pressure cuff and pneumograph tubes were attached to the doctor.

"Okay, Doctor, this a simple test. All you have to do is pick a color and don't tell me what color you picked."

Hardwood picked his color. John told him to write that color down on the piece of paper he gave him, and place it under his hand. John looked away as Hardwood complied with his request.

Half way through the test John noticed a spike in the galvanic skin response and the blood pressure. He also noted a smaller rise in all three testing elements on a different color. When finished, he shut the instrument down released the pressure in the cuff and shook his head slowly and slightly.

"What? Is there a problem? I knew it. I just knew it. I told you the thing wouldn't work on me."

"The instrument is infallible. It talked to me and proved you've read about the polygraph."

"What do you mean?"

"Examiners are trained and tried daily by people like you. I'm not trained or educated in your field of expertise. I couldn't begin to figure out what you do at work. Why do you think you are smart enough to best me at mine? I would think an educated individual would be smart enough to not even try."

"Try? Try what? What are you talking about? How am I trying to best you at your work?"

"You damn well know what I'm talking about. I'm talking about you squeezing your sphincter muscle. How can you not know that we are trained in countermeasures? This should be your first indication now that the polygraph works. If it is obvious to me that you're squeezing your ass, then it should be obvious to you the instrument works. I mean the instrument told me that."

Hardwood did his best to look shocked and indignant. "I don't know what you're talking about!"

"You told me you know all about the body. So, I think you do know what I'm talking about. You can't possibly be that dense and have the education you have. We'll try it again and I'd advise you not to do that this time."

The test began again. This time there was a lesser spike on the same color but the color that had a lesser spike the first time, now had a bigger rise this time. The instrument was shut down and the pressure in the cuff released.

John let out a sigh and looked at Hardwood. "Doctor, scrunching up your toes is as old as the hills. Of course we can identify that. You are attempting to deceive on the color yellow. Hand me the paper on which you wrote 'purple'."

The doctor looked genuinely shocked. Then he let out a sigh and handed John the paper on which he had written the word 'purple'. "You're good."

"Doctor, only guilty people attempt to manipulate the instrument. I ask you now. Did you kill Martha Hires?"

"No, I did not."

"Are you comfortable with that answer?"

"Yes."

"Now that you know the instrument works, are you willing to take a polygraph to prove your innocence?"

Hardwood let out a sigh and again looked down at the floor. Seconds passed. John waited.

chapter

NINE

"All right, all right, I'll take the damn test," exclaimed Hardwood. "But, no tricks, you understand?"

"You got it. I promise you, no tricks. Let's take a quick trip through your history. I nee…."

"Whoa, right there!" Hardwood interrupted John. "My history is not relevant to anything involved in this test. I don't know what you're trying to prove."

"There is no way I can test you without additional information. I need to know a little bit about you."

The doctor reached over on the desk and picked up his personnel folder. "It appears that you already know a little about me. Let's just get on with the questions you're going to ask."

"It's not ethical but we can try it your way. Let's start with some easy ones. Is your last name Hardwood?"

"Yes"

"Were you born in Sparta, Wisconsin?"

"Yes"

"Is there something else you're afraid I'll ask you, even though I told you I would not?"

"No"

"Regarding the killing of Martha Hires; do you intend to answer truthfully each question about that?"

"Yes"

"Did you kill Martha Hires?"

"Not only no, but hell no," stated Hardwood irritably.

"You have to answer the questions with only one syllable answers. Use either 'yes' or 'no' and make sure you keep the tone of voice the same."

"All right."

"Try it again," said John fighting hard not to show his frustration.

"Did you kill Martha Hires?"

"No"

"Did you cut Martha Hires with a knife?"

"No"

"Do you know who killed Martha Hires?"

"No"

John continued with a few more questions and then repeated them again to Hardwood. Then he attached the finger probes, tubes and cuff to the scientist.

He calibrated the instrument and began the test. After the third-chart he shut the instrument down and removed the probes. Hardwood stood, stretched and rubbed his arm. John removed the charts from the instrument.

Holiday, who had been waiting outside the office door with coffees, came in. "Is everyone ready for an eye opener?" He handed John his coffee then gave the doctor his. "How about it, John, have we found our killer?"

"Harry, do me a favor and take the good doctor out on the deck while I go over his charts."

"No problem, John. I'd be glad to." Holiday motioned for Hardwood to follow him. Hardwood knew he had no choice and quickly complied.

John went over the charts and there was something very wrong. He hadn't seen anything like this in six-years. He had to break the doctor and find the truth. Something bothered Hardwood more than the murder.

John looked up and out the window of the office at Holiday. He motioned him to come in and bring Hardwood with him. He placed the doctor in the straight-back chair in front of the desk, after which he rolled the desk chair around in front of him. Their knees were a foot-apart.

"What's up? I know I didn't kill anybody," said Hardwood, wide eyed. "Come on, I did not kill Martha."

"I don't know if you did or didn't," replied John. "But, there is one glaring lie on the examination."

"What do you mean?" Hardwood rose out of the chair. Holiday moved quickly and pushed him back down.

"I mean your psychological threat was so strong on other questions it masked the relevant questions."

"What in hell are you talking about?" The scientist began to squirm in his seat. "Say that in English."

"I'm talking about the name you gave me and where you were born. Who the hell are you?"

"I'm Paul Hardwood. I was born in Sparta, Wisconsin. It's right there in my file. Damn. If you can't figure that out, how in God's name are you ever going to find out if I'm innocent of murder?"

"There is no way in hell you're Paul Hardwood," accused John, "and God only knows where you were born."

John and Holiday interrogated Hardwood for eight solid hours. It was Sunday noon when thirty hours without sleep took its toll on the doctor. He finally broke under John's questioning.

"Paul Hardwood and I were best friends all through college. He was smart and had a great future. His parents died and left him a considerable amount of money while we were in school. We celebrated pretty heavy that night. I passed out. He must have passed out and dropped the bottle. It broke and he fell out of the chair onto it. Paul bled to death."

"What did you do?" asked Holiday.

"I sat and stared for an hour or so. I was the playboy. I owed money. A girl was suing me for support of her baby. My only money came from Paul as his assistant. We looked a lot alike. People thought we were brothers."

"So you decided to take up his identity?" questioned John. "For some reason, I can see that happening."

"It made sense. He didn't need it anymore. I decided that I needed his identity more than he did."

"What did you do with Paul's body?" asked Holiday. "How did you dispose of a corpse that you didn't want found?"

"You're right. I didn't want his body found. We were in Jacksonville, Florida, so I drove up to Manor, Georgia and slipped him in the crocodile infested Okefenokee Swamp. That was twenty-five years ago."

"Well, I guess at this point the main question is what is your real name?" demanded John.

"Jason McFee."

"Well, Jason, I'm going to test you again using your true identity and see how you do." John began to ready the instrument.

"I'll pass because I didn't kill anyone. That question was the only one that bothered me on the test."

John went through the testing procedure again, and as McFee stated, there was no deception indicated. Holiday took him down to the Maricopa County jail and put a hold on him for Homeland Security. Holiday called his second-in-command in D.C. to come and get McFee. They would sort out the mess in Washington.

John sat alone after Holiday and McFee left. *If the killer isn't here, then he must be at I and J's. It's 2:25 p.m., and since it's Sunday, the restaurant closed at 2:00. I'm too tired to redo the poly on Rachael today. I'm just going back to the room and sleep.*

"Rachael, I have something I need to tell you." Holiday rolled over on his elbow and looked at her.

"Oh, crap! You're married. I knew it," said a wide eyed Rachael. She sat straight up in bed. "Just when it was getting comfortable you come up with that."

"No, no way. That's not it. I'm definitely not married. God, no! I've never even been close."

"Whew. That's better. Why'd you scare me like that? I finally get comfortable with you and trust you...."

"Listen, I have to trust you. What I'm about to tell you, must remain between you and me, oh yeah...and John, too."

"Oh, crap! You and John are bisexual. I should have known. It's always the good looking ones."

"No, damn it. This is important. We didn't come down here to find Hires' killer." Holiday sat up beside her.

"Then why are you here? You sure have been putting a lot of time and effort into it. You could have fooled me."

"It's more of a matter of national security. Someone is breaking into the classified files at night."

Rachael wrinkled her brow and cocked her head to the side, "How could you possibly know that?"

"Hires called our headquarters and told us. But, before we could get down here, she was killed."

"Did she say who it was?" Rachael threw off the sheets and started to adjust her position.

"She knew and was going to tell me when I got here. I'm sure that's why she was killed."

"That's silly, Harry. None of the scientist nerds would have the backbone for something like that. If they see a spider they call me to kill it." Rachael turned and sat on her ankles facing Holiday.

Holiday's expression was serious as he held her shoulders in his hands. "What I'm saying is that I have to find out who is leaking classified information."

"I never had any indication of such a thing. Remember, I'm in charge of security in the lab. What made Martha think someone was getting into her files? How could she have known something like that?"

"She slipped a piece of paper between the file drawer and the cabinet when she left for the night. The next morning it it was on the floor."

"Hell, Harry, it could have just fallen out."

"That's possible, but she was adamant even to the point of knowing who it was. I've got to know for sure."

"I'll help any way I can. You know that. Now that they have placed me in charge of the files, I'm in a position to give you all the help you need." She leaned over on Holiday and pushed him down onto the bed. She lay on top of him as she said, "You know me. I'm good at positions."

———

John managed twelve hours of solid sleep. He awoke at 5:30 a.m. on a bright and sunny Monday morning. After a shave and shower and getting dressed he realized how long it had been since he had eaten. He rushed over to the Cracker Barrel across the street and ordered 'Uncle Hershel's' with extra grits and hold the gravy. He enjoyed eating alone. It gave him time to think.

He had the two lists given to him by Isabel. He read them over and over. He needed input on the names. I and J's didn't open until 5:00 p.m. on Mondays. He drove over to Wal-Mart, purchased a bathing suit then returned to the hotel. Swimming helped him clear the cobwebs from his head. He showered again, dressed and called Polly. They had lunch and spent the afternoon together.

Polly gave her opinions about the names on the list. There were a few she didn't know, but had seen in the restaurant on several occasions. There were five customers whose names were unknown to anyone. They had been taken from the reservation list. She was sure none of the people she knew on the list would have killed Hires.

They arrived at the restaurant at 4:30 p.m. Isabel was just unlocking the chain on the entrance gate. They followed five of the karaoke singers inside. It seemed several of the karaoke people would arrive early, so that they could get their names higher on the list of singers.

Isabel became occupied with taking people's orders. However, she took time to look at the list and mention that she had seen three of the no-names in before, but it was the first time in for the two men John and Holiday had encountered. John and Polly decided to wait to place their order. Holiday and Rachael came in just as Isabel left the table.

They were finishing their meals when the KJ, Arnie started the music for the night with 'Old Violin'. His wife, Sandie, the equipment operator, was next with 'Whispering Winds'. It was standard for the KJ and his wife to open up the evening. Sammy started off the karaoke singers, as usual, with an excellent rendition of a Frank Sinatra song.

The restaurant was occupied with about an equal number of singers and listeners. The din from the laughter and conversation was just a few decibels less than the music, yet most people managed to applaud after every singer, no matter how well they sang. All were enjoying food, drink, camaraderie and songs.

Julie just finished her version of 'When I Fall in Love'. Jasiu was chewing the last bite of his BLT sandwich when a commotion occurred on the dance floor in front of the KJ. Julie reached out to hand the microphone to Arnie.

An inebriated individual took the microphone before Arnie could reach it. The man said he wanted to sing. Arnie did his best to convince the man that he could sing, but he had to put his name on the list and wait his turn. The person would not listen. He was adamant that he was going to sing. The drunk became obnoxious and crude, using foul language.

Isabel called to José, who immediately came over to Arnie. They took the microphone from the man and with one on each side, took him out of the restaurant. Ira, wanting to assist, followed them out. Once out on the sidewalk, Arnie attempted to talk the individual into leaving.

He pulled loose from Arnie and swung at José. José moved enough that it was a glancing blow. Arnie swung quick and hard, but the drunk ducked and the punch landed square on the side of Ira's head. He went straight to the sidewalk. José started low and came up hard and fast connecting on the inebriate's chin. He fell backward and slowly slid down the side of the building and then fell over.

They helped the dazed Ira up onto his feet. Once they were sure Ira was stable enough to stand on his own, the two men sat the unconscious individual, on the sidewalk, up against the building. "Should we call the police?" asked Arnie.

"No, give the poor guy a chance to sleep it off and go home. If he comes back in, then we'll call the police," answered José.

They helped a shaky Ira back to his table. Isabel prepared a small bag of ice for the swelling on his cheekbone. Jasiu enjoyed Ira's story immensely. Every time he looked at Ira he would laugh.

"I've been coming here for five years, and I have never seen anything like this happen before," said Polly.

"It sure makes for an interesting night," offered John. "I don't want to leave. The idiot may come back."

"I've never seen that guy in here before," stated Rachael. "I'll bet he's not even a local dude."

"He's probably a winter visitor who came down a little early enjoying his visit a bit too much," murmured Polly.

"He's probably some swabby who escaped from his ship," offered John. His exaggerated smile received dirty looks from both Rachael and Holiday. "Well he sure wasn't Army. If he was, the three gentlemen who went out with him wouldn't have been the ones to come back in."

"Cut John off. He's drunker than the guy who just left," said Rachael. Everyone but John laughed.

The men who propped the drunk up against the building had no sooner returned to the restaurant than Jasmine parked in the lot next to the building. She was attempting to get in on the third round of singing. She usually came late and got in one song.

Jasmine was amazingly attractive for a seventy-eight year old. She still possessed the body of a school-girl and her energy was comparable as well. Her boyfriend was twenty years younger and had a hard time keeping up with her.

The lady hurriedly removed the key from the ignition and picked up her purse. She opened the car door and was shocked when it was snatched from her hand. Jasmine looked up just in time to see light reflect off the blade of the knife as it was on its way to her heart. There wasn't any time to cry out. She grabbed at her breast as the knife was slowly pulled from the soft flesh. The blood was wiped on the leg of her tight fitting white jeans. The door was closed and the assailant walked away.

After Jan, the tall, statuesque school teacher, sang 'My Man' in the second round, she gathered her music and purse and went to the register. Jasiu noticed she was leaving by herself. He rushed over and joined her by the door. He walked the strikingly attractive lady out to her car and saw her safely away.

John and Polly were swing dancing to 'Bad, Bad Leroy Brown' expertly sung by Pearl. Holiday and Rachael were deep in conversation when her cell phone rang. She looked at it and decided it was not important enough to disturb her conversation with this hunk, to whom she had luckily attached herself.

By nine o'clock Arnie finished the last song of the evening. There was an abundance of hugs and quick kisses among the singers as they prepared to leave. As usual, Fred had to visit with each one and he and Scooter were the last out.

Rachael and Polly waited patiently while John and Holiday remained to talk to Arnie and Sandie about their knowledge of the customers. Most had followed them from previous places in which they had performed. They've been at I and J's for the last five years and never experienced any problems involving customers before.

Julie came running in, yelling, "Call the police. Call the police. There's been another killing." It wasn't until most of the customers left after karaoke was over that Jasmine's car was noticed.

chapter

TEN

While the police and medical examiner were investigating and clearing the crime scene, John talked with Arnie, and Holiday talked with Sandie. They were questioned on their feelings about the regulars and any knowledge they may have about the newcomers.

Arnie was quite candid. He was absolutely positive none of the regulars would do such a thing and most couldn't do it. The majority of the clientele were senior citizens.

He went down the list: "Fred and Scooter are in their eighties; Big Jack is a typical New Yorker, who imitates Jimmy Durante and moves so slow the victim could be a block away before he got the knife out. Sammy is another New Yorker, but he's totally harmless. He and his girlfriend are always the first into the restaurant.

"Now, Jasiu, being ex-military, is physically capable, but he doesn't come here on Tuesdays and he's always with his wife. We had one killed last Tuesday. Ira has had massive heart surgery and couldn't do it. Little Jack wouldn't hurt a fly. Jerome and Pete always come here with their wives.

"These people have been coming here for years. They're like a family. In fact we call them our karaoke family. They care about and support each other.

"Oh yeah...there's fast draw Bo and his fast draw wife, Maurine. If either of them were to kill anyone, it would be with a gun. But there, again, they're the nicest people and have been coming here for years as well."

"Is there anyone not on the list?" asked John. "I'm sure it's possible that a new person comes in now and then. Someone you don't know."

"Certainly, customers come in every night that I haven't seen before. This is a busy restaurant. It gets a lot of traffic. Some of them are drinkers at the bar, others are diners and listeners.

"If they're singers, their names will be on that board. If your name is not on the board, you don't sing. There was a couple whose names I can't remember right now. But they're regulars and have been coming here for a long time and have never caused trouble. I haven't seen them in a couple of weeks." Arnie held his cup for Natalie to refill.

"How about your Tuesday night customers? Is it the same bunch or do you get a big turnover?" John took a drink of his iced tea.

"Pretty much the same crowd. A few only come on Monday. Most come both days. The biggest difference is the family."

"Family?"

"Yeah. Tyler and Sylvia bring three to seven of their family. They're all senior citizens. Tyler and Sylvia were married in this restaurant and celebrated their anniversary here. One of Sylvia's children was married here. There is no way they could be suspect. They're some of the nicest people you'll ever meet."

"It looks as though we need to look at the newcomers." John sat back in his chair and tossed his pen on the table. He couldn't help but smile remembering when Chief Ortega did that. *Oh my God, I'm starting to get just like him.*

"Like I said, most of our customers are senior citizens. However, there have been a couple of guys that show up now and then. They never sing. They just eat, watch and listen to the singers."

"Did you see them here tonight?"

Arnie paused for a moment and after much thought said, "No. I guess I didn't see them tonight."

"Arnie, Harry and I will be here tomorrow night. Would you point out anyone that you do not recognize or is not a regular?"

"Sure. I'll be glad to do it. Sandie and I will help any way we can. We don't need this kind of publicity for the restaurant."

Sandie's descriptions of the customers matched Arnie's. John and Holiday were interrupted and questioned by the homicide detectives. Rachael and Polly were more than ready to leave by the time all the questioning was over. Holiday went home with Rachael and John drove Polly home.

"I'm sorry we kept you out so late. You must be tired." offered John. "I should probably go back to the motel."

"Sometimes when you're tired you can still run the race. You just run it slower. A nice slow race can beat a fast one most of the time." Polly batted her eyes at him.

"I can do slow," said John grinning. "In fact, as the years pile on, I've noticed it just about takes me all night to do, what I used to be able to do all night."

"In that case, the race is on," announced Polly. John locked up the car and accompanied Polly into the house.

The slowness of the night's race was only surpassed by the intense slowness of the morning race. They were both impressed with each other's stamina. The two enjoyed a joint shower and then dressed. Polly prepared pancakes and bacon for breakfast. They chatted all through breakfast and doing the dishes. John talked about some of his cases and Polly talked about her life as a postal worker and poet.

Holiday went to work with Rachael. It was time he discovered the contents of the files. This would answer the question of the extent of the risk to national security. The information was shocking. He had no idea. His thoughts were interrupted with the ringing of his cell phone.

"Hey, Harry, where are you?" John pulled away from the curb and out into traffic.

"At the lab. I'm working. Where are you? Aren't you supposed to be working as well, old buddy?"

"I guess. I'm on the way to the lab."

"Good thinking. We need to put our heads together. It's important."

"On the way, wait."

John, Holiday and the young Sergeant Steel sat around the security supervisor's desk. The sergeant had his elbows on the desk and his chin in his hands. Holiday sat in front of the desk with his legs crossed and John stretched out in his chair.

John was the first to speak. "This is a top secret facility. No one knows it's here. The only way information could leak is from someone on the inside. That being the case, I think we are spinning our wheels nosing around the restaurant. Our killer has to be here."

"Unless there is more than one person involved. Like maybe a group. The person leaking the info is giving it to someone who killed Hires and is keeping up the killings to cover it up," suggested Holiday.

Sergeant Steel offered, "Yeah, that may be true and it could also be two totally unrelated situations."

"The last time this happened here, about six years ago, the chief of security was working with that foreign terrorist group," said John.

"Hey, Sir, let's not go there. I'm innocent." Sergeant Steel sat up wide-eyed and straight.

Laughing, John continued, "We know that, Sergeant. What I'm saying is some outside source is getting the information. Maybe we should look for the receiving source. The informant has to be getting the info to them somehow."

"John, I guess I could bring my team down and follow the employees for a few days," offered Holiday.

"That would take too long, Harry."

The trio tossed around ideas for the next hour. Rachael came up and said it was time for lunch. She recommended Denny's, because it was close and the service was fast.

Once they were settled in and the orders placed, the discussions started up again. "Wait a minute. I just thought of something. Didn't Hires say it was happening at night?" queried John.

"Yeah. So?" said Holiday.

"Isn't the key to the cabinet kept at the military police desk down stairs?" John continued.

"I see what you're saying. The leak could be one of the military policemen. They weren't polygraphed about the leak, only the killing. Damn, John, I think you're onto something."

"I don't like where this is going. You suspect one of my men as being the leak?" asked Steel with a frown.

"It makes sense," stated Holiday.

"None of my men have ever been in the lab. They wouldn't even know which files to look in."

"How do you know they have never been in the lab?" questioned John. "You're not here at night."

"It's simple. They have not been allowed access to the Iris Identification System. I am the only one with that clearance. Whoa." Sergeant Steel put both hands up in front of him as though he was stopping something. "Don't even think what I think you're thinking. I've never been in there at night. My men make me sign in any time I go in there."

"The Sergeant very seldom comes down there," added Rachael.

"Okay, how does the key get from the MP desk to the filing cabinet? Can you answer that?" Holiday slapped his hand down on the table.

The four of them sat in silence for a minute. Finally, John spoke up. "The MP is either friendly or in cahoots with someone who does have that Iris thingy clearance."

"Now I think we're getting someplace." Holiday reached for his drink as soon as the waitress set it down.

"How do you find the MP that's involved?" Rachael unwrapped her silverware.

"That's easy. It's called polygraph." John looked at Rachael and raised both hands above the table, palms up.

"When do you want to start?" questioned Holiday.

John turned to Steel. "When can you get the first body?"

"Start with me and then we'll do the remainder of the guys that are working. If you want to work late," Steel cleared his throat, "we can do the oncoming shift."

"Well, what do you say we start with the present personnel and see what happens," offered John.

The food arrived. Everyone became quiet as they consumed their orders. There was no room for dessert and they were soon on their way back to the warehouse. Rachael waved to the men as she headed down to the lab. The trio moved up the steps to the security office to prepare for the polygraphs.

The ten questions on the test were similar to the previous test that the MPs had taken. The relevant questions were quite different. The questions were:

"Did you ever give the key to the files to anyone who did not sign for it?"

"Did you ever allow anyone in the lab at night with the key to the files?"

"Do you know who entered the lab at night with the key to the files?"

There was no deception indicated with Sergeant Steel and the military police shift sergeants. John decided to do more on Wednesday. He wanted to get over to I and J's and watch out for the karaoke singers.

Holiday and Rachael found a table inside, but John elected to sit in the car outside and keep a lookout for the killer. Polly sat with him. No suspicious activity was noted until 8:30 p.m.

Two of the male singers came outside and engaged in a shouting match. It appeared that one of the men accused the other of stealing his song. Just as the men began throwing punches, Ira came out and tried to break them up. John couldn't tell which man did it, but Ira was struck in the face and wound up on the sidewalk for the second time in two nights. John jumped out of the car and ran over to him. The two-men saw John coming and left in a hurry. John helped him up.

"Thanks for the help, cowboy. This is getting to be a habit. It's almost like people are just looking for a reason to punch me out."

"What makes you think that? I've heard you sing and you're not that bad."

"Thanks...I think." Ira returned to the restaurant and John to the car.

A few minutes later, the skinheads, Tolman and Hobbs, parked the black Toyota Camry across from the entrance to the restaurant. After sitting for a few minutes they went inside. Tyler was just finishing a superb version of Elvis's 'Trilogy'. Of course Jasiu and his wife stood during the 'Dixie' portion of the song.

Holiday spotted the two guys as they entered. This time they went to the bar. After ordering, they turned and looked at Holiday and Rachael. Tolman nodded to them. Holiday and Rachael returned the nod.

John and Polly were especially watchful as the customers were leaving. He watched closely as the skinheads left. When it appeared all the singers and listeners left, they joined Holiday and Rachael inside.

"Harry, what do you think our hillbilly duo was doing here tonight?" was the first thing John asked.

"It was strange. It was as if they just wanted us to know that they're still around. I don't think we want to turn our backs on them."

"I agree."

"Did they leave or are they still out there?" asked Rachael.

"No, they're gone. At least they drove away. Of course they may have just circled the block and are out there waiting for us," suggested John.

"Thanks for that piece of information. Maybe we'll let you guys go out first and see what happens," said Polly.

John noticed the svelte body of Isabel approach. He turned to her and asked, "I know it's late and everything is shut down. Sitting out there all night made us hungry. Is there anything to eat?"

"How would you like to have a nice big piece of carrot cake?"

"Can I have iced tea with it?"

"Why, sure." Isabel gave a friendly smile.

"Make that two," ordered Polly.

Arnie and Sandie joined them and the conversation was again about the customers. Neither of them had any idea who the skinheads were. Isabel thought it was strange that they ordered one drink and left.

John and Polly finished their shower and were heading for bed when John's cell phone rang. "Come on. This is no time for a call." He looked at the caller ID and immediately opened the flap. "What now, Harry?"

"Steel just called. He said one of his MPs was just killed in a hit and run earlier this evening."

"Do you want me to go with you to talk to the investigating officers?"

"That won't be necessary. Steel and I can handle it. Get back to whatever you were doing and I'll fill you in tomorrow."

"Thank you for that. See ya *mañana*."

"John, I'm not really tired but I sure would like another one of those slow races." Polly strolled over to him and placed her hand on his chest.

"You're my kind of woman."

"And what kind would that be?" She looked at him with eyes filled with desire.

"A woman who isn't afraid to ask when she feels like a race."

———

Colonel Basset, Sergeant Steel, his shift sergeant and Holiday were in Steel's office when John arrived Wednesday morning. The meeting was somber. Sergeant Steel was preparing the 'Flash Report' for the Colonel to submit to his commander.

"Have you got the accident report?" asked John.

"It's on the desk. But I don't think it tells the real story behind the accident," advised Holiday.

"What do you mean?" John picked up the report.

"Witnesses said it looked like the driver lost control of the car and it swerved into the young man as he crossing the street. Then it kept going."

"Did they give any description?" John lowered the accident report.

"It was a black midsized car. They didn't get any of the license plate info." Steel was quick to offer that information.

John stared at the report for a few seconds and then looked up at Holiday. He gave a slight motion with his head indicating that he wanted Holiday to follow him out of the room and onto the platform. He made it a point to move away from the door.

"Harry, what do you want to bet this was the MP who could have told who was in the lab at night."

"That idea had entered my mind. I didn't give it much thought, but now that you mention it, I'm afraid you're right."

"What time did it occur?" John scanned the report for the time.

"The accident report lists the time at 7:48 p.m." informed Harry.

"We had a black midsize car show up at I and J's at 8:30 p.m."

"I forgot that our hillbilly buddies drove a black car. Good thinking, John. I'll call Francis and have her get in contact with Tennessee and Georgia and look for any vehicle registered to our southern gentlemen."

"Sounds like a plan. Oh, and Harry, we don't have any dates of birth but give her an idea of their ages and see if she can get anything on them."

"You got it."

John set up his polygraph and tested four MPs...none of whom, indicated deception. He sat staring at the floor after the last one left. *Whoever's doing this is thorough. They seem to be one step ahead of us all the way. Has the leak stopped? Is it still going on? Have they gotten what they need and it's over?"*

He put away his instrument and walked, with a slow, thoughtful pace, to the car. Holiday and Rachael had gone. He decided to have another health night. He picked up an order to go at Uncle Sam's Pizza and took it to his room. He opened a bottle of Lambrusco and ate his mushroom and sausage delight. His concentration never strayed from the mystery at hand.

chapter

ELEVEN

John rolled and tossed throughout the night. He felt as though there was something very obvious that he was missing. He was just as tired when he awoke as when he went to bed. His mind kept jumping from one thing to another. What was he missing?

He sat up and slid his feet to the floor. John rubbed his face and head as he sat there on the side of the bed. His eyes were dry and didn't want to open. Finally he strolled over to his shaving kit and found the bottle of 'Artificial Tears'. A couple of drops in each eye helped. He wondered why combing his hair, brushing his teeth, and shaving seemed like such a monumental effort this morning.

The Cracker Barrel was his favorite, but he felt like something different today. He headed for Denny's and the 'Moons Over My Hammy' sandwich. While waiting for his meal he noticed the two guys from Tennessee and Georgia. They either didn't recognize him or chose to ignore him. John watched closely as they left the restaurant. This time they entered a gray Dodge Avenger. John repeated the tag number over and over until he could get his pad and pen out and copy it down. The sandwich and hash browns arrived just a he was calling Holiday.

"Harry, those two skinheads are not driving that black car any longer. They're driving a gray Dodge."

"How long ago did they leave? Which way did they go? John, did you get the tag number?"

"Gee, I never thought of that…of course I got it." John gave him the number.

Holiday said he'd run it down. "When are you coming in?"

"I'm right in the middle of breakfast. I guess I'll be there just as soon as I finish eating. What's up?"

"I'm questioning the employees about the classified files."

"I'll hurry. See you soon."

———

"Hey, Al, did you see that dude who came into the café just before we left?" asked Tolman.

"You mean the dude with the Army baseball cap and the 'Oath Keepers' shirt? He looked familiar."

"Hell, he ought to. Him and that other guy are the ones that jumped us in the parking lot the other night."

"Damn! You're right, bro. Now that you mention it, I remember seeing him last night in the restaurant."

"Do you suppose he's following us?" Tolman took his eyes off the road and looked over at Hobbs.

"No, man, I checked him out. He was still in the restaurant when we left. I'm not sure he even saw us."

"Why don't we follow him, then? It would be interesting to see where he goes when he leaves."

"I don't know, Cleduus. What would it prove?"

"Think about it. He will probably go straight to work. We can find out who he is working for."

"You're right. That could be interesting. It might even tell us why he hassled us the other night."

Tolman took the off ramp from I-10 onto Avondale Blvd and turned west on McDowell. They turned into the parking lot off Litchfield Ave and parked behind Denny's. The two men didn't have long to wait.

John hurried out to his car. "The notebook, damn it. I forgot the notebook. Now I've got to stop back at the motel." John said aloud not caring who heard. He thought to himself, *Wouldn't you know it? When you're in hurry; you do something stupid like this.* His focus was on his mistake. He didn't look in the rearview mirror as he left the parking lot.

He parked close to the entrance and rushed in and over to the elevator. By the time Tolson parked and the two men entered the lobby, John had disappeared. They decided to stand by the elevator. Their plan worked. Within minutes the elevator doors opened and John started out. He was immediately shoved back in. Hobbs reached over and yanked the key out of John's hand.

"Cleduus, push number 4." Hobbs smiled at John. "You're gonna have a couple of visitors, good buddy."

The two skinheads led John back to his room. Hobbs unlocked it, opened the door and shoved John inside. The door was quickly closed.

"You and your buddy had your fun the other night. Now it's time for me and my buddy to have fun," said Tolman.

Hobbs swung a punch and hit John on the side of the head. "Now that's for not lying to us. You can imagine what's going to happen if you do lie to us."

John straightened, glared hard at Hobbs and said, "So, what in the hell do you want to know?"

"For starters, tough guy, who's trying to impress us with his Army hat," said Hobbs, "Who the hell are you?"

"Bodie. John Bodie's the name. Now, that didn't tell you a damn thing did it?" He was looking at Hobbs when Tolman hit him.

"We also inflict pain when you smart-mouth us, Bubba. If I were you, I'd make up my mind right now to talk real respectful like to us."

"Who do you work for?" questioned Hobbs.

"I'm a police detective in a little town in Washington State."

"What the hell are you doing down here, hassling us?"

"I'm visiting a friend."

"Give me your wallet, Mister Detective."

John handed over the credentials case that he used as a wallet. Tolman snatched it out of his hand. He flipped it open and saw the badge.

"Well. Old Bubba is telling the truth about being a cop. Now, tell me who your friend is you're visiting."

"He's a retired U. S. Navy S.E.A.L. and has some kind of government job down here now."

"You can do a hell of a lot better than that," said Tolman as Hobbs punched John in the stomach. John saw it coming and tightened his abdominal muscles. He barely felt it.

"You didn't hurt yourself, I hope," said John with a smile.

"I warned you about that smart-mouth, dude." stated Hobbs. "I want to hurt you some more. So watch what you say."

"Hell, it's some kind of secret job and he can't even tell me about it. I know better than to ask."

"That's a bunch of bull shit, Bubba." Tolman swung at John. John blocked it and hit Tolman square in the face with his elbow, splattering both of them with blood.

Hobbs moved in and John kicked hard and fast into Hobbs' crotch. He bent over and John lifted his knee as hard and fast as he could into Hobbs' face. Hobbs went flying backward and landed, unconscious, on the floor.

Tolman came at John and swung his right arm. John stepped inside and threw his left arm over, and encircled Tolman's right arm. He yanked up hard and John felt the dislocation as Tolman hollered out in pain. John punched him hard in the face and Tolman went down, holding his right arm.

John walked over to the night stand and lifted out his snubnose .38. "This is just to let you jerks know playtime is over." He called Holiday, who was pleased to say he was on the way.

"Now, BUBBA." John emphasized the word 'bubba'. "Why don't you tell me what you, and sleeping beauty over there are doing in this town? Don't give me that crap about vacation. That's my line. People on vacation don't concern themselves with who other people work for. They especially don't beat the hell out of them to find out."

"Screw you, man. I don't have to tell you nothin'." Tolman crossed his arms in defiance. He couldn't help wincing when he moved his right arm.

"You are so wrong, old buddy. You're going to talk...non-stop...before we're through with you." John pulled him to his feet by his right arm.

"Ow, damn it. Ow, that hurts," Tolman cried out. As soon as he was on his feet he backed away from John.

"When my Navy friend gets through with you, you're going to think water-boarding is just a facial massage."

"I don't know why you are doing this to us. We're the real Americans in this country. We're God-fearing, country-loving white Americans. Your kind has polluted this country with other races and religions. You've invited crime, drugs and civil disobedience to be part of our culture. You're the criminals not us. We're the true American heroes. We don't send our people out to be maimed and killed for countries that don't even like us. You never catch us burning the flag. When these other countries take over the United States and divide up into their territories, you'll wish you had supported us instead of condemning us. Mark my words it's a gonna happen."

"Now I'm beginning to get it. You're saying that you're an active member of the Aryan Nation."

Tolman clinched his fist and placed it over his heart and recited the Mantra of the Aryan Brotherhood: "An Aryan brother is without a care. He walks where the weak and heartless won't dare. For an Aryan brother, death holds no fear. Vengeance will be his through his brothers still here."

"Well, partner, you're right. You don't have to fear death. However, I would be a tad bit concerned about pain. My friend is good at that."

"You don't scare me. This government is a candy-ass when it comes to torturing people. Other countries laugh at this government, because you can't hurt anyone to make them talk."

"My friend is in a top secret organization that can do whatever it wants. You never hear of it because they bury anyone who can talk. I don't need to convince you. He will do that when he gets here."

John answered the pounding on the door. Holiday strolled into the room. He looked at the two men and broke out in a huge smile. "How in the hell did you catch these guys? I was all set for a major manhunt. This is just unbelievable." He walked over and pushed Hobbs with his foot. Hobbs did not respond.

"It was easy."

"From the blood on you and this guy, plus the unconscious fellow on the floor, it doesn't seem like it was that easy."

"I'm Army."

"Oh yeah, I forgot." Holiday laughed.

John brought him up to date on the information they had given him so far. Holiday said that he had already figured out that part. What he needed to know now is why they are here.

Tolman breathed a sigh of surrender as he explained, "Okay. Look, man...we don't need this cloak and dagger shit. We're an advance party attempting to establish a home for our organization in the area. We plan to do combat with the Mexican Mafia, *Le Eme.* They're importing tainted food. You've heard about the bugs in the rice. They're determined to take back the Southwestern United States.

"We also need to eliminate the African-American gang, 'The Black Guerilla Family'. They push more drugs than the Mexicans. We ain't no threat to you guys. Hell, white people are our friends."

"Why are you hanging around I and J's restaurant?" asked John. "I haven't seen one black or Mexican gang member in there."

"We're country boys. We like the music there. The food's good and the drinks are great and the waitress is cute too. Why not?" asked Tolman.

"Damn good argument, Harry." John went over and slapped around on the unconscious form of Hobbs until he woke up.

"Keep in mind, both my partner and I carry guns. We are excellent shots. And I'm licensed to kill. So stay the hell out of our way and if you happen to see us, make sure both your hands are empty...and smile." Holiday punched his index finger on Tolman's chest.

"Man, you don't need to worry none about us. We ain't going to be no bother to you," stated Tolman. "We got our own agenda and you ain't it. I promise we'll do our best to stay the hell away from you."

"I should turn you over to the FBI. Members of the Aryan Nation are considered to be terrorists. But we have other fish to fry. Get your butts out of here and don't mess with us again." Holiday opened the door. Tolman helped Hobbs up from the floor and they were gone.

"I don't believe this, Harry. Why in the world, are you just letting them go?" John looked at him quizzically.

"Think about it, John. If the gangs want to kill each other off, who am I to stand in their way?"

"I guess I can see the logic in that."

"Those were pretty big boys. What the hell did you do to them? I would have enjoyed seeing that."

"It's all in the wrist." John rotated his fist.

The remainder of Thursday and all day Friday John devoted his time to polygraphing the military policemen. All of them proved to be truthful. None of them had allowed anyone to enter the lab after the close of business. It became obvious the soldier was killed on purpose and not by accident.

Rachael decided to show Holiday around Yuma over the weekend. Polly had to babysit Friday night, but bright and early Saturday she and John left for the Tucson area. They spent most of the morning at the Desert Museum and the afternoon at Old

Tucson, the western movie studio. Late that afternoon they drove down to Tombstone and stayed at the Best Western.

After grabbing a bite to eat at the OK Café on Allen Street in Tombstone they checked a few of the shops as they were closing. They picked up a map and laid out their plan for Sunday. Returning to the room they showered and pulled out the bottle of Lambrusco and curled up on the bed. The glasses were clinked and the perfect night began.

———————

When Holiday arrived at the laboratory on Monday morning, John had his polygraph instrument set up and ready. "What's that all about?" questioned Holiday indicating the instrument.

"Think about it, Harry. We questioned the lab workers on killing Hires. We didn't test them on the main issue we came down here to do. Now we need to test them about leaking classified information. We probably should have done that to begin with. We might get a lead on the Hires killing that way, also."

"That's a great idea, John. However, Doctor David is becoming concerned about us disrupting his operation. He said he is at a crucial point and so close to wrapping it up that he needs his people. Right now, he's been friendly and cooperative. I don't want to mess that up if we can help it."

"What if I just do one in the morning and one in the afternoon? That shouldn't mess up his schedule too badly."

"I guess you're right," agreed Holiday.

"Can you ask him?"

"I'll talk to him. I think it's a great idea. There shouldn't be any problem selling it to him." Holiday left for the lab.

John proceeded to calibrate his polygraph instrument. Hopefully, he waited for a customer. He didn't wait long.

The doctor agreed to the polygraph schedule. The first of the eight laboratory personnel arrived within twenty minutes of Holiday leaving. Since the lab people had a pretest earlier, John skimmed over it and got right to the questions. The three relevant questions on the test this time were:

"Have you ever had unauthorized access to the classified files?"

"Have you ever given classified information to an unauthorized person?"

"Do you know anyone who gave any unauthorized person classified information?"

Both scientists proved to be truthful on the examinations. They were asked to refrain from discussing the test with other personnel. Doctor David scheduled two more examinees for Tuesday.

John packed up his instrument and waited for Holiday. Holiday arrived shortly after the last test. He was in a great mood.

Rachael had some errands to run. Holiday and John rode together back to the motel. Holiday discussed his idea for the night.

"Let's sit with the singers tonight and get their feel for what is going on. I still feel that even if the leak is at the lab, the killer is at the restaurant. Most of the personnel here are 'milquetoast' type."

"I think that's a great idea, Harry. It should be fun. Are we going to see our lady friends tonight?"

"Maybe after karaoke is over. I think we should direct our attention to the others tonight. We need to get to know the customers. For some reason I think our killer is one of the karaoke bunch."

"Harry, I was wondering. Is what I heard true? That the local cops are staking out the joint this evening."

"Yep, we can just relax inside. They will be out of sight. With any luck, they may catch our killer."

"You know. It should be real interesting to hear what the singers have to say about each other."

"You're right. It should be most interesting. Are they as close as everyone says they are?"

"Only the Shadow knows." John smiled menacingly.

chapter

TWELVE

John and Holiday made it a point to arrive early at the restaurant. It gave them time to meet with the singers sitting in the
lobby who wanted to get on top of the list to sing. Sammy and his
girlfriend Delta were already there. Attractive Pearl came in with
her cane, followed by Ira. John and Holiday no sooner sat down
than Scooter, Fred, Jasiu and his wife Demi came in. It was as if
these people hadn't seen each other in years. They were a huggy,
kissy bunch. One thing was obvious; their feelings were genuine.

They were curious about John and Holiday. They had seen
them in the restaurant but knew they weren't singers. The two explained who they were and what they were doing there. The atmosphere changed from the jovial greetings to a more somber mood.
The discussion was on the murders. It was a relief when Isabel
unlocked the gate and they all spread out inside the restaurant.

John made it a point to sit with Scooter, Fred, Ira, Jasiu and his wife, Demi. Holiday sat with Pearl, Sammy and Delta, who were later joined by Julie. All the singers scrambled to get their songs up on Sandie's counter in the order of their arrival. Sandie operated all of the karaoke equipment.

When John interviewed Scooter he found out that all the singers were either Angels or Saints. She and Fred knew the singers and most of the customers. Fred was quick to agree with her. Ira and Jasiu knew the singers too, but rated them more in the friendly category than celestial beings. Jasiu's wife never said much of anything other than an occasional nod but John noticed that for her mid-sixties, she sure had perky breasts. Ira said Jasiu was physically capable of stabbing someone but was so dumb he wouldn't know which end of the knife to use. Jasiu said Ira's singing was so bad the women probably stabbed themselves.

Sandie and Arnie joined them for a quick dinner before going to work. Everyone placed their orders. Jasiu was teased because he always ordered a BLT sandwich. As Sandie and Arnie left the table, Jerome and DeAnna joined the group. There, again, they had nothing but nice things to say about everyone.

John thought to himself, *This is the biggest mutual admiration society I've ever seen. Either that or they're blowing smoke up my chimney. If the killer is here he sure has them fooled. I hope Harry is doing better.*

Pearl was chatting away with Julie while Holiday talked with Sammy. Sammy told Holiday that he did karaoke in half a dozen places. He said, "I and J's is the most organized, best laid out and finest managed karaoke location in town. Sometimes the microphone isn't loud enough and the music is too low but that seldom happens. Arnie runs a tight ship. You damn sure aren't going to find anyone better."

Big Jack sat down with them. During the conversation, he said, "It don't matter how well you sing. We treat everybody as if they're a star. Wait till Jasiu gets up there. You'll see what I mean."

Pearl jumped on Big Jack, "That's a mean thing to say, Jack. The man tries. He's a nice guy."

"Yeah, he'd be a lot nicer if he didn't try to sing."

"Do you think he'd have any reason to kill anyone?" asked Holiday

"Jasiu? Oh, Lord, no!" returned Big Jack. "Like Pearl said, he's a nice guy."

The singing began and conversations became sparser throughout the restaurant. The lull was only temporary. It appeared that the singers who weren't singing were noisier than the listeners. Most of the time, they didn't even look at the person singing. They were too busy talking to each other. However, they applauded after each singer finished. The interest seemed to lie in the song they were going to sing as opposed to listening to other singers' performances. They were a strange bunch, thought John. However, he did notice the non-singing customers...the listeners... were attentive and enjoyed the mixture of talent.

Holiday found the singers all happy and enjoying each other's company, even more so than the song being sung. He did notice some singers were excellent and the crowd did stop and take notice. To him it was just one big good-natured family. It would be hard to find a killer in this bunch.

John was able to get Holiday's attention. He nodded toward the other side of the room, close to the door. Holiday did a quick scan of the area and located John's concern. The southern boys, Tolman and Hobbs, were seated in a booth. They noticed Holiday and John looking at them. They held up their hands to show they were empty, smiled and nodded.

Rachael, who had moved over to Holiday's table, got up and took the microphone from Jerome and did an excellent rendition of 'Guy's do it'. During the applause John noticed Hobbs leave the restaurant. Tolman went to the register and paid the tab and left. Holiday gave John a 'should we follow them' look. John shrugged and they let the two go, knowing the police were on stakeout by the restaurant.

Whether or not it had anything to do with the laboratory, John was positive the killer had to come from this restaurant. *Why does the killer just pick women? Why just the singers? Other women eat here as well. Why just this restaurant? There are many karaoke locations throughout the area.* John was staring at the singer but not seeing. His mind was racing with questions. *Did someone have it in for José? Did Isabel do something so horrible that somebody is trying to ruin her? Is the owner of the facility trying to get them out of the building? Is this location just convenient to the killer? There are over a hundred apartments in the immediate area. The facility is adjacent to a mobile home resort with hundreds of motor homes and trailers.*

He looked over the crowd of singers. It had to be a male. There is no way spunky little Julie, statuesque Jan, cute Pearl or pretty Delta could do it. The men had been coming here for years except for Jasiu and Jerome. They were relatively new. Both appeared healthy enough.

Jerome was a 'people' kind of guy. His smile was genuine and he enjoyed laughing. He had a beautiful wife who always accompanied him. The man had a great voice and sang songs everyone loved to hear. However, he was certainly man enough to do anyone in. He could probably whip any guy in the house. John didn't want to try it. His personality was not what you'd expect from a killer. This guy didn't seem to have a mean bone in his body.

Jasiu, on the other hand, had military training. He always came with his wife, but that didn't mean he couldn't step outside for a minute. Hell, how long does it take to stab someone?

"Hey, Jasiu. You were in the military, right?" asked John.

"You bet. In the Army."

Ira leaned over by Jasiu and butted in, "My cousin was in the Marines."

Jasiu looked at Ira with his face just inches from his and said, "I tried to join the Marines but they wouldn't take me."

Ira had to ask, "I don't doubt that. Why not?"

"My parents were married and my IQ was too high." John and everyone laughed.

"I'm telling my cousin," said Ira indignantly.

"You'll have to excuse Ira's interruption. Why do you ask?" questioned Jasiu.

John continued, "I was just wondering if you ever killed anybody."

"Of course I did. I didn't go to Viet Nam to hand out gift cards."

John laughed. "What did it feel like when you killed someone?"

"Man, that's a weird question. Nobody ever asked me that before." Jasiu set his glass of wine down and turned to John. "Most of the time you were just shooting into bushes and trees and didn't know if you hit anyone or not."

"Did you ever see anyone you shot?"

"Yeah, I did."

"Can you talk about it?"

Jasiu took a drink of his wine, placed the glass back on the table, and sighed. "I was on the way to make a payment to a Vietnamese family whose child was killed by friendly fire. As we drove around this curve there were three Viet Cong tax collectors on the road. They raised their weapons to fire. I was faster and shot all three."

"Wow! How'd that make you feel?"

"Euphoric. I mean, like it was the ultimate game of life and death...and I won. As we drove by them I even shot them again."

"So...killing actually gives you a high?"

"Let me finish, man. By the time we arrived at our destination, I was damn near in tears. I fought it back. I couldn't let my men see that. It hit me that those VCs could be someone's brother, father, and son. Their families would never see them again. You want to know how it feels to kill somebody; it's so horrible that it's indescribable. That's how it feels. That's why most of the veterans never talk about it."

"I apologize for asking. Thank you for your time, effort and the blood you sacrificed for your country. I'm proud to know you." John shook Jasiu's hand. *If this guy is the killer, he's one hell of an actor.*

"What's it like to actually sing a song in this environment?" John asked Jasiu.

"I guess 'frustration' would sum it up. You're really trying to do your best and maybe you see little Julie, your wife and Ira listening to you. The other eighteen to twenty singers are telling jokes, laughing loudly even shouting over from table to table. Sometimes their outburst makes you lose your place on the screen. They are so wrapped up in themselves and their conversations they haven't heard a word you have sung.

"I bet you can ask what the song was you just sang and they wouldn't have any idea. This is just social hour for them until it's time for them to sing. Then their friends will be quiet until they finish. They either don't realize how loud they are or they just don't care. You just have to make up your mind that you're here with the idea of singing the song for yourself and a handful of listeners."

Holiday had been looking at the men sitting at his table. Both Big Jack and Sammy were from the New York/New Jersey area. As far as Holiday was concerned, their compassion and sensitivity level wouldn't prevent them from killing anyone. Nevertheless, they were about as different from each other as could be.

Big Jack was so laid back that his idea to have a family would be to marry a pregnant woman. He did have one lust for life... the excitement of stamp collecting. Holiday decided that stabbing someone would be too much work for him.

However, Sammy was a different story. He was hype friendly to everyone and seemed to genuinely enjoy people. His promiscuity was a legend that was most recently cut short by the pretty Delta. The man didn't have a chance ... he was hooked. He was certainly man enough to do someone in. The man just didn't have any reason to do it. There was absolutely no motive.

Jasiu's glass was empty and he was tired of trying to catch Isabel's eye. He looked at John and said, "Watch this." He pulled out his cell phone and dialed. Isabel was at the register when she looked at her phone. She didn't even answer, her head snapped around and she looked at Jasiu. She just shook her head and laughed. Jasiu got his glass of wine within a minute.

A couple left after the second round and Polly who had been sitting at the bar came over and joined John. Ira began a conversation with her about his horse riding days.

When he finished, Jasiu stated, "One nice thing about egotists. They never talk about other people."

"You're living proof we evolved from apes, Jasiu. You just didn't evolve far enough," replied Ira.

"Hey. You've got thirty-two teeth, Ira. Do you want to try for none?" Jasiu looked Ira in the eye.

"The notification won't be hard. Your next of kin is already here," returned Ira staring back.

"Fred, are these guys always like this?" asked John.

"Actually, they've been pretty good tonight."

It was Jasiu's time to sing in the third round. He did Ray Stevens' version of the 'Haircut song'. Midway through the song loud laughter came from Big Jacks' table and caused Jasiu to miss a whole paragraph on the screen. He caught up and finished the song and returned to the table. Both Ira and Jasiu's wife had to calm him down.

The lack of courtesy from the surrounding tables was taking its toll on him. It was definitely time for him to leave. He waited for his friend, Jerome, to sing and was glad he did. He sang Jasiu's favorite song...The Ballad of the Green Beret. Fred, Scooter, Ira, Jasiu and his wife, Demi, all left afterward.

Holiday came over and joined John, Jerome and DeAnna. John introduced them. There were handshakes all around.

"Well, what's new, partner," asked Holiday. "I didn't learn a damn thing at my table. Everyone is cool."

"I thought I struck out, too. Now, I'm not so sure. I saw anger tonight that makes me wonder. I have a substantial subject. We have a singer with a temper and a possible motive. I'll tell you all about it later. We're going to need to do a background check on this guy."

Rachael finished her song and joined Holiday. John and Polly led them out of the restaurant. The four of them drove to Rachael's. She threw a pizza in the oven and they settled down for a nightcap and pizza. John expressed his concern over Jasiu.

Polly said, "Jasiu is the karaoke clown. He's not a singer. He's an entertainer. He makes people laugh. He's fun. Why would you even think of him?"

"Lady, you didn't see the look in his eyes, redness in the face and manner he slammed things down. He spoke loud enough for the people at Harry's table to hear him. What he was saying was not nice. It was more like mean and angry. If it hadn't been for his wife and his buddy, Ira, calming him down, there could have been real trouble tonight."

"I'm a little surprised. But, he's somewhat quiet; he very seldom smiles and doesn't really talk unless someone talks to him. He's certainly capable. There could be motive in the fact that he shuts people up that interfere with his singing," offered Rachael.

"I hate to say it, but Martha, Gwen and Jasmine were loud talkers. Martha and Jasmine were also continuous talkers. They never listened to the singers. They just liked to talk," advised Polly.

"I guess we had better bring him in and have a little discussion before we have another killing," suggested Holiday.

"Jasiu left with a crowd of people tonight. He's always with his wife. I doubt he is going to do anything now. Nevertheless, we have karaoke tomorrow night. That could be a problem. We'll pick him up tomorrow." John turned to Polly, "Miss Polly, I'm a little tense and somewhat sad. Is there any way you could help me with that problem?"

"I think I have sufficient experience to not only cure that, but I believe that I can make you forget your own name."

"Harry. See you tomorrow. We're out of here." John quickly led Polly from Rachael's house and straight to her house and within hours he not only didn't know his own name but didn't care.

Holiday picked up John the next morning to go to Jasiu's. John's legs were a little weak and there was effort to keep them from wobbling. "John, for crying out loud, get that smile off your face."

"I can't. I think I slept this way and it seems to be frozen."

"Well, I'm glad you, at least, slept."

John continued to stare straight ahead. "Does three hours count?"

"Oh, you're going to be in great shape to take this guy down if you have to."

"Harry, you get the big bucks. You take him down and I'll cheer you on. I really don't think I could whip my way out of a wet paper bag right now."

"What's with this woman anyway?"

"Harry, she said she had been saving up. I thought she meant money. Boy was I wrong."

"Well, get your act together. We're almost there."

"Does this dude have any guns?"

"He's ex-military. What do you think?"

"Crap, all we can hope is that ours are bigger." John checked the magazine of his .40 cal. Glock. "Should I go around the back?"

"Nah, we're just here to talk to him. He doesn't have any reason to run."

Demi, Jasiu's wife, met them at the door and seated them in Jasiu's office. The two men were quite impressed at Jasiu's awards and decorations from his time in combat. Jasiu had several computers and appeared to spend quite a bit of time on them. He was a member of the VFW, American Legion, Oath Keepers, Military Order of the Purple Heart and a number of other patriotic organizations.

"Hey, Jasiu, how are you doing this morning?" asked Holiday.

"Up until now I was doing great. What brings you gentlemen here?"

"I guess it's me that brings us here, old buddy," said John.

"Was it the way I acted last night?"

"You're right on. You seem to have a sense of violence toward some of the singers. The fact that some of the singers have been killed at that location makes us want to talk to you."

"John's right," agreed Holiday

"Yep," John said as he cocked his head to the side.

"Listen, gentlemen. My idea of dealing with people who anger me is not killing them. Once you kill them, it's over. That is totally unsatisfactory to me. I like for them to remember that they did me wrong. A quick knee to the crotch followed by a quick knee to the chin as they bend over in pain lasts for a while. A black eye lets them know they wronged me. The same with a bloody nose or a swollen cheek or even a missing tooth.

"Those things last for a while and the individuals have to live with it. I'm definitely not into killing. It's over too quick. Their hurt doesn't last long enough. My wife will tell you I can't even kill an animal. After my outburst last night I don't blame you for coming here. But trust me, I'm no killer."

chapter

THIRTEEN

"I guess we can scratch Jasiu off our suspect list," said Holiday sliding onto the driver's seat.

John froze at the passenger door. "You've got to be kidding. That gruesome sucker is more than capable. Hell, Harry, he has killed before. He has a temper, especially about loud people. You heard what Polly said. Those three women, who were killed, were loud and inconsiderate. I think you are making a big mistake writing him off." John got in the car and closed the door.

"John, that was Polly's opinion about those women. Loud and inconsiderate to her may not have been the same to Jasiu."

"I don't know, John, he sounds pretty much against killing to me. I think he had enough of that in Nam."

"What do you expect him to say Harry? 'Killing is my hobby'. Maybe he'd say, 'Killing is good because it relieves tension'."

"Get serious, John. Everybody likes the man. They say he's the clown and a fun person."

"I'm sure he is…until you cross him. I'm telling you Harry the guy scares me. I think he has a screw loose."

"He makes sense to me. If somebody pisses you off, you just want to hurt 'em not kill 'em."

"Crap, now you're scaring me." John gave him an exaggerated look of fear and slid closer to the passenger door.

"But it's true. When someone pisses you off, don't you want to just go over and smack them?"

"Harry, have you considered going to an anger management course?"

"All right, John. I'll call Turner and have him run the guy."

"Good. How are Tom and the rest of team doing anyway?"

"They're pouting because they're not down here."

They drove back to the laboratory John polygraphed his two scientists. Both proved to be truthful. The instrument was quickly packed up and put away.

They decided to have dinner at I and J's. It was Tuesday night and there would be some different customers and singers there tonight. John dropped Holiday off at Rachael's and went to Polly's house. It was four o'clock and wine time to John. Polly met him at the door with a glass of chilled Lambrusco.

It was five p.m. when John and Polly entered the restaurant. The laughter and camaraderie was already in full swing. Most of the singers present were already eating their meals. They had an hour before they began singing.

"Polly, are they always this happy?" John led her around the tables and across the dance floor.

"John, it's a family. It's a loving bunch of people that truly enjoy each other. You will never find atmosphere like this in any other karaoke establishment. You think singing is what it's all about. That's only a part of it. Friendships made here will last forever. The chemistry between Arnie, Sandie, Isabel and José is like a magnet to these people. They're drawn to it every week."

"You may be right but one of them is a killer." They were summoned over to Fred and Scooter's table. This time there was a table pushed up against it and Tyler with Sylvia and her dad, mom, aunt, brother, and his wife were there. Another couple who was there, were obviously from the south. Their accent was pleasantly charming. Jasiu and Ira were arguing about something when Arnie came over and asked Ira if his car was parked in Arnie's parking space. Ira smiled sheepishly and admitted that it was. Arnie just smiled and nodded as he walked away.

The singers came early so they could be finished with their food before time to sing. It was an hour before karaoke began and already there were more than a dozen singers present. John decided he would spend time with Tyler, Sylvia and the southern couple, Jaime and Ilene.

John could sit and listen to her talk all night. She was a real Georgia Peach with a great personality. Jaime was retired Air Force and he too, had a great sense of humor. He told great stories and loved to laugh. Both sang well and left after two songs. The couple sang at several locations around the area. They very seldom came to I and J's. It was obvious they were no threat to anyone.

Sylvia was absolutely beautiful and sang like a professional. She was upbeat, cheerful and a real pleasure to be around. Her husband Tyler was a good looking, rugged type. He had a great personality and could easily sing professionally as well. There was no doubt he could cause the demise of any person in the restaurant. He was certainly man enough. The only problem being the family man he was. He was always with his family and never spoke a bad word about anyone. He never even complained about Jasiu's silly songs. The other singers had great respect for him.

John kept a close eye on Jasiu. He was playing it too cool as far as John was concerned. The man was quiet and attentive when others sang except for the few times he was picking on Ira. Jasiu kept his arm around his wife, Demi, or at least held hands with her throughout the night. He was careful not to display any suspicious activity. He was conscious of the concern John was giving him. This made John more determined to get him on the polygraph.

Holiday got John's attention and directed him to the other side of the room. John was quick to notice Tolman and Hobbs sitting in one of the booths. After the first round of singers finished and the second round began, both men paid their tab and left. John followed them out the door and watched them leave. Upon returning, John smiled when he noticed Rachael didn't sing but spent her time cuddling up to Holiday. He had never seen the big man this relaxed.

After Sammy and Delta sang, they were followed by Sammy's lady friends who were called Sammy's Mammies by the other singers. John was absolutely convinced the only person in the building that would have what it takes to kill someone would be Jasiu. He relaxed and enjoyed the singers for the remaining part of the night.

After waiting for all the singers to leave, Rachael led Holiday, Polly and John out of the restaurant. They stood outside and watched Jasiu and Ira walking around the parking lot. Polly hollered out to Ira, "What are you guys doing out here?"

Ira scratched his head and yelled back, "I'm looking for my car."

"Where did you park it?" shouted Rachael.

"I parked in Arnie's parking spot and it's not there."

"It might pay you to go back in and make nice to Arnie and promise never to do that again," bellowed Rachael as she and the others laughed.

"Harry, let's call this Jasiu tomorrow and have him come in for a polygraph. I really want to do this."

"You know I think John's got something. Jasiu is relatively new to our group. We really don't know much about him. He's certainly not a karaoke singer. He does mostly talking songs and funny ones. I don't think he can carry a tune," informed Rachael.

"John, we have to finish up with the scientists first. That's our top priority. You know that, as well as I do," insisted Holiday.

"Okay, I'll do the scientists. Then can I have him?"

"What are you going to do if he refuses to take one? You know you can't force him to do it."

John looked at Harry and shook his head. "I know they are totally voluntary. If he refuses, then we need to really focus on him. In my experience, only the guilty would refuse a polygraph. Why wouldn't an innocent man take one?"

"Fear, you fool. The damn things are scary. There is a lot of information against them and an innocent person wants to stay innocent. He's afraid the polygraph doesn't work and he's going to get hung for something he didn't do."

"I know all that." John raised his hands over his head in exasperation. "I'll just have to use my powers of persuasion. I can pretty well talk people into doing stuff."

"Ain't no lie about that," agreed Polly with a large smile. Everyone laughed and headed for the cars and privacy of their rooms. It was a tough case but a great investigation for Holiday and John.

———

John took plenty of time with the two-scientists. Both men proved to be non-deceptive. He spent the remainder of the day putting together the test for Jasiu. If he was guilty he didn't stand a chance of beating the test. If he was innocent, John intended to prove it beyond a doubt.

———

Jasiu, who was practicing a karaoke song in the front room, rushed over to the phone, "Hello, this is Jasiu."

"Hi there, this is your neighbor. Scooter and I are going over to the motor home resort for karaoke this evening. Do you guys want to come along?"

"I don't know, Fred. Let me ask the boss." He turned toward the kitchen and looked at his wife. "Demi, would you like to go out with Fred and Scooter to karaoke tonight?"

"Sure. Why not?" yelled back Demi.

"She said sure. What time?"

"It starts early, so we'll pick you up at 3:30 pm. It runs from 4 to 7."

"You got it. See you then."

He no sooner hung up and resumed practicing than the phone rang again. "Hello, this is Jasiu."

"Jasiu, this is John Bodie. Would you mind if I come over this evening and talk with you?"

"I didn't kill anybody if that's what you want to talk about. And if that's what you want to talk about then the answer is yes. I would mind."

"I want to prove that you didn't kill anyone and remove all suspicion. I can do that if you give me the chance."

"Well I'm not going to be available. I'm going to karaoke this evening. How about tomorrow?"

"Where do you go to karaoke on Wednesday? Isn't I and J's closed?"

"It's at a motor home resort."

"Okay, let's get together tomorrow. I know I can help you. All you have to do is give me the chance."

"Fine, I'll see you then."

Holiday, Sergeant Steel, and Rachael were having coffee in the room when John hung up.

"Damn, I almost had him tonight."

"Who?" asked Sergeant Steel.

"Jasiu, he's one of the singers at the restaurant where Hires was killed. He's going out to karaoke tonight."

"I bet I know where he's going. He's going to the motor home resort," said Rachael setting her cup down.

"I bet you guys know the entire local karaoke circuit." John started looking for his tea cup.

"Pretty much," answered Rachael.

———————

Jasiu followed Fred and Scooter in the singing order. He had just finished 'Minnie the Moocher' in the third-round and headed for the small building that contained the restrooms. Madeline, one of the motor home resort residents, who had been seated at the table on the patio behind Fred and Scooter, also left for the restroom. The restrooms were up the stairs and out of sight of the patrons on the patio.

Darkness had arrived and provided the perfect cover for the figure waiting in the shadow of the building. Madeline stepped out of the restroom and as she turned to leave, a hand grabbed her chin from behind. It closed her mouth as it jerked the jaw up. She was dragged into the shadows next to the building. A hand swung around and the blade quickly entered her body over her left breast and penetrated her heart. She was gently lowered to the ground and the blood from the blade was wiped onto her sweater. The assailant waited as someone entered the building and then casually walked away. Madeline was found the next morning by the cleanup crew.

———————

John finished with his first polygraph of the day and was talking with Holiday when Holiday's cell phone rang. "Holiday here."

"Agent Holiday, this is Detective Rodriguez with Surprise P.D. We met earlier about the Hires' case."

"Yes Detective, I remember you. What can I do for you?" Holiday gave John a look of surprise. "Have you discovered additional information?"

"Not about Hires. Since you have shown such an interest in the killings at the restaurant, I thought you might be interested in the killing of another female. This one was killed by the same M.O."

"I and J's was closed yesterday. How could that have happened?" Holiday walked over and sat down.

"It wasn't at the restaurant. It was at a motor home park close to there. It happened last night but the victim wasn't found until this morning."

"Is this the one that had karaoke last night?"

"That's why I'm calling you. They all seem to happen at karaoke events. This is the first one that wasn't at I and J's."

"That is extremely interesting. I may have a lead for you. Let me check it out and I'll get back to you."

"I would appreciate anything you have." They hung up and Holiday sat there with a stunned look.

"Wow. Harry, who was that and what was that all about?" John was concerned about the look on Holiday's face

"I hate to admit it, John. You may be right. I can't believe I could be that wrong." Holiday looked up at John.

"What are you talking about?"

Holiday told John of his conversation with the detective. He also reminded John that Jasiu had been at the motor home park last night. Now, it was John's turn to stand there with a stunned look.

"Oh, whoa, Harry. Did you tell him about our suspicion of Jasiu?" asked John as he sat down.

"Of course not. It's too early. I don't want to take any chances of somebody messing up our case."

"When do I get him? I've spent most of the day putting together an examination just for that guy."

Holiday stood and said, "What are you waiting for?"

"Harry, the poly is set up and ready. Are we out of here?"

"Damn right."

They decided not to call Jasiu and ask him to come in. They didn't want to give him any warning. Holiday wasted no time in driving over to Jasiu's house. He found Jasiu with his white Bischon Frise in the front yard. The animal began a continuous barking. Jasiu made no effort to quiet the dog.

"It would be a lot easier to speak with you if you would put the dog inside," advised Holiday.

"Why should I make it easy for you to talk with me? I can tell by looking at you I'm not going to like what you've got to say," replied Jasiu.

"Then you obviously know why we're here." stated John.

"Yeah. You still think I killed those ladies at I and J's. I said it before and I'll say it again. I didn't kill them."

"How about the one last night?" questioned John.

"Excuse me! What the hell are you talking about?" Jasiu's jaw dropped and his eyes widened.

"We're talking about the woman at the karaoke party last night. We know you were there."

"Yeah, so were a hell of a lot of other people. How's come I didn't hear about this killing until you guys show up?"

"You're right. There were a lot of people there last night. But we've sort of taken a liking to you," said John.

"Well, I don't know anything about somebody being killed last night. You guys ain't cops so go away and quit annoying my dog."

"It appears that you need a reminder. We are Federal Agents and Federal Agents can arrest anyone we please. It just so happens that it pleases us to arrest you and your damn dog if you don't get rid of it," announced Holiday.

"On what charge?" demanded Jasiu as he placed his hands on his hips in a defiant gesture.

"Let's see; murder of a federal employee. Oh yeah, how do matters pertaining to national security sound?"

"Sounds like you're out of your mind. I fought and bled for my country. I'm a loyal patriot. I've never given anyone any reason to doubt that. Where the hell are you coming up with these trumped-up charges?"

"How about it, pal? Are you willing to take a polygraph to prove your innocence?" asked John.

"Hey, PAL, that all depends." Jasiu opened the front door and put his dog back into the house.

"Depends on what?" inquired John.

"Who the examiner is that's giving it; how good his credentials are; his knowledge of the issue being tested; but, mostly whether he believes I'm guilty before he even does the test."

Holiday looked at John. John glanced over to Holiday and then back to Jasiu. He smiled. "Those are all valid concerns. They're excellent indicators of an innocent man. I don't think you'll have a problem. You appear to have knowledge of the polygraph methods and procedures."

"Why do you say that?"

"Because most people aren't smart enough to ask those questions. I think we're going to get along fine."

"Who is going to test me?"

"I will be giving the test." John proceeded to advise Jasiu of his credentials and experience. "...and after hearing your concerns you're going to have to prove to me that you're guilty...not innocent."

Jasiu told his wife he was leaving. Holiday breathed a sigh of relief. John had a good feeling about Jasiu's innocence.

While John talked to Jasiu, Holiday made a quick, important call to Sergeant Steel. They loaded Jasiu into the car and drove to the secret facility. When they arrived John was surprised to find the usually locked gate open and no guard in the guardhouse. The entrance door to the warehouse was unlocked and the civilian-clad military policemen were moving boxes around.

"What is this place?" asked Jasiu.

"It's a warehouse of a friend of mine. He's letting me use it while I'm down here. It's cheaper than renting office space," answered Holiday.

"With all the money the present administration is spending, they pay people not to work. They give billions of dollars to countries that actually hate us. Their corruption gives billions to corporations that file for bankruptcy. Are you telling me that they won't even provide you with office space?"

"I take it you're not happy with the present administration. I thought you were a patriot, Jasiu," stated Holiday.

"I am a patriot. I'd fight for this country again in a minute if they'd have me. But that doesn't mean I have to accept this shambles that's governing our country."

"Wow, Jasiu! Don't hold back. Tell us how you really feel," said John

"Hey, I love my country...but I fear my government."

"Whoa. You just stole my line, Jasiu." John gave Jasiu a surprised look.

John did his pretest interview with Jasiu and was impressed with his background, education and military history. Jasiu answered all the questions without stuttering or hesitation. John began to think he had been wrong about the man.

chapter

FOURTEEN

Rachael reached inside the small holster on her belt and re-moved the ringing cell phone. Taking a quick look at the cover to see who was calling, she flipped it open. With a smile in her voice she answered, "Well, good afternoon, girlfriend. How are you do-ing this fine day?"

Polly returned the greeting with an equally cheerful voice. "Lady, I've never been better. I don't know how much longer this is going to last but I'm going to make the most of it while he's here."

"I'm not exactly sure what you're talking about. But, whatever it is, I'm damn glad you've got it."

"Honey, I never met a man with an implant before. For the first time in my life, it's not a matter of how much he wants, but how much I can take. I love it. I'm like twenty years old again."

"Girl, don't be stupid. If you find someone like that, keep your mouth shut. You don't advertise it. There are enough women out there, like me, who would be giving you a run for your money. To be this age and find something like that, you keep it to yourself. I get nervous, even when you tell me about it."

"I wouldn't look for us at I and J's tonight, Rachael. I'm feeling especially energetic today."

"You mean horny."

"Horny, sexy, needy, you can call it what you want, but I mean I'm going to whip his butt tonight." Polly raised a clinched fist.

"Okay, Miss Braveheart, you go ahead and challenge him. Don't come crawling to me tomorrow and say you lost."

"Sugar, if I lose, I won't be able to crawl to you tomorrow."

"You know, Polly, I've always heard the stories about redheaded women. I guess they're true."

"I've never had a complaint since I was a teenager. As you know, that was a few years ago."

"Quite a few years ago," said Rachael laughing.

"Watch it, girl."

"You need to think about this and be careful. He may not want to go home when the time comes."

"Now, you're getting the idea."

"Good luck, Polly. Have fun. What do I tell them tonight when you don't come to the restaurant?"

"Just tell them something got into me and I'm trying to shake it off. I think I should stay in bed until I whip it."

Rachael laughed until she coughed. "You are so bad. That's exactly what I'm going to tell them."

———————

After the pretest interview and the questions involved, John started with the ten questions to be asked on the test. It had to be explained to Jasiu that all answers on the examination had to be one-syllable…"yes" or "no". Of course, they had to be in the same tone of voice. There could be no emphasis placed on any answer.

He told Jasiu that they were going to discuss each question that was going to be asked on the examination. They would be the only questions asked during the test. However, the questions would be mixed up when asked.

"Now, Jasiu, we discussed all but the last three questions on the test. These are what we call 'relevant questions'."

"These must be the ones that ask if I killed anybody," mused Jasiu.

"You're correct. How did you know?"

"It figures. You haven't asked me that yet."

"Have you ever killed anyone?"

"Of course; and I got paid to do it, too."

"Who might that have been?" asked a surprised John.

"They were called Viet Cong or VC."

"Of course you have. I should have known. Thank you for your service and your sacrifice."

"It was worth it."

"Okay, are you ready?"

"Lay it on me."

"Did you kill Martha Hires?"

"No."

"Did you kill Martha Hires with a knife?"

"No."

"Do you know who killed Martha Hires?"

"No."

John watched Jasiu closely as he asked the questions. His kinesics behavior appeared to be that of an innocent man. Such as his looking up to his right as opposed to his left when he answered. The polygraph would give him the answer. John attached pneumograph tubes, the finger probes and the blood pressure cuff to Jasiu. He turned the instrument on and adjusted the pens.

"The test is about to start." John watched the chart go by, and fifteen seconds later he asked the first question. He continued through the test asking a question every fifteen seconds. Fifteen seconds after asking the last question he shut the instrument down and released the pressure in the blood pressure cuff. The blood pressure cuff was massaged to insure all the pressure was gone.

As most examinees do, Jasiu complained about the pressure in the cuff. He didn't even ask how well he did. John had him relax and pumped up the cuff again. The instrument was turned on and the second chart was started. The procedure on the second chart was the same as the first. After the break at the end of the second chart the third chart began. It differed only in the rearrangement of a couple of questions.

The charts were pulled from the polygraph and spread across the sergeant's desk. John picked up his sheet for marking the results of the test. He grabbed his pencil and began scoring the results of the test. Sitting back in the chair after he completed the scoring, he stared quietly at Jasiu.

Jasiu still did not question how he did on the test. He just stared back for a moment. Finally he asked, "Can you take me home now? This whole thing was interesting but I'm tired of it."

"You bet. There's no question about that. You have a score of plus twelve. That is an indication of a very truthful person."

"What is a truthful score?"

"Plus six or higher."

"Seems like I doubled the score," said Jasiu proudly.

"Yep. But you know it still doesn't clear you of the one at the resort or any of the others at the restaurant."

"Crap, how many of these tests do you want me to take? There've been several women killed."

"I think we can do it with one more test."

"How?"

"I know you killed men in Nam. That's a soldier's job. But have you ever killed a female?"

"I can't answer that question. How do I know who I shot in the jungle? The Cong used women, too."

"All right. Let's try this question and see what happens. Have you ever killed a female in the United States?"

"Of course; a few doe, fish, squirrels, opossums…."

John interrupted him with, "Have you ever killed a female human being in the United States? Wrap your mind around that."

"I like that. I can truthfully say no to that question. That is, as long as thinking about it doesn't mess me up."

"Hell, I couldn't even pass the test if thinking about it would have anything to do with the results."

"So that's a no?" asked Jasiu.

"Absolutely. Only the act itself is what we test on. Thoughts, intent or dreams play no part in the examination."

"Fine. Hurry up and let's get this over with. I want to go home. I love my wife but I miss my dog."

"I can fully understand that."

"That's right. You met both of them."

"That's not what I meant and you know it. I mean if I had a wife and dog I'd probably feel the same way."

"Yeah, right."

John thought for a moment and then prepared a list of nine questions this time. The two relevant questions were:

"Did you ever kill a female human being in the United States?"

"Have you killed any female human being in the last month?"

Jasiu answered both questions with, "No." After the three charts were completed, John scored them. He sat back and smiled at Jasiu.

"Okay. I apologize, old buddy. I honestly thought I had nailed the killer. I couldn't have been more wrong. You are definitely off the hook."

"Thank you for that apology. However, know this; if anything bad ever happens to Ira, I refuse to take a polygraph."

John laughed. "That's true friendship. Should I polygraph him if anything happens to you?"

"You wouldn't have to. He's such an idiot he'd be bragging about it. He does like to talk you know."

"Well let's hope nothing happens to either one of you. I enjoy both of you at I and J's. He has a great voice and you have a wonderful sense of humor. I don't know where you find those songs you do. But they're great. You should go on both Monday and Tuesday. People seem to like you."

"Hey man, that's like fifty dollars a shot, for the tea, wine, food and having to feed that woman that goes with me. You think she would ever order a BLT. No, she has to have prime rib, flat iron steak or salmon and at least two glasses of wine plus coffee. If we went out just two nights a week it would be a hundred dollars a week or four or five hundred dollars a month. That would more than pay for a red Ford Ranger." Jasiu continued to rub his arm from the aftermath of the blood pressure.

"I guess I can see why it's once a week."

"Of course, when she goes back to Arkansas or up to Washington State, I go out twice as much...but I have half as much fun."

"Sounds like you're a good husband."

They both turned to the door as Holiday entered. "Well, John, do I go for the cuffs or a handshake?"

"Definitely a handshake. I tested him on Hires and the other women and he is most assuredly innocent of all those killings. He's really a great guy. Kind of reminds me of myself."

"That's good news. Now that we know who didn't do it. It should be simple to go out there and find out who did do it," said Holiday, as he raised his hands out to his sides at shoulder level with the palms up.

John shook his head, stared at Holiday for a second or two and said, "You are a sarcastic sucker sometimes, Harry."

"I know." He smiled at John.

John closed up his instrument, looked at Jasiu and said, "Come on and I'll take you back home." John led him out to the car.

As soon as they entered the vehicle, Jasiu cleared his throat and asked, "John, can I ask you a question?"

"Certainly. I damn sure asked you plenty of them today."

"Are you or Holiday married?"

"I have been, but not now. I was married several times as a matter of fact. Marriage is kind of a place you like to visit but you wouldn't want to live there. Holiday has never been married that I know of. Why do you ask?" John turned onto east bound I-10.

"Well, the karaoke group noticed that you two have become quite cozy with our friends, Polly and Rachael. Those ladies are sort of special to us and we don't want to see either of them hurt."

"Tell your group that neither Harry nor I are married. We are enjoying the ladies' company and I believe they are enjoying ours. We're not really looking for anything serious nor are they. We'll be leaving as soon as this case is solved. The ladies are well aware of that.

"I have to admit that I am somewhat 'in like' with Polly. I will unquestionably miss her when I leave here. I will never, ever, forget her and will always cherish the time we had together."

"Wow! I expected you to tell me to mind my own business. I never expected such honesty."

"I'm a polygraph examiner. I firmly believe in honesty." John sped up to get over in the outside lane and ramp to the 101 freeway.

"I'm glad to hear that."

"Holiday and I are not gigolos. We are federal investigators under a lot of pressure and often find ourselves in life-threatening situations. This is the first time that we have experienced such an escape from our normally dangerous operation."

"We may be overreacting to the friendship offered by Rachael and Polly. Tell your friends that they have nothing to worry about. The four of us are being totally honest with each other and understand that this a temporary fling that we'd be foolish to pass up. It's something that will bring smiles to our faces for years to come."

"Thank you for that information. It changes my opinion of you guys. When the karaoke group finds out, I'm sure the two of you will be better accepted. You'll probably be part of the family."

"That would certainly be helpful in this investigation. Tell them if they have any further questions to talk to Rachael and Polly and get their side of the story. Harry and I wouldn't mind at all." The two of them swapped a few war stories and memories of Viet Nam for the rest of the trip.

John and Jasiu shook hands as he left the car. *Wow! Why did we have to have that conversation? Now, I'm really confused. Why am I into this relationship? I know it can't go anywhere. I don't know if it is going to hurt her when I leave. I know damn well it's going to do damage to me emotionally. She is such a neat lady.*

———

John parked in front of Polly's house. He sat there deep in self-analysis. He was fighting an approach/avoidance conflict. He wanted more than anything to have what that woman offered, but he didn't want the sadness of separation after he left. The man felt something for the lady that he couldn't ignore. At the same time, there was a tinge of guilt about the one he left behind in Vallejo, even though he knew she was playing the field.

"What the hell. I'm sure Dede has found some 'dog barking up her tree' by now. After all, she said she was looking. If things are too miserable when I get back to Vallejo, I can always come back here. I've got to admit, I like the weather," John said loud and clear as he exited the vehicle. He decided to take Polly out to dinner and dancing tonight. *Hell, we might even go to a movie.*

She must have anticipated me, thought John as Polly opened the door for him. "Your red hair seems to glisten tonight. Your face makes your makeup beautiful. I actually have eye-candy to show off tonight," John said, admiringly.

"I don't know how to tell you this, lover, but no one else will see it tonight. You've been to the Orient on several tours of duty. It's time you showed me what you learned." Polly dropped her robe to the floor.

John's jaw dropped at the same time. He couldn't help but stare at her nude presence. He experienced every reaction that one feels when 'fight or flight' occurs. He had a quick intake of breath, his heart sped up and all the pores in the skin popped open at the same time. There would be no fighting or running but he knew he was going to need extra muscle for something.

The thoughts raced through his head. The young, sun-baked, hard, curvaceous bodies lying around the pool were nice. Most of them felt they were doing you a favor by making love to you. It was like they were built for speed and endurance. However, he saw what younger men see in older women. She, too, knows she's doing you a favor, but realizes she is also going to receive some of the benefit. The, soft, nude, body of a mature female is built for comfort and comes with superior experience. The more he looked, the more he wanted comforting.

John left a trail of clothes from the door to the shower. There was a trail of dripping water from the shower to the bed. Where the trail ended...comfort began. It did not begin with the wild abandon of sexual gymnastics. There was no hurry. Time was not important. Instead, the wet kisses and warm embraces led to the slow and sensual pleasures of making love.

Their movements were those of synchronized lovers, each more concerned of providing mind altering bliss to the other than to their self. No sensual areas were left unexplored or un-stimulated. Every position involved in an amorous endeavor met with increased fulfillment. Love had never been more intense yet the word was never mentioned even as they lay, spent, watching the sun as it slowly rose.

John knew it was time for him to prepare for work. He began kissing Polly and proceeded to kiss her all over her body. He settled in on one particular spot until the neighbors could hear her cry out in ecstasy as she climaxed for the final time that morning.

John jumped up and headed for the shower. He dressed and gave Polly a last kiss. He was amazed how rubbery his legs felt as he walked to the car. He was going to stop by Walgreens and get a couple of those five hour energy pepper-uppers.

Polly thought, *win lose or draw...I'd have to call tonight one hell of a draw.* She rolled over and cuddled with her pillow and savored the aftermath of good loving.

chapter

FIFTEEN

Holiday was deep in thought as he stared at the crowded freeway rush-hour traffic on I-10. His concentration was interrupted by Rachael as he drove to the laboratory on Friday morning.

"Harry, I just can't believe Jasiu is innocent. Are you sure John knows what he's doing?"

He turned his head quickly and looked curiously at Rachael. "Excuse me, girl. What in the hell are you talking about?" He'd come out of his concentration to pick up on her last sentence.

"I mean everything points to Jasiu. Like he's been present every time someone was killed. He was even at the motor home resort when that lady was killed there. You've got to admit that's quite a coincidence, isn't it? John says he is innocent. Are you sure John knows what he's doing?"

"Lady, you don't know John. I've worked with him on many occasions. He's never been wrong yet. I can understand your concern. Hell, the first thing I thought about when I heard Herman Cain passed his sexual harassment polygraph was who the examiner was and what were his qualifications or credentials. But I guarantee you if John says Jasiu is innocent, then, by God, the man is innocent."

"Okay, Okay. I guess I'll have to think about who else it could be. I do have a couple in mind."

"Already?"

"You're damn right. I've been thinking about him for some time now. Jerome used to be a firefighter."

"What's does being a firefighter have to do with anything? The victims were stabbed not burned."

Rachael turned and gave him a disgusted look. "Damn it, Harry. Think about it, will you?"

"For one thing, he's new to the group. Another thing, being a firefighter, he's had some medical training. That man would know exactly where to place the knife blade for an instant kill. Man, you've seen him. That guy is big and he's strong. Hell, he's man enough to do anybody in."

"I hadn't thought much about Jerome. He's always with his wife. I suppose it wouldn't hurt to check him out."

"I wouldn't stop there, either. While you're at it, you should definitely check out his wife, DeAnna."

"Why? Was she a firefighter, too?"

Rachael gave Holiday a dismayed look. "No. But you should see what she can do with a knife. That woman is an artist with a knife."

"What...does she throw them or swallow them? What in the world does she do with a knife?"

"Get serious, Harry, like I said, she is actually an artist. Her house is full of figurines that she has carved and painted. I mean she gets down to the finest detail. Her work is absolutely amazing."

"So, she is good with knives. Big deal! However, I think it's more for carving than stabbing."

"Maybe she's super jealous and she didn't like the way the victims were looking at her man. The guy is good looking. I bet his mustache tickles, too," Rachael couldn't help but giggle.

"Remember; curiosity kills," said Holiday glancing over at her.

"I didn't say I was curious. I just made a statement. I'm sure most of the women in the group wonder about that."

"They seem to be a warm and friendly part of the karaoke family now. The group seems to really like them."

"Yeah, but they are the newest addition to the group. What do we actually know about them? These killings didn't start until after they started coming to I and J's."

"All right, woman. I guess it wouldn't hurt to sit down with this Jerome guy and have a little conversation. However, in the meantime, I'll discuss this idea with John and get his feelings on it."

"You depend a lot on John, don't you?" Rachael slid out of the passenger seat and closed the door.

"We're a team, Rachael. I don't believe this case can be solved without him." Holiday pushed the button to lock the car and Rachael jumped as she walked in front of the car when the horn sounded.

"You think he's that important to the case? Do you believe this case will never be solved without him?"

"There is no doubt in my mind that without John and his polygraph this case couldn't be solved."

"Huh," mumbled Rachael.

John, super relaxed from the night before, drove up to the facility just as Holiday and Rachael entered the gate. They waited for him. John had to make a special effort to walk with a firm gait.

"We missed you at I and J's last night. Polly told me she had some big plans for you." Rachael couldn't hold back an ear-to-ear grin. "How did that go? I have to admit that I'm somewhat jealous."

"We had a most enjoyable evening...uh and night...and morning." John looked sheepishly at her.

Rachael punched Holiday on the shoulder and said, "Sounds like they had a good time, sugar. I think maybe we should try that." She entered the building laughing and headed for the lab.

John casually followed Holiday to the sergeant's office, dreading the stairs he had to climb. Upon entering the sergeant's office, John said, "I guess we're back to square one, old buddy."

"John, it looks to me like we're going to have to go through all those people at the restaurant."

"As much as I hate to say it, I agree with you. I really feel the killer is there. We just have to find him."

"John, you once told me that women are more likely to kill with a knife than with a gun, right?"

"That's what the statistics say."

"Maybe we should start thinking along those lines. There are plenty of women in that karaoke group."

John sat on the corner of the sergeant's desk. "I hadn't really thought about it. That's a good idea."

"What kind of woman would do this? What kind of woman could do this? Maybe we should look for a strong woman?"

"Harry, sometimes strength is not a factor, especially when you have the element of surprise."

"You've got a point."

John finished testing the scientists. Again he found no deception. He was packing up his instrument when Harry returned from the lab. He sat the instrument behind the sergeant's desk.

"Hey, buddy boy, are we going over to the restaurant tonight?" asked Holiday while doing a little dance.

"This is a bad night to go. You know the place is packed. They turn people away on Friday night."

"They won't turn us away."

"Don't matter. You can hardly move on that dance floor because it's so crowded. All you can do is stand and hug to the music. If you're extra lucky, you might get a little swaying room."

"Damn, John! What's wrong with you?" questioned Holiday. "A little hugging set to music is good."

"I'd rather go over to that ex-firefighter, Jerome's house. We need to talk to him. Rachael might be on to something."

"Okay, John. You can take him in one room and I'll take his cute wife in another and we'll see if there is enough suspicion to polygraph either one of them. We know they are both knowledgeable of anatomy and physically capable with weaponry."

"Then let's do it."

"Can we eat first?"

"Sure where do you want to go?" asked John.

"I and J's is a long haul from Avondale. We should probably eat down here. What do you think?"

"I suppose we could do that. But, I think we should eat some place close to their house."

"I only have one problem with that, John. Where in the hell is their house?" asked Holiday with a blank stare.

"You're the Government Agent. Find it. You're supposed to be trained to do stuff like that."

Holiday made a few calls and drove to Jerome's home. The couple met the investigators at the door. Jerome and DeAnna were surprised but pleasant. The two men were escorted to the summer room. The planter shelf went from one end of the room to the other with carved figurines butted up against each other. Other walls and tabletops held additional, beautifully, carved wooden figurines. It was definitely evident that DeAnna was extremely talented with a knife.

After some small talk, John and Jerome moved to the winter room. They settled down on the couch. Jerome appeared completely relaxed. He was quick to answer the questions. There was humor in some of his responses. His kinesics mannerisms were indicators of an honest man. He was a hardworking owner of a transmission repair shop. He hardly mentioned his days as a firefighter.

"We've been talking to a lot of your karaoke friends. In fact, we've just finished testing Jasiu. Would you be willing to take a polygraph?"

"I've always wondered about those things. If you're sure it works, I think it would be fun to take one." Jerome appeared sincere to John. Nevertheless, he wondered how Jerome got on the fire department without taking a polygraph.

John decided it would be a waste of time to polygraph either one. He talked to Holiday, apologized for bothering the couple and headed for the car. They drove south on 99th Ave. to Union Hills then east to 91st Ave. to a Chinese restaurant.

While John was waiting for his shrimp fried rice and Holiday was looking forward to his Mongolian Beef, they sat in deep thought. John started to say something but changed his mind. A few minutes later Holiday broke the silence.

"You know, I've been thinking. There are a couple of professional fast-draw experts in the crowd."

"Harry, our victims were stabbed not shot."

"Hell, I know that. What I'm saying is they are fast. They could stab someone before the victim could even defend themselves."

"From what I've learned about them, they usually sing one or two songs and leave. They sit at their own table and don't really seem to socialize. They're friendly to everyone. Ira told me that only one time had he ever seen them move to the other side of the room to get away from the loud talkers at the next table."

"All right, you come up with someone. You obviously aren't going to agree with any of my suggestions."

"You know, Harry, we've lost sight of why we're here to begin with."

"What do you mean?"

"How do we know that government secrets aren't still going out the laboratory door?" John arched his back and stretched.

"I forgot to tell you." Holiday leaned back to allow the waitress to place his Mongolian Beef on the table. "Steel and I installed a surveillance camera; it's focused on the filing cabinet. He checks it every morning."

"Super. How come you didn't tell me?"

"I just forgot it. So far there's been no action on it."

"How close are they to finishing the project?" John picked up his chopsticks and started in on his Shrimp Fried Rice.

"They are close, very close. I think it's ready for testing."

"You can't tell me what it is?" John frowned as the rice fell from his chopsticks.

"I wish I could, John."

"You know, it's funny that there's been no further attempt to get information since Hires' murder." John grabbed his napkin and wiped the rice grain from his lip.

"None that we know of anyway."

"Oh, yeah."

———

John continued to think about it while dancing with Polly at I and J's. Polly could really tell his mind wasn't on the dancing. Something was bothering him.

"John, you aren't into dancing tonight. I can tell something is bothering you. Would you like to leave?"

"You can tell?"

"Yeah. You seem distant. Have I done something?" She stopped dancing and stepped back with a concerned look.

"No. Absolutely not. Don't even think that. I've never been happier with anyone." John pulled her close to him.

"Is it something I can help you with?" she asked as she rubbed the back of John's neck while following his lead in dancing.

"I suppose I've thought about it long enough today. I bet you could help me get my mind off it." He looked into her eyes and smiled.

"Honey, you're in luck. I have a special talent that can drain all your memory. But it won't work with your clothes on."

"Grab your purse, young lady. We're the hell out of here." John led her over to the table. He grabbed some bills from his pocket and threw them down on the table in front of Holiday.

"What's this for?" asked Holiday looking up from his chair.

"It will help with the tab. We're leaving."

"Why? Where are you going?" questioned Rachael.

"I have to go forget something," answered John, leading Polly away.

"What did he say?" asked a confused Holiday.

"It didn't make much sense. I think he said he had to go forget something," repeated Rachael.

The automatic sliding doors slid open as the two entered the night air. They had their arms around each other. They were almost awkward, trying to hang on to each other and walk at the same time.

John heard a car engine start. There were no headlights but the motor was coming closer. He looked back over his shoulder in time to see the pistol pointed at them from the passenger window. A shot rang out.

chapter

SIXTEEN

The din from the music, singers and talkers prevented Ira from hearing what his wife was saying on his cell phone. He hopped up from the table and headed for the exit. As the sliding glass doors opened, he heard a gunshot. Looking down the street, he saw a car with the lights turned off speeding away. He flipped the phone shut and looked to his left. There was nothing of note there. He walked to his right and when he reached the corner of the building, he saw John and Polly.

John was kneeling and holding Polly in his arms. Ira rushed over to them as John said, "Call 911." He shifted his position and held her tight. He rocked back and forth with her while softly reassuring her everything would be all right.

"Let me help," said Ira bending down. He attempted to take Polly away from John. John held tight.

"No, call 911. We need an ambulance. Come on Ira, we need medical assistance here."

"John, let's get her inside before whoever shot her comes back." The two men carried Polly into the lobby and placed her in a chair. Ira sat beside her with his arm around her and called 911.

John rushed to the restroom and grabbed a handful of paper towels. He brought them back and placed them on Polly's chest. He applied pressure to slow the bleeding. Her entire chest was covered with blood.

"It's my shoulder, you idiot," said Polly through gritted teeth. "Or are you just copping a feel?"

"I'm sorry. I couldn't really tell where the wound was. I can open your blouse and find it."

"Ordinarily, sugar, I'd encourage it. Since we have company, I think I'll just direct you to it."

Ira finished his request for the police and ambulance. After putting his phone away, he noticed blood dripping from John's fingers on his left hand. "Oh my God, John, you've been shot."

John had been too absorbed in Polly's injury to notice. He removed his shirt. His injury was no more than a flesh wound. Ira ran to the restroom and brought back towels for John's arm.

"Ira, do me a favor."

"Sure, John. Whatever you need."

"Go inside and get Holiday for me. Keep it quiet. We don't want to cause a panic in there."

"You got it."

"Oh, and you better inform Isabel what's going on. Let her know the cops and ambulance are going to be here any minute. She may want to make an announcement to keep everyone inside so they won't get in the way. Let everyone know there is no further danger."

John sat by Polly and held her. He kept assuring her that the wound wasn't life threatening. She did her best to smile at him.

Holiday came out immediately. He looked the situation over and made a mad dash for his car. He retrieved John's and his weapons. After giving John his gun, he took a position by the sliding doors to await the police.

The police were the first to arrive. They immediately drew down on Holiday when they saw his gun in his hand. He produced his credentials and announced that he was a federal agent. He also informed them that John was with him.

When the medics arrived, John stepped back while putting his shirt on and gave a quick statement to the officers. Then he entered the ambulance with Polly and accompanied her to the hospital. Ira gave his statement to the officers as well. Holiday and Rachael then drove the few miles to the hospital.

Isabel thanked everyone for remaining inside the restaurant. She assured them there was no further threat to anyone. The owner even offered a free dessert to anyone who wanted it.

Once it was decided that it wasn't a life-threatening wound, her surgery was completed. Knowing Polly was sedated, John had Holiday drive him back to her car parked at I and J's. He drove back to the motel, showered and slept for a few hours before returning to the hospital.

"Hey there, girl, did you get a good night's sleep?" John questioned as he entered the room.

"Gee, I don't know, kind sir. I didn't wake up to find out." Polly was finishing up her breakfast.

"How are you feeling?" John leaned over and kissed her forehead.

"I'm fine. I think. With these drugs they're giving me, my shoulder hurts but I don't care."

"When are they going to let you go?" John sat on the side of the bed and took her hand.

"I'm just waiting on the paperwork. They said it shouldn't be long now. I should be released within the hour."

"Seeing how it's Saturday, I think I'll take the day off and take care of you. How's that sound?"

"I knew something good would come out of this. Why don't you move your stuff out of that motel? You can bring it over to the house? I might need a lot of taking care of. Maybe even for days."

She did her best to look sexy. The effort fell short. But John still welcomed the message.

"I'm not sure that's a good idea."

"Why not, John? You spend most of the nights over there anyway. Besides, I want to keep an eye on you." Polly squeezed his hand and gave him a disappointed look.

"If somebody is gunning for me, I don't want you shot again. Besides, I can move faster alone."

"So you're saying you're going to stay away from me?" Polly gave John a look that made him feel sad.

"No way, young lady. It's just that when we're out and about I don't think you should walk with me."

"So come on over to the house and I promise we won't do much walking." She gave him a sexy grin.

"I may do that. In the meantime let's get you home and tucked in. I will be your waiter today."

Holiday and Rachael followed John and Polly to her house. John kept alert for any suspicious activity along the way. He closed the blinds on all the windows. They made Polly comfortable on the couch and settled in for an enjoyable visit. Holiday drove over to Kentucky Fried Chicken and brought back lunch. That evening Holiday barbequed steaks and they broke out the Lambrusco.

John left Holiday with Polly and drove over to the motel. He was carrying a suitcase to the car when he saw movement out of the corner of his eye. It was a natural reflex for him to drop to his knees and grab his gun at the same time. The crack of the bullet was loud as it passed over him. He spun and fired. The figure hollered out in pain and ran away between the cars in the parking lot.

John rose and looked in the direction the person ran. The thought of going after him was quickly squelched. The danger of exposing his body to a hidden gunman was not a good plan. He threw his bag in the car and drove back to Polly's. He kept an eye on the rearview mirror and made several turns to see if he was being followed. He felt safe in the fact that he was not followed.

What's going on? Why have I, all of a sudden, become a target? It can't be because I'm close to the killer. I still have no idea who the murderer is.

John told Holiday and the ladies all about the incident. They all agreed it was because they were closer to finding the killer than they realized. It was now apparent that Holiday's safety was also at stake.

———————

Big Jack entered the emergency room at the Banner Del E. Webb Medical Center. The nurse questioned his problem. Big Jack responded with, "I have a hole through my shoulder muscle."

The intern came over and removed Jack's shirt. "Let me have a look at that shoulder."

"Easy, boy. It's sore," complained Big Jack.

"Wow! It looks like a GSW to the deltoid muscle." The intern looked surprised. Then he examined it closer.

"What the hell is a GSW to the deltoid muscle?" asked Big Jack. "You can speak English to me, son."

"Sir, that looks like a gunshot wound to your shoulder muscle. The wound goes all the way through."

"Young man, there is an entrance and exit wound. It went in the back and came out the front. But I assure you it was not caused by someone shooting me. I'm a friendly person and everyone likes me."

"Let's not make a mystery out of it, if you don't mind. Just tell me how you received this wound." The intern was quickly becoming somewhat annoyed with his patient and his arrogance.

"I was carrying a concrete block in the back yard. A snake came out of a rosemary bush right at my feet and startled me. I backed up and tripped over a garden hose. I fell backward onto a four-tine cultivator. The tines are very sharp and one of them punctured my shoulder."

"What is a four-tine cultivator?"

"It's sort of like a rake with longer tines...what the hell difference does it make? Just fix the thing. I'm, like, hurting and I came here with the idea you people would fix it. Will you please do that?"

"Please calm down, sir. We'll clean that wound, stitch it up and have you out of here in no time." The intern took Big Jack to one of the beds and began to work on him. He was going to pay for his arrogance.

———

By Sunday afternoon, as usual, the word spread throughout the karaoke family, about Big Jack in the hospital with a puncture wound to the shoulder. Polly heard it when Isabel called her. *Is it possible that it was Big Jack that John shot?* Polly sat and stared at the telephone.

Polly hung up the phone and called to John in the kitchen. He came and helped her on with her robe, then her sling and led her out to the kitchen. He was making ham and cheese sandwiches for lunch. She sat at the table and looked up at him. He could tell by her expression that she was bothered by something.

"What's the matter, young lady? Are you hurtin'? Why are you looking at me like that? What is it?"

"My shoulder is certainly hurting that's for sure. However, John, that's not what's bothering me."

"Talk to me, honey. Have I done something to upset you?" John sat down at the table with her.

"No, you haven't done anything wrong, silly. You said, when you shot last night, you think you hit the guy. Is that right?"

John looked at her in surprise. She looked at him as though there was more to say. John leaned on the table.

"I would bet money on the fact that I shot him. I heard him yelp. I'm pretty sure I hit him. Why do you ask?"

"Big Jack went to the emergency room last night with a puncture wound to the shoulder."

"Whoa! I would have never thought of him." John sat and looked at her in total surprise. "I guess I had better get a hold of Harry and go to the hospital and find out what time he was in there. Was it before or after I made the shot?"

The two of them sat silent for a few seconds. They looked at each other still in shock. Polly felt a certain sadness. However, John felt elation in the fact they may have found their killer.

"John, I can't believe Big Jack would be involved in anything like this. He's been around for years and never been a problem. He's one of the nicest guys you'll ever meet. I'll be real surprised if it's him."

"Hopefully, before this day is over, we'll know for sure. It seems to me we're a lot closer than we thought."

Holiday answered John's call and picked him up. They drove over to the hospital. After Holiday produced credentials, they were granted access to Big Jack's emergency room medical records.

"The timing is right. It's about thirty minutes after I made the shot." John looked from the medical folder to Holiday.

John broke out in a large smile. Holiday nodded and smiled as well. They did a high fives hand slap.

"We just might wrap this thing up this morning," said Holiday. "Jot down his address and we'll pay him a visit."

John copied the address from the medical form. When they returned to the car, they checked their weapons and headed for Big Jack's. As they arrived at the gated community, the guard stopped them at the gate. Holiday again had to produce his credentials. Holiday refused to tell the guard whom he was there to see. The guard started to argue as Holiday drove away. John looked in the side view mirror and saw the guard standing in the middle of the street with his hands on his hips staring after them.

They found Big Jack in his driveway getting out of his car when they arrived. His left arm was in a sling. He watched them curiously as they exited the car. He began walking over to meet them.

"And a good Sunday afternoon, gentlemen. To what do I owe this unexpected visit?" Big Jack greeted the two men with a smile.

"Well, partner, truthfully, we're here to question you about the hole in your shoulder," informed Holiday.

"Boy, news travels fast. How in the world did you hear about that? Was it on the eleven o'clock news?"

"I don't think so. It appears that the karaoke grapevine is working overtime today," said John.

"Why would you be interested in my shoulder? What does that have to do with anything?"

"About thirty minutes before you entered the hospital, someone shot at John. John shot back and wounded the individual. I think now, you can see why we're interested," stated Holiday.

Big Jack gave out with a genuine laugh. "You think I'm the one who shot at him. That's funny."

"Sorry, but being the one shot at, I fail to see the humor. Would you be willing to take a polygraph about the incident?" questioned John.

"Not only no, but hell no."

"Why not? If you aren't involved in the shooting, why wouldn't you take the polygraph?" asked John.

"Because, they're not a true science. Their accuracy, reliability and validity is questionable. They are intrusive and damn sure inconvenient. In short, I flat-ass don't trust them. Are those good enough reasons for you? If not, I'm sure I can come up with more. If you keep asking me, I will damn sure come up with more."

"Wow, Big Jack! Don't hold back. Tell us how you feel," said John with an exaggerated smile.

"Look, guys; I fell on a four tine cultivator. Please, come on back and I'll show you exactly what happened." He led the two men into the back yard and demonstrated what happened.

"It's a lot to ask, but would you allow me to examine the wound? I'll be careful," John asked as nicely as he could.

"What would that prove?" Big Jack looked suspiciously at John. "All you're going to see is a hole in my shoulder."

"After looking at that tine, I can see that it's small. My bullet, however, is probably a little bigger. The size of the wound should answer the question."

"All I've got to say is you're just damn lucky the wound is in the shoulder and not my ass."

Big Jack complied. It possibly was too small to be a bullet wound. It was hard to tell. Both John and Holiday apologized. They were back to square one.

"That's quite all right guys. I know you've got a job to do. You can just buy me dinner at I and J's and we'll call it even." Big Jack walked them back to their car with his typical jovial demeanor.

Polly answered the rapid knock on the front door. "Hi, Rachael. Your knock sounded urgent." She led her over to the couch.

"Polly, I know that John winged that guy last night. Then Harry told me Big Jack had been in the emergency room last night with a shoulder wound. Curiosity is killing me. I thought I'd come over and see if you've heard anything new." Rachael sat on the couch and pulled one leg up under her.

"I haven't talked to them since John left. I have a real hard time believing that Big Jack would be involved in this," said Polly. "That man doesn't show any interest in anything other than stamp collecting and singing karaoke." Polly plopped down in the over-stuffed chair across the room from Rachael.

"Well, you never know. It could be anybody. It could even be Tyler. He's physically capable."

"Come on, Rachael, what possible motive would Tyler have? He's devoted to his wife and he goes out of his way for her family. He sings great and she sings just as great. He enjoys all the karaoke people and they enjoy him. There is no possible reason for him to do anything like that."

"I'm just saying it could be anybody."

"My question is why have they stopped killing karaoke singers and started trying to kill John? Would you like some coffee?" Polly rose from the couch.

"You bet. Maybe they think John is getting close to the real killer and they are trying to take him out?"

"Hey, why aren't they trying to kill Harry, too? They're a team. He and John work together," Polly said as she proceeded to the coffee pot.

"That's a good question. Maybe he's going to be next." Rachael followed Polly into the kitchen. "Hey, girl, I can take care of the coffee. I have two good arms. You go back and sit down."

———

Holiday was concentrating on his discussion with John and didn't notice the car in his rearview mirror. It had followed them since they left the 'Traditions' housing community. Holiday stopped for the light by Sam's Club on West Bell Road. The car following them pulled up alongside. Holiday glanced over just in time to see the barrel of the pistol.

Holiday pulled his shoulder up and tried to duck as he accelerated. The shot caught him in the shoulder and the back of the head. His car veered right and up onto the sidewalk and into the lamppost. He fell forward, unconscious.

chapter

SEVENTEEN

John fought with the airbag while recovering his weapon. By the time he was in a position to return fire, the assailant's vehicle was gone. He scrambled loose from his seat belt. The door was jammed. Rolling down the window and crawling out of the car, he ran around to the driver's door. After some considerable struggle, the door was yanked open. Holiday was unconscious and bleeding from the shoulder and the back of the head. John was able to release the seat belt.

As he reached for his cell phone, a man ran up and said, "I've already called 911. I'm an off-duty medic with the fire department. Let me in there. I was behind you when you left the roadway."

John moved away and allowed the medic in. His mind was racing. He knew that he needed to call someone, but whom? He had to calm down and start thinking straight. The authorities were on the way. Now what should he do? Harry's office needed to be notified. He didn't have the number.

"Excuse me, buddy. I need to have his cell phone before they take him way." John moved in front of the medic and reached across Holiday and pulled his phone from its holder. He stepped away from the car and began to scroll down. The first name to appear was "Francis".

John recalled Holiday mentioning her. He pushed the send button. It was two rings later when John heard, "Office of the Director of Homeland Security."

"Is this Francis?"

"Yes it is. How may I help you?"

"I'm John Bodie...."

"Yes Mister Bodie. I've heard a lot about you. What can I do for you?" The voice was warm and friendly.

"I have some bad news. Harry's been shot."

There was a gasp at the other end. "I knew I would receive this call some day. How bad is it?" Francis' voice was shaky and weak.

"I don't know yet. It's a head wound and he's unconscious. I have medical help. Hold on a minute."

The medic had just reclined the seat and repositioned Holiday. He stepped back and straightened up. John grabbed him by the arm. "Can you leave him long enough to talk on the phone?"

"Yeah, I've done all I can for him. Who am I talking too?" The medic wiped the blood from his hands onto his pants.

"This man is a very important person. I have the Department of Homeland Security on the phone. They want to know how bad the injury is." John handed the medic Holiday's cell phone.

"Hi. I'm an off-duty medic with no equipment. I did what I could for him while we're waiting for the ambulance."

Francis tried not to sound impatient, "We certainly appreciate that. Please tell me about his injury."

"He has a gunshot wound that passed through the shoulder and grazed the occipital bone. It's hard to tell at this point if the occipital lobe was damaged. He has lost an awful lot of blood."

Trying her best to fight back panic, Francis said, "If the lobe was damaged, what does that mean?"

"He could lose his sight. Blindness could occur. I have to go. The ambulance has arrived."

"Sir, I thank you for the information. Would you please put the other man back on the phone?" The medic motioned to John and handed him the phone.

"John here."

"I don't know what you two have gotten yourselves into. Harry hasn't kept me informed. It's obviously serious. I'm going to get Turner on a flight this evening. Can you pick him up at Luke?"

"I'm afraid when Harry was shot he wrecked the car. Can Turner pick up another one at the base?"

"I'm sure he can. How can he contact you?"

"I have Harry's cell phone. Have him call and I will guide him in. I'll probably meet him at the hospital."

"Thanks Mister Bodie for holding this thing together until Turner arrives. Harry is lucky to have you. I'm glad to finally meet you. It's a shame we had to meet under these circumstances."

"I agree, Miss Francis. Thanks for your help. I'll look forward to seeing Tom again. Bodie out."

John jumped into the ambulance with Holiday. He sat in the emergency room of the Banner Del E. Webb Medical Center. With shock wearing off, he remembered he needed to make a phone call.

Polly saw the identification of the caller as she opened the flap on her phone. "It's about time you called. We've been worried about you two. You should have been here hours ago. Is everything all right?"

"I'm afraid not."

"What do you mean 'not'?" Polly sat straight up on the couch and looked over at Rachael.

"Harry's been shot. I'm at the hospital up on Grand Avenue. It doesn't look good, Polly."

"Oh, no! How bad is it?" Polly bent her head down and brought her left hand up to her face.

"I don't know yet. I'm still waiting in the emergency room and no one has told me anything."

"Was he conscious? John, please tell me he was."

"No."

"Oh, my! Where is the wound?"

"Wound," repeated Rachael, as she moved closer to Polly.

"It's a head wound. He was really bleeding. If he lives, the medic said he could be blind."

"Oh my God! I can't believe it. Poor Harry. I'll have Rachael drive me over there. I'll hurry."

Polly was almost in tears when she told Rachael. She was shocked that Rachael wasn't more emotional about it. "What's wrong with you, girl? It's your boyfriend we're talking about."

"I'm sorry to hear it. I feel bad for him. But face the facts, Polly. These are just play-toys for us. They're going to be leaving soon. They won't even remember our names in a few weeks. I'm warning you now; do not get too attached to them. All that's going to do is break your heart."

"Wow! You're one cold calculating bitch." Polly glared at Rachael. "John is not just a play-toy. He is a human being who I happen to care very much for. I intend to keep in touch. Who knows what the future holds." Polly hurriedly dressed, and led Rachael out the door.

When the ladies arrived, they found John still sitting in the emergency room. Polly hurried over to him. He gave her a warm embrace. Rachael leaned in between the two and also hugged John.

"Have you heard anything new?" asked Rachael. "Have the doctors been out? Did they tell you what's going on?"

"They haven't said a word." John sat back down with the women sitting on each side of him.

"I guess you two have the killer worried. It appears that he's not going to give up until you guys are out of the way," said Rachael.

"What the dumb ass doesn't realize is that this is a national security problem and even if he gets us, more will come. In fact, the idiot has pissed off Homeland Security now and they are sending down more people. He has really crapped in his hat this time. We are really going to work now. The whole damn TACT may show up."

"What's a TACT?" asked Rachael.

"Terrorist Activity Control Team. It's a team that is made up of military specialists. I've worked with them several times and they have never failed in any endeavor they've undertaken. It's just a matter of time."

"God, I hope so," said Polly. "I'm tired of being afraid. I mean afraid for myself, you, Rachael and all the karaoke singers."

"Well, it definitely looks as though it's coming to a head." Rachael nodded while staring at the floor.

"Excuse me. Are you the gentleman that came in with the gunshot victim?" inquired the intern.

John and the women stood as soon as the intern approached. "Yes, I'm John Bodie, Mister Holiday's partner."

"I'm his girlfriend," said Rachael not noticing Polly's dirty look. John put his hand out and stopped Rachael from getting between him and the intern.

"I'm afraid the bullet fractured the cranium. We're not sure, at this point, how severe the damage is to the occipital lobe. We're still working with him. The injury is not life threatening. We are concerned about damage to his vision. We'll let you know as soon as we know." The intern mouthed "Sorry", turned and left.

John fell back into his chair. The women remained standing and looking down at John. He shook his head and looked back up at the women. "I'm going to kill the son-of-bitch. I've got to be the one that gets him. That man's career is his life. If he loses his eyesight, he loses his career."

Tom Turner, the second-in-command of TACT, was an ex-special forces' 'A Team' member in Iraq just before the war broke out. He stands six-two, weighs 180 pounds and is good looking with his black hair and brown eyes. He's a clean-shaven, non-smoker. Even at forty-six years of age, he only carries four percent body fat. He's one of the toughest members of the team.

"Tom, I've got you a flight out of Andrew's AFB. You're going to have to step on it. The pilot wants to return here this evening," said Francis over the phone.

"I'm almost out the door now. I'll call you if I get any additional news about the chief." Turner grabbed his suitcase and utility bag with the tools of his trade: various weapons, wrist-ties, marking devices, explosives and other exciting things.

His fellow team member, Charles Avery, an ex-Air Force special Ops member was waiting outside with the car engine running.

Turner threw the bags in the back seat and Avery wasted no time accelerating away. As soon as they pulled onto the tarmac, the pilot fired up his engines. Once Turner and his baggage were aboard and the door was closed, the plane taxied to the runway.

Turner called Holiday's phone as soon as they touched down and talked to John. A GSA car was waiting for him. John guided him to the hospital. Rachael was asleep, curled up in the emergency room chair. John and Polly rushed over to meet Turner as soon as he entered the door.

It was like old-home week for the two men. They had worked closely together on several cases. They had a high regard for each other. John brought him up to date on the case from the first day to the present.

Rachael woke up rubbing the sleep out of her eyes. She strolled over to the group and was introduced to Turner. She shook hands with him. She held the handshake a little too long.

She looked at Polly and said, "Damn, where do they find these guys? They just keep getting better."

"Rachael!" hollered Polly. "What in the world is the matter with you? You're acting so weird lately."

"I'm kidding. Harry's still my man. You're cute, honey. But Old Harry has beaten you to me."

"Huh?" uttered Turner.

"I'll explain it later," advised John.

"John, based on what you've told me, I wonder if we should bring the entire team down and get this thing over with?"

"What do you mean 'entire team down'? How many are you talking about?" asked Rachael.

"Ma'am, I'm sorry but that's classified. Nevertheless, it would damn sure clean this mess up in a hurry. We would find the leak at the laboratory and the killer and be home in no time. Our guys are that good." Turner looked her in the eye with a typical military determination.

Rachael looked over at John as if to say, "This man is scary." She swallowed and said, "If that's what it's going to take, what are you waiting for? Get your men down here. You should do it."

They were interrupted by the approach of a doctor. "Who should I talk to about Mister Holiday?"

John advised the doctor, "I'm Holiday's partner, but Turner here should probably be the man to talk to." The doctor nodded and asked Turner to come with him. The remaining group looked at each other with Polly saying what the group was thinking. "That's not good. No, that's not good."

They all sat down and waited for Turner's return. No one felt like talking. No one knew what to say.

chapter

EIGHTEEN

John was sitting and staring at the floor. He was wondering what to do next. Polly reached over and touched John's arm. He looked up to see Turner returning. The three remained seated while Turner stood in front of them.

"Well, like the old saying goes, we have some good news and some bad news," announced Turner.

"What's the good news?" asked Rachael.

"The good news is he's going to live," replied Turner

"The bad news?" questioned John.

"The bullet did fracture the occipital bone. The occipital lobe also got some minor damage."

"In English please?" requested Rachael.

"He has a skull fracture in the lower rear of his head. And the lobe that handles vision was damaged."

"Will this result in his loss of vision?" asked John. "Please tell me the man isn't going to be blind."

"They don't know for sure at this point. But he could have blurred vision," informed Turner.

"Like for the rest of his life?" questioned Rachael.

"They don't know for sure. It's possible that the condition could be temporary. Only time will tell."

"Can we see him?" asked Rachael.

"I'm afraid not. He is heavily sedated. He's going to have one hell of a headache. He won't be able to have any visitors until tomorrow afternoon." Turner reached into his pocket and brought out his car keys. "Let's get me bedded down for the night. This has been one hell of a day."

"I have an extra room," offered Rachael. She moved over to him. Both John and Polly gave Rachael a dirty look.

John took Turner by the arm. "Come on, Tom. I'll get you checked in at the motel with me."

———

As usual, the sun was bright and the smell of desert dust was in the air when Rachael rushed off to work on Monday morning. John prepared breakfast for the one-armed Polly and made sure she was set for the day. He borrowed her car and drove over to the motel to get Turner, who followed John back to drop off Polly's car. It was easier than trying to give Turner directions to Polly's house in Sun City West. From there they drove over to the hospital.

The hospital medical staff refused to allow John and Turner access to Holiday. Turner produced his credentials and mentioned national security. They allowed them five minutes with Holiday.

The first question John asked Holiday, due to the limited time, was, "Did you see the shooter?"

The heavily sedated Holiday managed to get the message across that he only saw the gun. Turner talked to him and he complained that it seemed like he was looking through water. He also told them he was having the worst headache of his life. They let him rest and decided to return later in the day.

They returned to the laboratory and Sgt. Steel introduced Turner around. He was familiar with the lab. He recalled vividly the terrorist attack that killed several military policemen several years ago. The same terrorists also stole a highly classified secret weapon and led TACT and John on a cross-country chase. After the howdys and handshakes, Turner and John went to lunch at John's favorite, Cracker Barrel.

While waiting for their food to arrive, Turner said, "I know you and the chief have been working on the murders. It seems to me that the important mission is stopping the classified leak. Have you guys lost sight of that?"

"Tom, the murders and the leak are all tied together. We find the killer, we solve the leak."

"With all the time you've been spending looking for the killer, how do you know that the information isn't still going out?"

Steel and John looked at each other. "I guess we don't," said John, "but we do know that no unauthorized person is getting into the classified cabinet. In fact there is only one person that goes into that file. It's her job. Sergeant Steel set up a surveillance camera. He checks the video every morning."

"That's good to know. I was just told they are about to wrap up the project. If any of this classified info gets out now, it could be a catastrophe." Turner leaned back to allow the server to set his plate down. "Do you have any leads on who this killer might be or his connection with the lab?"

"We have good reason to believe that a karaoke singer is involved. You'll have to come to karaoke with me tonight. It's a tight-knit bunch of people. I'd like to get your read on the group."

"I don't know. I'm not into listening to a bunch of amateur singers struggle through their songs. I do like a good drink, though."

"You need to hear these people sing before you judge them. You're going to be surprised. Not only are they good, but the food is great and the waitress is pretty. I think you're going to enjoy it."

"I'll trust you, John. What time do we go?"

"I and J's opens at five but they let the singers start coming in at 4:30. It's good to be there early and listen to the conversations. They're a pretty cool group." John put his fork down and took a big drink of sweet tea.

After lunch John and Turner went to the hospital. Holiday was still heavily sedated but more coherent. He still complained about blurred vision and the worst headache of his life.

"I have tried to remember if I saw the shooter. All I really remember is that damn gun. I keep getting flashes of a face looking at me, but it doesn't stay with me long enough to make it out."

"Don't worry. If we have to bring the whole team down here we'll get the person who did this. He's a dead man walking." Turner moved over to the bed and patted Holiday on the ankle.

After twenty minutes, Holiday told them he was getting tired. "We'll let you get some rest. I'm going to take Tom to karaoke tonight. I want him to look the group over and see what he comes up with."

"Are you taking the girls, too?" ask Holiday.

"I don't think so. It's just Tom and me tonight. Actually I don't know if they're coming or not. I didn't ask them," explained John. "It's probably not a good idea. I want to set a good example for Tom."

"It's too late for that. Tom's worked with you before." Holiday tried to laugh but flinched with his headache.

"Serves you right, Harry. We'll talk to you later. Don't go anywhere." John laughed and left the room.

John and Turner arrived in the lobby of I and J's and found the chain still around the gate and seven of the singers were already there. Ira and Jasiu were arguing about who got there first.

"You just don't want to follow me because I set the standard too high for you," announced Ira loud enough for all to hear and laugh.

"That's not true at all Ira. I want you to follow me because just before I finish my song I intend to pass gas and hand you the microphone," said Jasiu. Everyone broke out in laughter that included John and Turner.

Isabel unlocked the gate and the singers started in. Turner saw Isabel and mumbled, "Wow!"

John caught him by the arm. "Let me warn you, good buddy. You can look but don't touch. Flirting is even dangerous. You are one of the toughest men I know. But you ain't seen José."

"Thanks for the warning." Turner just nodded as he entered.

John didn't sit with the singers this time. The two men sat across the dance floor from them. Just as they were finishing their meal Rachael came in with Polly. They joined John and Turner.

The women had to catch up on Holiday's condition. Polly wondered if they had any new leads. Rachael decided, since Turner was there, she would sing tonight.

Rachael put her name up on the counter in front of Sandie. Sandie filled out the singing order and Jasiu jumped up, took the list and wrote the names on a large board. Rachael was number eight on the list of twenty. Arnie, Sandie's husband, the karaoke jockey, didn't allow anyone to sing out of order like some of the other KJ's. If you were number ten then you sang in the number ten spot. Nobody was allowed to squeeze in front of you. If you came when the last person on the list was singing, you waited until the next round.

John, kidding and joking with the women at the table, stopped abruptly. The quick change in his manner was noticed by Turner. John sat back, looked at Turner and nodded toward the door. Both

John and Turner rose from the table and Turner followed John out of the restaurant.

Once in the lobby John said, "There're two 'good old boys' that just came in and are sitting in a booth behind us. Harry and I had a physical encounter with them a week ago. I had another one with the two of them a few days ago.

"They're self-admitted Aryan Nation. Those two come in here every so often. One's from Tennessee and the other is from Georgia. According to them, they're some kind of scouting party or advance party to the area. They intend to establish a foothold in the Phoenix area and open a chapter here.

"These guys usually leave in the middle of all the singing. When they're here they spend most of the time watching our table and less time looking at the singers. I don't like them being behind us. We'll have to change places with the women. I'm going to listen to the first round of singers and then leave.

"I'll wait in the shadows across the parking lot. One usually comes out ahead of the other. I'll watch him and you can follow the second one out and see what he does. Is that Okay with you?"

"John, until I get a little more into the game down here, you are more than welcome to call the shots. This could get exciting and I damn sure could use the exercise. I'll follow your lead, buddy."

"The younger one is Hobbs. I don't remember the other guy's name. My adrenalin pumps anytime I see them. Be prepared for trouble. Harry warned them to stay away from us. If they do run into us make sure their hands are empty."

Turner smiled and nodded showing he understood. John led him back into the restaurant. It confused the women, but they didn't complain when John made them change places.

The singing began as normal with Sammy leading off followed by his girlfriend Delta. Scooter was next with Fred after her. Ira took the mic from Fred and sang 'If You're Gonna Do Me Wrong, Do It Right'. Jasiu did an outstanding job with 'Keep on Rockin'. When Rachael's turn came she sang Patsy Cline's song 'Crazy'. When she finished, John was surprised to see Hobbs leave the booth and go out the door.

John rushed to the bathroom and found it empty. Then he ran outside just in time to see Hobbs enter a car. John moved quietly and quickly into the shadows across the street and waited.

Ira came outside on the sidewalk to use the cell phone. He casually walked around the side of the building as he talked. Tolman, the man from Tennessee, almost knocked him down as he ran past him.

"Hey, you stupid son-of-a-bitch, watch where you're going. The least you could do is apologize."

"Screw you, old man."

"Old man, my ass. You asshole, you need a lesson in manners." Ira began to run after him.

Tolman dropped down on his knees and reached under the dumpster and pulled out an envelope. As he straightened up, Ira caught him with a right cross. He put all his weight behind it, and the man went over backward and the envelope went sailing off in the middle of the alley.

Tolman jumped up and started for the envelope when Ira caught him again with another right cross. Tolman grabbed Ira and tried to hit him. Ira ducked and held onto him. During their wrestling around, Turner arrived and not fully realizing what was going on separated the two men. Ira told Turner to stay out of it. Tolman moved over toward the envelope.

Hobbs started the car and drove over by the activity. John ran over there as well. They got there at about the same time.

"Stop that guy," hollered John as he approached. "Don't let him get away. We need to talk to him."

Tolman grabbed up the envelope and started for the car. Turner, in his unsuccessful attempt to tackle Tolman, caused him to lose his hold on the envelope. Tolman kept running and jumped into the car with Hobbs, and the car sped away.

"Damn. Ira that was a pretty brave thing you just did." John came over and patted Ira on the back. "He was a big guy. He was also a young guy."

"I don't care about his size. He might get a meal, but I was at least going to get a sandwich," said Ira.

"That guy is a real bad ass. I don't care what you say, that was still brave," continued John.

"Brave? Hell I just wanted to teach him some manners. That butthole needed some educating."

Turner opened the envelope and said, "You did a lot more than teach him some manners. You may have solved our case."

"What are you talking about, Tom?" John moved over by Turner.

"You're not going to believe this, but this happens to be some very important paper work. It's the kind we've been looking for." He looked at John with a big smile.

"What was it doing under the dumpster?" questioned Ira.

"I'm not sure, Ira. I have an idea it was placed there for that guy to pick up," informed John.

"You say that I may have solved the case. Does that mean you know who the killer is now?"

"It's damn possible Ira. You might've just met him," stated John.

"Holy crap! I think I need a drink. I'll be inside if you need me." Ira turned away in shock and walked slowly back to the restaurant.

"Keep this to yourself for now. Don't tell anyone about this. It must stay our secret," Turner hollered.

Ira held up his hand to show he understood.

"John, let's go into the lobby and have a look at this. From what I can tell so far, these are classified documents from the lab."

"Why were they here?"

"That's a damn good question. What were those dudes doing with them?" questioned Turner.

"Yeah, and who put them there?"

The two men entered the lobby and sat down in the armchairs by the planter. Turner read the three pages and looked at the two pages of drawings. He shook his head and put them back in the envelope.

"I'm sorry, John. I can't even show them to you. They are classified documents from the laboratory. I'm not even sure if my clearance is high enough to look at them. I think it is. I'm not sure."

"What the hell are they doing here, Tom? And why would they be hidden under the dumpster?"

"You said this place and the killings were tied to the documents. It proves that your suspicions are correct."

"But that's all it proves."

Turner placed his hand on John's shoulder. "I think it proves who the killers are."

"I'm sure those guys are the killers. Since they don't have access to the lab, then their supplier has to bring them here for the pickup. I wonder how they knew the documents would be under the dumpster tonight."

"But why here? In all of Maricopa County, why I and J's?" John shook his head and stood.

"You said that Hires sang here. Do you suppose she was the original leak?" Turner looked at John quizzically.

"I don't think so, Tom. She is the one who discovered the leak. She was murdered not twenty-five feet from that dumpster. That woman wanted to tell Holiday who the person was that was going into her files."

"Maybe she got cold feet and wanted to stop?"

"If that's the case why did she call you guys?" John wrinkled his forehead and squinted his eyes.

"Yeah, I guess you're right."

"What's the date on those documents?"

Turner opened the envelope and looked in. "Last Friday. Why?"

"I bet if we check the closed circuit video, you'll find only one person has been in that file. We have our leak and possibly our killer as well."

"Are you saying it's Rachael?"

"This is going to kill Harry. He really likes her. She is retired military. What would make her turn against her own country?"

"John, it's probably as simple as money."

"Money and two hot young studs. She does like to play around."

"How do you think we should handle her?" questioned Turner.

"If we don't say anything and I can get her on the polygraph tomorrow, we could get all kinds of information."

"That's a good idea except for one thing."

"What's that?"

"Those two dudes are going to tell her what happened. When that occurs you will have seen the last of her."

"You're absolutely right. I guess we should take her to the lab and go to work on her tonight."

"That goes without question. Let's go do it." Turner stood and started for the door with John following.

As they approached the table they noticed Polly sitting alone. John stood next her and asked, "Where did Rachael go?"

"She got a call on her cell phone and said she had to go to the ladies room. That was about five or six minutes ago."

Turner turned and headed for the ladies room. He opened the door and hollered inside, "Rachael." He repeated two more times and then asked, "Is anyone in here? A man needs to come in. Holler if anyone is in here." When there was no answer, Turner entered and checked out the stalls. The room was unoccupied.

He rushed back to the table. John saw the look in his eyes. He sat down next to Polly and asked, "Did you or Rachael drive tonight?"

"Because of my arm, she drove."

Turner heard this and asked Polly to show him where Rachael had parked. Polly led them out to the parking lot by the side door. Rachael's car was gone.

chapter

NINETEEN

"You idiots! How could you screw this up? We were so close," Rachael hollered into the cell phone. "If we don't get the rest of the documents, we're dead. You hear me? You have no idea how much trouble you have put me in." She swerved around a car on Bell Road as she headed for the freeway.

"There wasn't nothin' we could do. Those guys jumped Cleduus. We had to get out of there. They already threatened us once. What are we going to do? We have to have those documents," said Tolman.

Hobbs pulled over on El Mirage Road and parked. They had no idea what to do next and were depending on Rachael for an answer.

"I have to get to the laboratory before the guards find out about me. I can get another copy of the documents you lost."

"Should we come with you?" asked Tolman as Hobbs started the car and slowly pulled away from the curb.

"You're damn right. What I want you to do is park within view of the laboratory and cover my ass."

"Why? The guards don't know nothin'. They ain't going to be bothering you," said Tolman.

"God, you two are so stupid. I don't know why I teamed up with a couple of country bumpkins."

"Rachael, you don't have to go and start calling us names. We couldn't help what happened."

"Use your head, Cleduus. Think about it. Did you warn me about this mess on the cell phone?"

"Yes, ma'am. We done good."

"Well, stupid, don't you think they can do the same thing with the lab? They could be on the phone with the lab right now."

"Hmmm, I see what you mean. Where are you now?"

"I'm on Bell Road heading toward 101 and then I'm going straight south to the laboratory."

"Hobbs and I will beat you to the lab. We'll be set up to take care of you. Don't you worry none."

"Yeah. Right." Rachael continued to speed to the freeway. "Keep out of sight and don't spook the guard."

"John, you know that woman better than me. What do you think she is going to do now?" questioned Turner.

"My guess is she will go straight to the lab and try to get a duplicate copy of that classified document before the military police find out about her. She knows by tomorrow everyone will be looking for her."

"We need to notify them," advised Turner.

"John, I have a little problem. I don't have a ride home now that she's gone," mentioned Polly.

"Tom, can we drop Polly off at home on the way to the lab?"

"I wish I could. We just don't have the time. I'm sorry. Let's get back in the restaurant and gather up our stuff. We need to get moving."

"Here sugar." John handed Polly a twenty dollar bill. "Call a cab and I'll be over as soon as I can."

"Be careful. I want you back in one piece." She smiled, spun around and returned to the restaurant.

"You have Harry's cell phone. I think he has Sergeant Steel's number in there. If he does you should call him and have him alert his M. P.s," directed John. "She could be there any minute."

The two of them returned to the table to see if they had forgotten anything. John threw some bills down and they rushed out to the car. Turner handed John Harry's cell phone. He wanted to concentrate on his driving. John scanned through the list of saved numbers but was unable to locate the sergeant's number.

"Steel's number is not in here."

"John, try information."

John dialed information and was informed the number was unlisted. When John told Turner this, he took the phone and gave his identification and a code number to the operator. A few seconds later, he told John to start writing. John wrote the phone number down. He pulled his phone from the holster and quickly punched in the numbers. "Sergeant Steel," was the reply.

"Bodie here, buddy. We have an emergency and need your help."

"Name it."

"Call your military policemen and warn them that Rachael Holmes is the spy. She is not allowed in the facility. In fact since it's a national security threat, they are to apprehend her. We are on the way to the laboratory now. You might want to do the same. We should be there in ten or fifteen minutes."

"Rachael Holmes, I'd never have guessed that. Do you think she is going to go there this time of night?"

"We have good reason to believe that she may almost be there now. So please get on the horn and advise your troops."

"Wilco and out."

Turner did a quick glance at John. "What did he say?"

"He said he will comply. I'm sure he's making the call now."

"John, the more I think about it the more I hope we're wrong about her going to the lab," stated Turner.

"Why? If she does we may catch her," responded John. "This case could be just as good as over."

"Those MPs could be caught off guard. These people are killers. I don't want to see anything happen to them."

"You may be right. We're going to be there shortly. I'm sure Steel has alerted them by now as well."

———————

The military policeman at the gate had just hung up the phone. He hadn't had time to alert the interior guard or the guard at the lab door when Rachael pulled up at the gate. He stepped out of the guard house and walked over to the gate.

"Good evening Miss Holmes. This is a surprise. What can I do for you?" asked the guard.

Good. He hasn't been notified yet. This may go smoothly after all. "You won't believe this. I forgot something in my desk and I need to run in and get it. Would that be Okay?" questioned Rachael.

"No problem ma'am. Just let me unlock the gate." The guard opened the gate.

Rachael thanked him and smiled as she started to enter. She had only taken a few steps, when the MP spoke.

"Sorry ma'am." The MP reached under his shirt and produced his issued weapon. "But I have orders to stop you from entering the lab. If you don't mind, I need you to walk over to the guardhouse."

"You've got to be kidding. Who would give you those orders? I'm cleared to work here and you know that."

"No ma'am, I'm not kidding. I'm serious. I also have orders to detain you until my sergeant arrives."

"Let's move, Al. The word's out. The guard has her at gunpoint," said Tolman as he opened the car door. He was careful to close his door as quietly as he could. He drew his weapon and moved along the fence toward the MP.

Hobbs quietly jumped out and moved, with stealth, down the street out of the MPs vision. He didn't want to shoot and alert the guard inside or anyone else for that matter. Tolman moved closer.

When they were as close as they could get without being seen, Hobbs stepped out and shouted, "Drop the gun, dude, or die. It's your choice, buddy." He took aim and tightened up on the trigger.

The Military Policeman spun around and saw the two men with their guns drawn. He thought fast and made his decision. "If you don't want this lady dead, I suggest you drop your guns."

While his weapon was pointed at Rachael and he was looking at the two men, Rachael reached into her purse and took out her .25 cal. automatic. "Sorry, soldier, but this woman isn't going to die."

He turned back to her. His expression changed from surprise to pain as she shot him three times. She told the two men to follow her, but stay out of sight. Rachael threw open the facility door as the interior MP arrived.

"What the...."

She interrupted him. "Hurry. Your buddy needs you." Rachael stepped aside and the MP ran out into the two waiting attackers.

Tolman swung his pistol striking the MP in the back of the head and rendered him unconscious. Then Tolman and Rachel raced over to the Conex container door. Rachael left Hobbs behind to watch the front entrance door. She opened the Conex door and ran down the ramp with her weapon drawn. The MP looked up to see her running down the ramp. Before it registered with him there was a stranger with her, she displayed her gun.

"If you even move you're dead. We killed your buddies and you're crazy if you think we won't kill you," announced Rachael. The MP held his hands in the air and followed her orders of not moving.

She took the keys from the MP's desk drawer, then entered the lab and ran directly to her office. After unlocking the classified document container, she removed several folders.

Tolman struck the MP over the head with his weapon. He fell unconscious to the floor as Rachael rushed from the lab and up the ramp. Tolman made sure the MP wasn't moving, and then followed her.

As Rachael ran from the facility, she glanced down at the MP, who was dying, and continued to her car. She slammed the door and turned on the ignition. Hobbs and Tolman ran for their car.

Turner and John saw Rachael drive away from the gate and started to give chase. Hobbs and Tolman both opened fire on Turner's vehicle. One of their bullets flattened the right front tire causing the vehicle to veer to the curb and up onto the sidewalk.

John was first out and returning fire. Hobbs went down and Tolman jumped into the car. Hobbs grabbed his leg and tried to make it to the car. Tolman floored the vehicle as Hobbs screamed for him not to leave him.

Hobbs threw down his gun and raised his hands. He was down on his knees. John's first shot caught him in the left thigh.

Sergeant Steel arrived at the gate. Even before he stopped he saw his downed MP. He ran from his car to the dying man.

"Oh my God, not again. Please Lord, don't let this happen again." Steel began reliving the nightmare of the terrorist attack of a few years before this. He was trying to shake those visions from his head as he dropped down by his buddy.

The MP attempted to smile but death stopped it and a fixed stare occurred instead. Steel couldn't stop the tear that formed in his eye. Turner rushed over to him and left John to guard Hobbs.

"Hang tough, Sergeant," encouraged Turner. "We'll check on the others. Take your time."

Turner turned and saw the prostrate body of the other MP by the door. He was first to reach him. Kneeling down, Turner checked his carotid artery and felt a strong pulse.

"Thank God," exclaimed Turner.

"Is he alive?" queried Steel.

Turner looked at the blood on his scalp. "Yes, but he's going to have a headache. He's going to be Okay. We need to check inside. We can help him later."

The two men noticed the Conex door open and hurried over to it. They rushed down the ramp and found the other unconscious MP. After determining he was alive, they continued on through the open door to the classified document container.

"Damn it to hell, it appears the bitch cleaned it out," exclaimed Turner

Sergeant Steel entered the lab and met Turner coming out. He could tell by the look on Turner's face the news wasn't good. He stopped by the door.

"Sergeant, get on the phone and notify all law enforcement agencies of Holmes' description and the information on her car. Is that information here? You do have a file on her, right?"

'You bet. We have files on all the employees." Steel hurried over to the personnel files. "I'll be go to hell."

"What's the matter?" asked Turner

"Guess who's file is missing?"

"All right, let's take the guy we got upstairs and get some information from him. That should give us something to go on. I'll leave you here to help your MP. I'll go out front and help the other one." Turner started for the door.

"I'd appreciate that, sir. I am kind of worried about them."

"After we get them on their feet, we'll get down to business with our wounded friend. I'm good at getting down to business. So is John."

"I can't wait to watch, Sir."

The two men worked on the unconscious soldiers. Once they were up and around, the sergeant took them up to his office. He called the next shift to come to work. As soon as they arrived, he was going to send the two men to the hospital for observation.

"Well, old buddy, it appears that your friends have flat-ass abandoned you. Don't you worry. We'll stay with you. I promise you won't be bored. We have lots of plans for you," advised Turner.

"Hey, dude, did you forget you shot me? I'm bleeding here. I could bleed out and die, damn it," whined Hobbs.

"Oh you mean like the poor soldier by the gate. I'm sorry, pal. We just can't seem to get a case of the sympathies for you. Try plugging the hole with your finger. It may make you last a little longer," said Turner faking concern.

"I just thought of something, Tom."

"What would that be?"

"If you don't have a file on Rachael, why don't I question someone who has lived with her for the past couple of weeks? I have a feeling Harry would have a wealth of information. Even Polly may help us."

"I hate to break the news to Harry this way."

"Tom, he is one tough old bird. We're talking a pot-load of classified information floating around out there."

"You're right. I want to lean on this dude before he bleeds to death. Why don't you go ahead? Take Steel's car and go on to the hospital and get what info you can. We've got to get that bitch."

"Hey, assholes, I'm dying here. You can't just let me die. You have to help. It's your job to do something."

"Oh, don't you worry. I intend to do something." Tom gave an exaggerated smile. "Every time I think of that dead soldier out there, I think of something else to do."

John and Turner helped Hobbs into the facility and placed him at the foot of the ramp leading up to the sergeant's office. John continued on up and got Steel's car keys and hurried out to his car.

"Listen, dying man, I would take you up to the office and make you comfortable, but I don't want you to bleed all over it and mess it up." Turner pulled an empty crate over and sat down.

"You can't leave me here. I'm in a lot of pain."

"That's another reason I can't take you up to the office. I need you to be in pain so that you'll talk to me. If I did take you up to the office, there are a couple of soldiers who just lost a comrade and I'm sure they would put you out of your pain before I could stop them."

chapter

TWENTY

Rachael's car turned off of Avondale Blvd. onto the eastbound ramp of I-10. Once she was on the freeway, she crossed over to the inside lane and pressed on the accelerator. The speedometer was passing eighty-five miles per hour.

Pushing the speed dial button on her cell phone, she heard Tolman's voice and asked, "Where are you guys?"

"I'm just a couple cars behind you, Rachael. I'm by myself. I'm afraid Hobbs didn't make it."

"What the hell do you mean he didn't make it? How did he not make it?"

"He was shot and couldn't get to the car." Tolman passed the remaining car that separated them.

"So you just drove off and left him? I don't believe you did that. What is wrong with you?"

"Rachael, honest to God, I didn't have a choice. You know damn well I didn't want to leave him."

"Well, if he lives he can talk. If he talks, you and I both have had it. You'd better pray he's dead."

"He's my buddy. I don't want him to be dead." Tolman had difficulty holding back a tear for his buddy. "Where are we going?"

"Where are you, now?"

"I'm the car that's right behind you." Tolman blinked his headlights.

"Stay with me, because we're going to the movies." Rachael turned north on 101 and came off the ramp at ninety miles per hour. She left the freeway at Thunderbird and drove north on 83rd Ave to the multiplex theater.

"What are we going to do here?" queried Tolman.

"The last show's just started. It will be more than an hour before people come out and look for their cars."

"So?"

"God, you're dense. We're going to find us a car. They've seen ours. They're giving that info to every law enforcement agency."

"Oh, yeah. Sorry, I didn't think of that." They parked in the lot and began walking around.

Rachael moved swiftly. She pulled on door handles and looked in car windows. Tolman followed her around.

"What kind of car are we looking for?"

"One that's unlocked, fool. Do me a favor and don't talk to me. Just go someplace I'm not and check for an unlocked car."

In less than five minutes she located a vehicle that someone neglected to secure. She hollered for Tolman. He came running.

"Can you hotwire this thing?" Rachael asked as she looked around the lot for anyone that might see them.

"Hell yeah. I've been doing that since I was a teenager. Hotwire is my middle name. That's one thing I'm good at."

It was an older model Plymouth. The ignition was not complicated. Within three minutes he had the engine running. They drove out of the parking lot north to Bell Road.

John had a twenty minute drive to the hospital. He had to overcome the objections of the medical staff in order to get in to see Holiday. When he finally made it, he found Holiday awake and lucid. However he kept squinting in his attempt to see John clearly. He still suffered from blurred vision.

"Hey, John, what in the world are you doing here at this time of night?" He looked over at the clock on the wall and noticed it read 9:25. "Did you guys just leave I and J's? Did Tom enjoy it?"

John sat down on the corner of Holiday's bed. "Harry, we have a lot to talk about and very little time to do it."

"What's up? You look serious. At least I think you look serious. I can't really tell. But you sound that way."

"I'm very serious. The situation is deadly serious. It's the old story of good and bad news."

"Let's not play games, John boy." Holiday sat up and scooted back in his bed. "Just lay it on me and tell me how I can help."

"Tom, Ira and I, caught one of the killers as he retrieved a classified document. He dropped the document and got away. So now we know who the killer is and the spy's connection."

"That's great news, John." Holiday smiled, then frowned, "Damn, Tom would be the one to catch the bad guy instead of me. Other than the fact that he got away, what's the bad news?"

"The tall, older Aryan Nation dude is the one that got away. The shorter one was driving the car. So now we know both those guys were involved. I guess they have been involved all along."

"Damn, John, we sort of figured that much. Where was he when he tried to get the document?"

"In the rear of I and J's. It was under a dumpster."

"You guys not only saved the classified info, but you've identified the perps. I still don't see the bad news."

"Harry, here's the bad news. I am so sorry to have to tell you this. The spy is Rachael Holmes."

Holiday froze. His jaw dropped and he stared hard at John. "That's crazy, John. What makes you think that? Hell, Rachael has been nothing but helpful."

"Think about it. She was helpful when it came to pointing the finger at all those other people."

"Was she there tonight?"

"She brought Polly, and they sat with us."

Holiday's voice lowered as he asked, "Did you apprehend her?"

"By the time Tom and I returned to the table, Rachael was gone. When those Aryan jerks drove away, they must have called her on her cell phone and alerted her to what happened. She left before we could get back."

"What tipped you it was her?"

"Tom and I checked the dates on the documents and they were dated last Friday. She was the only one that had accessed the container. That's why Steel hasn't been seeing anyone on his CCTV."

"I can't believe I was so stupid. She was right under our nose. Hell, she knew every move we were going to make before we even made it." Holiday slapped his hand down on the bed.

"Don't feel bad. She fooled me too, Harry."

"Oh man, I see it now. That's why they have been trying to kill you."

"Huh?"

"She asked me if I could solve this case without you. I told her, 'no'. We needed your polygraph. Sorry, buddy."

"That's fine. Don't worry about it. But, we do have a problem. Her personnel file is missing from the lab. We need you to give me all the identifying information about her that you can remember. We need to put out an APB on her."

"Wow! Let me think."

"Oh, I almost forgot. I did shoot the smaller one in the leg. He couldn't make it to the car and Tom has him."

"I thought you said he was driving and they got away."

"Oh, no, that was from the restaurant. Crap! I guess I forgot that, too. Rachael or one of the Aryan guys, after they left I and J's, killed the Military Policeman on the gate at the lab. They didn't kill the other soldiers, but they did knock them out. Then they broke into the lab and cleaned out the classified files from the container."

"Uh, John, that was rather important to know. You mean the files are floating around out there someplace now?"

"I'm afraid so; all of them. That's why we need the info on Rachael. We don't know how much time we have before she hands them off."

"All right. First of all she is a natural brunette."

John laughed, "Okay Harry, that's good to know, but we're going to need a little more than that."

"I'd say she is six foot tall, with brown eyes. She's forty-five years old with a thin build. The woman doesn't smoke or wear glasses but does like to drink. As far as her car is concerned, call the sheriff's department and they can get that info for you from her name. Don't worry about her address. She won't go back there."

"I'll get this info to Tom right away. I guess we can get her picture from her driver's license."

"The sheriff will be able to help you with that. God, John I should have known. I just should have known."

"There was no way. It's probably my fault anyway."

"Why would it be your fault?"

"I forgot to get her back on the polygraph. If I could have done that, the case would have been over."

"Hell, I forgot that she hadn't been polygraphed again."

"I should have remembered."

"I should have picked up on her guilt right away," said Holiday.

"Why?"

"The damn broad was not only an atheist she was a Democrat and from the northeast part of the country at that."

"I think it's time for your medication, Harry. I'm going to get back to Tom. I'll try to remember to bring you your cell phone next time, also."

———————

"Man, you've got to get me to the doctor. I feel weak, already, from the loss of blood. I'm not kidding, dude. I'm dying here."

"Yep. I know. Just like the soldier outside. There may be hope for you if you decide to tell me a story. One I want to hear," said Turner.

"What do you want to hear, man?"

"Let's start with how this operation of yours worked. Who did what? How long have you been doing it? Who are the people involved? Where are the people involved? You know, 'man', like that kind of stuff."

"Like, we met this broad at a bar. She took us home. We drank a lot and had a few threesomes. She was a cool gal. Then she said we could make a lot of money if we helped her."

"How long ago was that?"

"About two months ago. She said that she would leave a package for us under the dumpster at that restaurant. The package would be there every time she sang this particular song."

"What were you supposed to do with this package?"

"We would take it the next day to a restaurant out west on Bell Road. I would go in at exactly 11:a.m. I'd enter a stall in the bathroom and lay the envelope on the floor close to the next stall. A hand would reach over and take the envelope. This hand would stick another envelope back over with money for us. Then Cleduus and I'd leave. I never saw who took the envelope or paid us. We knew better than to look."

"Did you kill Martha Hires?"

"No, sir. I ain't never killed nobody in my entire life. That first woman who was killed, was killed by Rachael. Rachael told us that she found out about what was going on with the envelopes. She didn't have no choice. She didn't want to do it, 'cause the woman was her friend."

"Did Holmes kill all the other women?"

"No. She told Tolman how to do it and made him kill them. She was trying to cover up why that first woman was killed. I guess when you guys showed up, she knew she was in trouble and tried to make it look like that first woman was killed by a serial killer."

"Why didn't Holmes just give you the documents? Why all the hiding under the dumpster crap?"

"Come on, man, get me some help. I'm starting to get dizzy. Please, I don't want to die."

"If you expect to get any help, answer my question. Why didn't she just give you the documents?"

"She didn't want to have any contact with us. She knew you guys were investigating, and she got scared."

"So you don't know who wound up with the classified information. You never saw him or heard his name?" Turner gave him an unbelieving stare.

"No, man. Come on and help me."

"Does Holmes know the man's name?"

"Of course. She knows the person. She knows who it is because she works for him. How do you know it's a man?" Hobbs looked at him with surprise.

"Didn't you just say you made the hand off in the men's room?"

"Uh, yeah. It must be a man."

Sergeant Steel came down the ramp. He walked over and looked down at Hobbs. He kicked him.

"Which one of you bastards killed my soldier? Tell me the truth." Steel's face was the face of a man who wanted to kill.

There was no question in Hobbs mind. He didn't waste any time in answering him. "Rachael shot him. She shot him three times. I guarded the door. I don't know what went on inside."

Turner turned to the sergeant and said, "That's good to know. Sergeant, will you call the Sheriff's Department and also call for an ambulance for our wounded spy? I need him kept under guard and held for Homeland Security."

"Wilco. It's a good idea to get him out of here before my men get a hold of him. I have a new shift arriving any minute."

Turner's cell phone rang. He removed it from the holder. "Turner here."

"Tom, here's the info on Rachael." John repeated the information from Holiday.

"I'll see that this gets out right away. How did Harry take it?"

"He took it better than I thought he would. He's mad at himself for not figuring it out before now. He looked good but still has blurred vision. I hope to hell it's not permanent. It could be the end of a good man's career."

"I know. Are you on your way back?"

"You bet. Did you get anything out of the one you had?"

"A lot. Rachael was the one who killed Hires. She, also, is the one who shot our MP. I'll tell you all about it when you get here."

"Holy crap, you did get a lot out of him. I'm peddling as fast as I can. Steel has a great car."

"Don't get caught for speeding."

chapter

TWENTY-ONE

As the Plymouth accelerated westbound on Bell Road, Tolman asked, "Where are we going now?"

"We're going to get out of sight. By now every law enforcement agency in the country is looking for us."

"That sounds like a good idea. What are we going to do with all the stuff you got from work?"

"We have to get it to the commander. We're going to be in real trouble with the commander after what you two pulled tonight." Rachael gritted her teeth and slapped the steering wheel.

"Who is this commander?" asked Tolman.

"The commander is my boss and the person who has been paying you."

"Maybe the commander don't know what happened yet."

"The commander was singing at karaoke when you two bumbling idiots caused this mess." Rachael turned north on Grand Ave. and pulled into the first motel she found.

The lady behind the counter at the Hampton Inn greeted them with a smile. She said, "Hi there. I'm Pat. How may I help you?"

"My son and I need a room for the night." Rachael patted Tolman on the shoulder and smiled at him.

Son, my foot. If I ever saw a cougar, she's one, thought the clerk. The clerk checked them in and gave them the key. Rachael thanked her and they headed for the room.

Once in the room Rachael told Tolman to drive back down the street to the pizza place and get them something to eat and to pick up some beer. He was quick to comply and they settled in for the night.

While eating and drinking the beer Tolman asked, "What's in those papers? I know they must be important for us to kill for."

"You're right. They are important. That's why you made the money you did." Rachael put her pizza down and took a drink of beer.

"So; what's so important about them?"

"I guess it won't hurt to tell you." *Because when I deliver these papers you're a dead man, anyway.* "There are actually two items involved in these papers. One is a specialty gas, and the other is the antidote."

"What's so special about this gas?" Tolman put both his pizza and beer down and stared at Rachael.

"This gas has an immediate effect on the motor cortex and somotosensory cortex of your brain."

"Does it kill them?"

"No, not at all. It actually paralyzes them. They have no motor ability. They can see and feel, but their muscles are useless."

"What good is that?"

"God, you're dense, Cleduus. Think about it. You want to rob a bank. You want to rob a police station. Hell you can rob anything."

"I'd have fun at a bathing beauty contest."

"Yeah, you pervert, you're getting the idea. Think what one government could do to another."

"Yeah. These papers tell you how to make that stuff?"

"Pretty much. There is only one more set of documents needed to finish it."

"How are you gonna get them?" Tolman started back on his pizza and beer.

"I guess the same way we got these."

"Won't they be ready for you the next time?"

"I'm sure they will. That's one of the things we're going to talk to the commander about, Cleduus."

The owner of the Plymouth reported it stolen. Several hours later, the midnight shift sheriff's patrol spotted the vehicle in the parking lot. When they called it in they found it possibly connected to the two vehicles Peoria police found at the theater. All of which were involved in a murder of a warehouse employee in Avondale. All were to be reported to Homeland Security and left alone.

——— ——— ———

Turner called John's hotel room. "Is it time to rise and shine already?" asked a sleepy voice on the other end.

"John, it is 6:45 a.m. I think we may have found that murdering bitch and her hillbilly boyfriend. Do you want to go with me?"

"Hell. Yes! Where are they?"

"They're at a motel up on Grand Ave. At least the car we believe they stole is up there. They're probably sacked out. If we go now we may catch them by surprise."

"I'll meet you at the car. Give me fifteen minutes."

"You got it."

——— ——— ———

"Good morning, sugar. Would you like a little wakeup sex?" questioned Tolman.

"Get serious, stupid. The need to give you sex is over. I'm not even sure why I still have you around."

"Damn, Rachael, I said I was sorry."

"You dumb bastard; you've cost me my career and any possibility of a future. After I get this stuff to the commander, you and I are parting ways."

"That ain't no way to be."

"Just get dressed and go get me some morning sweet stuff like donuts." Rachael rolled out of bed and started for the bathroom.

"They got stuff downstairs. I saw their breakfast area last night."

"I don't want you seen downstairs. I don't want to call attention that we are here. Go someplace like the bakery or grocery store and hurry up."

Tolman got out of bed and began to dress. "All right, I'll go."

Rachael hollered out from the bathroom, "And bring lots of coffee."

Tolman finished dressing and checked his money. He opened the door and looked both ways in the hallway and headed for the elevator. He kept his head down and hurried through the lobby. Once outside, he ran for the car.

John and Turner had just parked and started for the motel lobby when they saw Tolman running for the car. "There goes our man," hollered John.

"Are you sure that's him? It was dark last night when I saw him and I'm not sure."

"Move it, Tom. I'll drive. You can shoot legally in any state. I can't." John jumped into the driver's seat and Turner the passenger seat.

Tolman was looking right at them when he left the parking lot. *Holy shit, how did they find me so quick? I've got to make a run for it. Rachael is on her own.*

"We'll be Okay if he doesn't get on his cell phone," said John, speeding out of the parking lot.

"Don't waste any time catching him," advised Turner as he rolled down the window and produced his weapon.

"Hang on to your seatbelt, Tom. We're going for a ride." John mashed the GSA car's accelerator to the floor.

The Plymouth's exhaust was smoking as Tolman accelerated south on Grand Ave. He was weaving in and out of traffic at a dangerous pace. His car leaned hard when he turned right by the Golden Corral and then again to the left onto Litchfield Ave. He clipped the front fender and bumper of a Cadillac attempting to turn right onto Litchfield.

The Cadillac continued to roll into the intersection, barely missing the GSA car as John maneuvered around it. Turner leaned out the window and tried for a shot. Due to the amount of traffic and pedestrians, he couldn't take the chance. The traffic signal had just turned from yellow to red as Tolman made his left turn onto eastbound Bell Road.

John began blowing the horn to warn the cross traffic as he approached the busy intersection. He managed to bully his way onto Bell through the symphony of blowing horns. He grimaced at the sound of screeching tires as a car skidded sideways to a stop just before hitting him.

Both Tolman's and John's vehicles went airborne when they crossed the railroad tracks. They were both weaving in and out of traffic on the six-lane divided road. John became trapped between two vehicles that refused to move at his incessant blowing of the horn. Turner watched as Tolman turned south on El Mirage Road.

John was too busy fighting with the two cars in front of him to notice. The traffic stopped for the light at the Bell Road-El Mirage intersection. Turner hollered for John to take the shoulder and turn south.

John maneuvered between cars to the shoulder and turned south. Tolman's car was nowhere in sight. They could see for at least a mile down El Mirage Road. John gunned the engine. All of a sudden he slammed on the breaks and slid to a stop in front of the entrance to the mobile home park.

"Tom, he killed a woman in this park. He must be familiar with it. Let's try it. I don't see him down the road."

"John, it's up to you. You're driving. What you said makes sense. Do it."

John made a left turn dangerously close to oncoming traffic. He pulled up next to the gate shack and noticed the wide eyed guard. Turner displayed his badge, and John asked if he saw the Plymouth. Jim, the guard peered in at Turner's badge.

"Hell, yeah, I saw him. The bastard came through here like an Indian going to shit. He didn't even slow down."

"Which way did he go?" asked John.

"He turned left at the fork down there. I was about to call the police. Are you going to get him?"

John said, "Dead or alive."

"I'm hoping for the first one," announced the guard. "I'll close the gate. This is the only way out."

John made the turn at the fork. He drove slowly looking down the small streets between the permanently-placed mobile homes. The road continued in a large circle. There was a huge auditorium, a couple of swimming pools, a large outdoor seating area and a Hawaiian style food and drink booth.

About a third of the way around the circle, Turner hollered. "There's the car!"

John looked over to his right and noticed the Plymouth with the driver's door open. It was parked by the entrance to the auditorium. The vehicle was empty.

John parked crossways up next to the rear bumper. Turner jumped out and ran toward the auditorium. John pulled the keys from his vehicle and got out slowly. He looked around the area. Once he was satisfied that Tolman wasn't waiting outside for both of them to enter, he followed Turner inside.

———

Tolman slid to a stop, piled out of his car, and ran for the auditorium. He thought about hiding up on the stage and shooting his two pursuers. Then he worried about the sound of the gunshots bringing the police. He continued to run across the facility and out the other side.

Running down the street, he had no idea what he was looking for. He had to find something and figured he would know it when he saw it. He wound up at the rear of the complex where the transit motor homes and trailers were parked.

A middle-aged lady picked up her small Terrier dog and opened her trailer door. Tolman didn't break his stride as he turned from the street and pushed the lady and dog into the trailer. Her rather large husband jumped up from the dinette table and started for the door.

Tolman displayed his pistol and said, "Don't make me kill both of you. I've killed in this park before and I don't mind doing it again."

The husband picked up his wife and sat her on the chair by the table and he sat back down as well. The miniature little silver poodle began to bark. Tolman kicked the animal all the way back to the rear of the trailer where the dog lay whimpering. The man started to rise from his chair.

Tolman said, "Don't even think about it."

———————

John and Turner searched the auditorium to no avail. Turner walked around outside of the building in one direction and John did the same on the other side. They looked around the hundred or so trailers, motor homes and permanent mobile homes.

"John, it's useless. He could be in any one of these places. We'd be endangering the residents if we did find him."

"Tom, we have a killer of at least three women someplace in this park. There is no way in hell we can give up."

"Since the guard has the gate secured, why don't we turn it over to the Surprise Police Department? They can take their time and search the resort. We can go back to the motel and look for Rachael," offered Turner.

"That sounds good to me. Let's do it. If you want to wait out here, I'll bring the car around." John jogged back through the building to the car.

They drove back to the gate and talked to the guard. He agreed to call the police and look people over when they left. Although, he said the guy went past so fast he didn't get a look at him. He would detain any strangers for the police. John warned the man that Tolman was armed and dangerous.

"How are we going to handle the hotel when we get there?" queried John. "Should one of us wait outside while the other checks with the clerk?"

"We'll play it by ear when we get there," responded Turner.

———————

"I need to use your cell phone," said Tolman.

"We don't have a cell phone. They're a nuisance," replied the husband.

"Okay, buddy. Here's what we're going to do. You're going to go out there and throw your belongings into the trailer. Then you're going to hook up your truck to this rig and drive us out of here."

"And why would I do that?" questioned the man.

"Now, that's a stupid question, Bubba…to keep me from cutting your wife's throat."

"All right, I'll do it."

"Now, I have a question. Should your wife and I ride back here in the trailer until we're out of the park or in the truck with you?"

"Mister, the guard might think it's funny that I'm pulling up stakes and leaving without my wife."

"Then I'll ride in the truck with you. I'll have my knife blade pushing against her side. If you try to tip off the guard...she's dead".

"What if the guard recognizes you?"

"He won't. I came in too fast for him to identify me. Don't worry about that. You just worry about getting me out of here."

"After we're out of here what are you going to do with us?" asked the wife.

"I'll take your truck and let you go."

"How do I know that you won't kill us?" questioned the husband.

"If I was going to kill you I would have already done it. I could drive the rig out myself. Why would I want to kill you?"

"To keep us from telling the police the description of the truck you're driving," said the husband.

"Hell, I can tie you up. By the time you get loose, I'll be driving a different vehicle. So see; if you play your cards right you're going to live." Tolman smiled at the couple and patted the wife's shoulder.

"Stupid jerk. He should have been back by now. I'm starving. What the hell is he doing? All he had to do was pick up some pastry and get his butt back here." Rachael was walking the floor of her hotel room. She walked over by the window and looked out at the parking lot.

"I've waited long enough." She lifted the box springs up and stashed the classified documents on the floor beneath it. After checking herself in the mirror, she grabbed her purse and room key and left the room.

She waited patiently for the elevator, then rode it down to the lobby. She did a quick look around. There were several people seated at the tables, one at the waffle machine and another at the coffee urn. Seeing nothing that presented a threat, she headed for the coffee and powdered donuts. After filling her cup she began to stack up the powdered mini-treats on her paper plate.

She took a quick bite and the white powdered sugar stuck to her lips. Picking up the cup, she took a most pleasing sip. With the donuts stacked up on her plate in one hand and the coffee cup in the other, she turned around in search of a vacant table. She couldn't help but gasp as her eyes went wide.

chapter

TWENTY-TWO

John parked under the portico of the entrance to the hotel. Turner slid out and John came around the front of the car to meet him. They entered the lobby and looked over at the people enjoying their free breakfast. Turner saw the sausage patties and scrambled eggs. John noticed the biscuits and gravy. Then they both saw the familiar figure at the pastry bar.

John couldn't help but smile as Turner grabbed his arm. They quietly but hurriedly moved over behind her. There was one on each side of her as she turned around. Both men were grinning.

"Good morning, Miss Rachael. Would you mind if we joined you for breakfast?" asked John.

"We'll even buy," said Turner.

Rachael's heart was pounding so hard her hand shook to the point that donuts were dropping. John took the plate with the few remaining mini-donuts, and Turner took her coffee. They led her away from the other patrons to a table in the corner of the room. The two men were not too gentle in sitting her down.

"Oh, thank God. I've never been so scared in my life. You have no idea what I've been through."

"You're right. We have no idea. You see we've never been a spy for a subversive element against the United States. We've killed people. But unlike you, we never murdered anyone. Much less an innocent civilian, excellent government worker and a patriotic U.S. soldier," said John.

"Wait just a damn minute! What the hell are you talking about?" questioned Rachael indignantly.

"Oh. I see. We're going to play games now. Listen, you murdering bitch. You killed an innocent woman and a good soldier. I'm in no mood for any of your crap," announced Turner.

"I didn't kill anybody. You've got to believe that." Tears began to form in Rachael's eyes.

"We have witnesses, Rachael. So knock off the act." John stared at her with his hands on his hips.

Rachael lowered her head and remained silent. John waited for a response. Seeing none was forthcoming, he turned to Tom.

"Tom, would you like some coffee? I'll even get some more donuts." John left Turner guarding Rachael and headed for the coffee and tea.

Tolman sat inside with the wife as the husband picked up outside. The lawn chairs and potted plants were placed in the trailer. The rolled up outdoor carpet followed. The trailer hitch was put into place on the truck and the stabilizing jacks were removed from beneath the trailer.

The husband backed the truck up to the trailer and connected it to the hitch on the trailer. He connected the sway bar. The safety chains were attached to the truck. He plugged in the trailer brakes and lights.

Tolman followed the woman into the truck. The husband pulled out of the trailer slot and onto the narrow side street. He slowed to a stop at the gate as the guard approached.

"I see you're leaving us. You didn't by any chance see a stranger running around back there did you?"

"No, I didn't see anyone. I've been busy getting the trailer ready to go. Is there a problem in the resort?" asked the husband.

"Don't worry about it, now that you're leaving. You drive careful and we'll look forward to your return," stated the guard. The police car drove up to the gate as the husband pulled out onto El Mirage Road.

"You did real good, bubba. Looks to me like you got out of there in time," said Tolman.

"Where am I going?" questioned the husband.

"Just drive north and we'll pull over on the side of the road after we get a little ways up on the highway," answered Tolman.

They drove a mile up New El Mirage Road when Tolman said, "Pull over on the shoulder. Make sure you're far enough off the road."

The man did as he was told. He stopped the truck, turned off the engine, and asked, "Now what?"

"Now, you unhitch the trailer. While the missus and I sit here. You two are still alive. If you want to keep it that way don't try to signal anybody or pull any funny stuff. You got that?"

"Yeah, I got it." The man got out and began to crank the hitch down. After he unhooked all the devices he took the block from the bed of the pickup, placed it under the hitch and raised the trailer from the truck. Once they were separated he came around to the passenger side of the truck.

"Back off, bubba and let me get out." Tolman slid out of the seat with his hand and gun in his pocket. "How about you and the woman opening the trailer and going in?"

The couple led Tolman back to the trailer. As soon as they entered, the woman started crying. Her husband hugged her.

"What the hell are you crying about," asked Tolman.

"You; you're going to kill us," cried the wife.

"Hey, bubba, do you have anything to tie you up with?"

"I don't know."

"Let me put it to you this way. It's either tie or die. Now, do you think you can find something to tie you up with?"

The man opened the door and walked out along the side of the trailer to a small storage area in the rear. After rummaging around for a minute, he returned. "Here; this will work, I'm sure."

Tolman stepped over the cowering dog as it moved slowly to be with the couple, took the heavy twine and ran it through the refrigerator door handle. Then he tied the man's hands behind him. He pulled the man up against the refrigerator. Then he pulled the lady over to the appliance and tied her hands behind her.

"Since you two have been so cooperative, I've decided not to cut your throats. Yes, I'm going to let you live. Do not even try to get loose for the next thirty minutes. You owe me that for letting you live."

Tolman left them and entered the black 1500 Dodge pickup. He let out a sigh of relief. The truck pulled back onto the highway and headed for the hotel. *Rachael needs to know what's going on.*

———————

"What did you do with the classified documents?" asked Turner.

"I'm telling you they forced me to take them. I didn't want to do it. I didn't have a choice."

"That's bullshit," said John. "You ran from us when we arrived. You knew we were there and drove away as fast as you could."

"I was trying to get away from them. Besides, I didn't really know who was behind me. All I knew was that there was a car that pulled up. Next thing I heard was a whole lot of shooting."

Tolman parked the truck so that it was concealed among other cars in the hotel parking lot. He hurried to the entrance of the hotel. Once in the doorway, he stopped and looked around. He froze when he saw Turner and John talking to Rachael.

At first he was confused. *Is she in cahoots with them? She seems so relaxed? What do I do?*

Rachael saw Tolman. She jumped up from the table and ran toward the elevator. John dove at her and missed. The coffee cup in front of Turner exploded at the same time he heard the shot.

The patrons in the dining area screamed as they scattered for cover. Turner dropped to one knee and immediately located Tolman in the doorway. He quickly drew his weapon and returned fire, splintering the door jamb. John rose from his attempt to tackle Rachael to a kneeling position and shot at Tolman also. Tolman backed out of the doorway and ran for the pickup truck.

The two men gave chase. John stopped at the GSA car and Turner continued to chase Tolman. Tolman made it to the truck and was able to start it and put it in drive. Turner fired at the truck but had to jump out of the way as Tolman sped from the parking lot.

John drove over to Turner. The GSA car's wheels were spinning before Turner could close the door. John had the pickup in sight and the pedal on the floor. This time, Tolman turned north on Grand Avenue away from the heavy traffic. John still had to maneuver between cars and even do some shoulder driving. It paid off. He was closing the gap between them.

"Hey, Tom; didn't we just do this a little while ago?" asked John. "Is it me or is it déjà vu?"

"Yeah, and it looks like we're doing it again." Turner rolled down the window and rested his arm and weapon in the opening.

"The way we're going, I should be able to get close enough for a safe shot in a minute or two. We're closing pretty fast."

"John, I'd like to take him alive...if we can. However, it's not absolutely imperative. I'm getting tired of chasing him."

"If I can dodge enough traffic, I'm sure I can get close enough for you to take out a tire."

"Partner, if you do at the speed we're going, he'll probably roll. I doubt he took time to put on a seat belt. I don't think we'll be fortunate enough to get him all in one piece."

"Maybe if you put a couple through the window it will scare him enough that he'll give up."

"It might be worth a try. However, the problem with that is the vehicle in front of him. I can't take the chance."

"Don't worry. He's about to pass that car. You'll have your chance in just a few seconds."

———

Rachael waited for the elevator while watching the entryway for either John or Turner to return. The doors slid open and she bumped into an elderly female. She caught the lady before she fell. Apologizing, she pushed the button to her floor, ignoring the looks and comment from the old woman.

The doors opened and she ran down the hall and rushed into her room. She lifted the box springs and grabbed the documents. Placing the files under her left arm, she placed her right hand in her purse and closed her fingers around her gun. Leaving the door open, she hurried to the stairwell and descended to the lobby.

Rachael opened the door from the stairwell and cautiously looked out. People were milling about talking about the shooting. She could hear the sirens in the distance. There was no way she could remain at the hotel. She walked rapidly through the lobby and out the front entrance.

A young man in his late twenties was just getting out of his car in front of the hotel when Rachael came out. She walked over to him. Pressing her body against his hid the .38 cal. revolver pushed into his stomach.

"Now, sugar, you do as I say and you may live to drive this little beauty." Rachael smiled at him.

"Lady, I just got this Porsche. I'm bringing it here to show my girlfriend," said the terrified driver.

"Give me the keys and you slide across. We're going to go for a little drive. You can tell me all about your car as we go." Rachael took his keys and forced him to climb across to the passenger seat. She followed him in and adjusted the seat.

Rachael drove out of the parking lot as the two police cruisers arrived. Turning south on Grand Avenue, she asked, "What's your name?"

"Franklin," answered the wide-eyed man.

"Hi, Franklin. I'm Rachael. We'll be traveling together for a bit so we might as well get to know each other."

"Lady, are you a criminal? Were those cops after you?"

"I guess they want to talk to me. Enough about me, tell me about this beautiful car."

"It's a 2012 Porsche Cayenne."

"What's the horsepower of this baby?"

"It's got a V6 300 HP."

"That's good. I'm looking for something that's fast. How far will it go on a tank of gas?"

"On the highway it's close to 500 miles. Tell me you don't plan to drive that far. What are you going to do, anyway?"

"We're going to spend some time together. I have to make a delivery this evening. After that I won't need you."

"I promised my girlfriend I'd pick her up at noon."

"Let's not whine, Franklin. You're a man. You're an attractive man I might add. I'm sure your girlfriend can take care of herself. Who knows? Before we're through, you might find me more enjoyable."

The highway smoothed. John closed the gap and Turner leaned out the window. He carefully aimed two shots through the rear window of the truck. Holes appeared in the rear and front glass of the truck. Tolman felt the shards of glass and heard the crack of the bullets as they passed through.

His leg was cramping from pressing so hard on the accelerator. The pulse rate was over a hundred as he felt his heart pounding in his chest. His hands were shaking and his entire body vibrated with fear. *Which is better, jail or certain death? I know I'm going to die if I continue to run. But, I'm afraid to stop. God, I don't want to die.*

"Tom, he's not going to stop. It looks like you're going to have to go for the tire and pray the kid makes it."

"I'm afraid you're right. I hate to do it. Get ready to maneuver when he rolls or you're going to be right on top of him."

"I got you covered. I'm ready."

"Hell, here goes." Turner leaned out the window again and set his sights on the right rear tire.

I'm going to surrender. Jail is better than death. Just as Tolman lifted his foot from the accelerator he heard the exploding tire and felt the rear of the truck veer to the right. He fought the steering wheel as the truck violently fishtailed. He lost the battle and the truck began to roll.

Turner and John watched the body inside the cab as the windows rolled by. John pressed his brake and steered close to the rolling truck. The various configurations of the body as the windows appeared made the two men cringe. Finally the door flew open and Tolman was thrown from the vehicle.

"He hit the pavement hard, Tom."

"John, look out! You're going to hit him."

John stomped on the brake and slid to a stop short of running over Tolman. Turner was first out of the car and over to the bleeding body on the roadway. John noticed the blood seeping out from beneath Tolman's head onto the road.

Tolman surprised them by being conscious. His voice was weak but clear. They leaned over him to hear.

"Please don't let me die. Call an ambulance. Get me help. I don't want to die," begged Tolman.

"I'll call an ambulance as soon as you tell us where those secret documents are," bargained Turner.

"I don't know, man. Rachael's got them."

"What's she going to do with them?" asked John.

"She's going to give them to some guy called the 'Commander'. Please call the ambulance."

"Where is this hand off to the 'Commander' guy going to take place?" questioned John.

"She told me he was at that restaurant last night."

"He was at I and J's?" asked Turner.

"Yeah, I think she's going to give him the documents tonight. I think she plans to meet him there. Come on guy, ca, cal...." Tolman went quiet. His blank stare was accompanied by his sardonic grin in death.

John looked at Turner and said, "It's sad for death to come to someone so young. It's such a waste."

"Try to look at it this way, John. At least he won't be causing the death of anyone else."

"True. Boy, did we mess up."

"How did we mess up, John?"

"We had her. By having her we had the documents. We let all that go just to chase this guy."

"You're right. We have absolutely no idea where the hell she is now. All we can do is go back to the hotel and start from there."

"We don't know where she is now. But, we have a good idea where she's going to be tonight."

"Yeah. You're right. And with the documents," said Turner as he stood and dialed 911.

"Yep. And possibly with the man behind all this crap as well." John reached over and closed Tolman's eyes. He stood and began directing traffic around the accident scene.

chapter

TWENTY-THREE

Rachael drove around Surprise, Sun City West and Sun City Grand trying to think of what to do. The young man continued to whine and complain about not picking up his girlfriend. He was cute and appeared to be a real stud but he was getting on Rachael's nerves.

She entered an alley behind a restaurant in Sun City West. Placing the hand with the gun into her purse, she ordered him to get out of the car. Rachael exited the car and walked around to the passenger side. While doing this, her hand changed from holding the gun to holding the small hunting knife.

"Okay, Franklin. I'm going to let you drive," she said as she walked up to the unsuspecting car owner.

He turned to walk away. Rachael quickly pulled the knife from her purse and grabbed him by the hair on his head. Before he could react, the knife slashed across his throat. He spun around with a shocked expression that suddenly turned blank as he collapsed to the ground.

Rachael looked around and saw that no one had witnessed her murder. She reached into his pocket and removed his wallet and any other items that might identify him. The dumpster made a good hiding place. Grunting and straining she placed his body behind it. There was nothing she could do about the trail of blood.

She couldn't go back to her apartment. Nevertheless, she needed to change her bloody blouse. If she tried to buy a new blouse the clerk would become suspicious. What to do?

———————

Polly had just finished making the bed when the phone on the nightstand rang. She eased onto the bed and reached over for the receiver, hoping it was John. She was smiling when she answered.

"Polly, this is Rachael. Have you heard from John or Tom either last night or this morning?"

"I'm worried about them. I haven't heard from them since he gave me money for the taxi last night. Have you heard anything?"

"Listen I'm on my way over. I'll tell you all about it when I get there. It's a long story."

"All right, I'll put on a pot of coffee. Are you hungry?"

"I could have something to go with the coffee, if you're sure it's not too much trouble for you".

"No trouble at all. I've wanted some cinnamon toast anyway. Is that all right?"

"You bet. I'm on the way."

Rachael arrived at Polly's house ten minutes later. The Porsche parked in the driveway. She hopped out and entered the house without knocking.

"Come on back," hollered Polly, "I'm in the kitchen. The coffee is done, and I just finished making the toast."

When Polly saw Rachael's blood-soaked blouse, she pulled her hand up to her mouth and gasped. "My God, gal, are you all right?"

"It's not my blood. It's one of those men who forced me to go with them last night."

"I wondered why you just took off. You left me stranded. I knew something wasn't right."

"Yeah, I finally got away from them. Do you have a blouse I could borrow? I need to get out of this oversized band aid."

"Sure. Take that off and throw it in the sink and I'll soak it. Come on back to the bedroom and pick out something."

Rachael did as Polly asked and followed her into the bedroom. She picked out a blouse and was buttoning it up as she entered the kitchen. Polly was just pouring the coffee.

"That cinnamon toast looks good." She was just on her second piece when Polly's cell phone rang.

Polly rushed back to the bedroom, hurried around the bed. She snatched the phone from the nightstand on the far side. She smiled when she heard the voice at the other end. She sat on the bed.

"Hi there, young lady. Sorry I haven't called before now. We have been super busy today."

"Tell me. Tell me all about it. What's happening?"

"First of all have you heard from Rachael?"

"She's here now." She stood and started for the kitchen.

"I'm on the way. If you have a gun, go get it. Rachael is a killer. She killed her friend Hires."

"Oh, my Lord. When are...." Polly stopped dead still and looked over toward the kitchen.

Rachael stood in the kitchen doorway with her revolver pointed at Polly. "Hang up, NOW!"

Polly snapped the cover down on the cell phone. She slowly lowered the phone. There was no way she could hide her shock.

"You know?"

Polly slowly nodded. "Why, Rachael? How could you?"

"Why do you think? Money. There's lots of money involved. A hell of a lot more than Navy retirement gives me."

"Are you going to kill me?"

"Not if I don't have to. It kind of depends on you. Now that you know what I'm capable of, maybe you won't do anything to make me kill you."

"What do you want me to do?"

"I'm not sure yet. Is John on his way over here?"

"He said he was. He knows you're here."

"I guess I don't have much time to make a decision." Rachael looked around the kitchen.

"I don't know how far away John was when he called." Polly's nervousness was beginning to show.

"The way I figure it is either to tie you up, kill you or take you with me. I don't think there's time to tie you up." Rachael pulled the hammer back on the revolver.

"I'll go with you. It probably wouldn't hurt to have a hostage. I won't try anything with you."

Rachael lowered the pistol and let the hammer go slowly forward. "You just saved your life."

"You won't be sorry," said Polly attempting to smile.

"I will kill you. You know that."

"I know. Don't worry you won't have to."

"Well, let's get the hell out of here." Rachael had Polly lead her from the house and out to the car. Once Polly was in, Rachael hurried around and slid onto the driver's seat.

"God, Tom. Rachael is in the house with Polly. She didn't get a chance to finish the conversation with me. We've got to step on it."

John and Tom turned the corner onto Polly's street as Rachael turned the opposite corner. They jumped out of the car and hurried to the wide open door. "Damn, this doesn't look good," said John.

Entering the house with caution, they checked each room. John's heart sank as he announced, "It looks as though she has a hostage."

Turner returning from the bedroom said, "Look on the bright side. At least she's still alive."

"God knows for how long," stated John.

"It appears we're back to square one again." Turner put away his weapon and followed John over to the kitchen sink.

"Oh, man, this can't be good." John pulled the blouse up and out of the bloody water.

"Just pray that blood isn't Polly's," said Turner.

"For Rachael's sake, I hope it isn't either. I would like to see her taken alive. If something happens to Polly, I promise there won't be a need for court." John put his weapon in its holster and led Turner back to the car.

"We might as well head back to the hotel. It's obvious that Rachael has a set of wheels. We need to know if anyone complained about a missing car," advised John as he sat back and watched Turner drive.

"He's almost an hour late. It's not like him. Something's wrong," said Cathy as she walked back and forth in front of the hotel check-in counter.

The clerk, Cathy's co-worker, said, "Why don't you call the dealership and see if he picked up his car yet. He may still be there."

"That's a good idea. Give me the phone book." Cathy reached over the counter for the book.

"Relax girl. I'll pull it up on the computer. Which dealership are we talking about?"

Cathy gave her the name of the dealership. The clerk gave Cathy the number. She was dialing the number as Turner approached the counter.

"Excuse me," Turner displayed his credentials, "Could you tell me if anybody has reported their car missing?"

"I know something's wrong. The dealership said Franklin picked up his car a couple of hours ago." The young woman looked first at her co-worker and then at Turner.

Turner introduced himself and asked, "I see you're troubled. You're not, by any chance, missing an automobile, are you?"

"Hell yes. Complete with boyfriend. He was supposed to be here an hour ago and he hasn't shown up."

"That's not good," said John."

Cathy turned to John and repeated, "That's not good? What do you mean 'that's not good'?"

"It's probably nothing. We're looking for a person who might be driving a car taken from this hotel."

"Are you saying my boyfriend might have been carjacked?" Tears began to form in the young girl's eyes.

"We don't know that," offered Turner.

"What kind of car does he drive?" asked John.

"He went to pick it up today. It's brand new. I haven't even seen it yet."

"What kind of car did he buy?" questioned Turner.

"He bought a Porsche."

"What dealership did he buy it from?" queried John.

The young woman told them the name of the dealership. Turner got the phone number from the note that the clerk had given Cathy and called them. John continued to question her about her boyfriend. Once they had the description of the boyfriend and the car, Turner called his headquarters and had them send the information to all the law enforcement agencies in the area.

———

The busboy carried the large container of lunchtime trash out into the alley. He set it down in front of the dumpster. Before he could open the lid of the large trash container he saw, what appeared to be blood. His curiosity got the best of him and he followed the trail around the dumpster.

He let out a loud gasp and jumped back when he saw the body. He stood frozen in place for a few seconds. Then he ran back into the restaurant.

The manager and cook immediately came out to confirm the young busboy's finding. Opening his cell phone, the manager called 911. The busboy was told to stay with the body until the police arrived.

———

Police unit 1210 was jotting down the descriptions of the missing vehicle and driver when he got the call. He was the closest car to the scene. He arrived at the same time as his sergeant. They examined the scene and called for the detective unit and the medical examiner.

"Sarge, did you get the description of the missing car and driver in that last message about fifteen minutes ago?" asked the officer.

"No. I was out of the car. What about it?"

"It's hard to tell from the position of the body, but I think this might be the missing guy."

The sergeant checked the victim's pockets. "He may have been robbed. His wallet's gone."

"Should we let dispatch know that this may be the missing person?" asked the officer.

"Sure. Whoever did this probably took his car. If this is the guy they're looking for, then the driver of his car is a killer and our units should be notified to approach with caution."

The officer pulled out his notepad and looked at it again. "The message said to notify Homeland Security if the car or driver is observed. They requested no contact be made, but keep them in sight until the HSD unit can relieve them."

"There may be more to this than we realize," said the sergeant.

"Wow! Look at that dust cloud. We better find a place to park until it passes. We damn sure can't drive in it," said Rachael.

"It looks like a giant wall coming at us," replied Polly

"It'll be impossible to drive in."

"Where are we going?" asked Polly

Rachael looked over at Polly and said, "I'm thinking,"

"How long do you plan on keeping me hostage?"

"I'll let you go this evening. I have to meet someone at I and J's. After that, we'll part company."

"I bet every police department in the area has your picture by now. You might even be on TV."

"I hope the picture is flattering. I do photograph well, if I do say so." Rachael made a special effort looking around for any threatening vehicles.

Polly snapped her fingers and looked at Rachael. "Why don't we go back to the house?"

"What? Are you CRAZY?"

"Not at all. Think about it. They have already checked there and found us gone. Why would they come back?"

"You got to be kid.... No; wait. That makes sense."

"They don't know this car. I'm not that friendly with the neighbors. No one should be suspicious."

Rachael pulled into a Fry's grocery parking lot, made a "U" turn and drove back in the opposite direction. "That's a great idea. Polly, I know you're scared and you should be. But I appreciate your helping me."

"When we get there, I'll take my car out of the garage and you can put this one in."

"Nice try, Polly. I'm not going to let you drive away in your car. I'm not that stupid, lady."

The cloud was just arriving as they approached Polly's house. Visibility was extremely limited. The smell of the desert dust was strong and made coughing necessary.

They parked in Polly's driveway. The two held their breath and ran. Rachael followed Polly into the house, shook her hair and said, "That storm will keep the cops busy. There'll probably be an accident on every corner."

"I'll turn on the TV." Polly hurried over to the remote control.

"I'm starving. What have you got to eat?"

"I'll make us a couple of ham and egg sandwiches. I never did have breakfast and it's past time for lunch."

"Polly, I'm not going to be so complacent that I'll let you get away. Don't forget the gun in my purse."

Opening the refrigerator, Polly looked around the door at Rachael and said, "You don't have to worry about me forgetting about the gun. I'm not going to give you any reason to kill me."

"That's good. I've probably killed enough for one day. I have a feeling though...the killing isn't over."

chapter

TWENTY-FOUR

"Holy hell, John. What is this?" hollered Turner.

"It's a dust storm. I saw one on TV before."

"We ought to make a run for the hotel."

"Get serious, Tom. You can't even see the hotel. We're sitting right in front of it."

"What are we going to do? Just sit here?"

"Smell that dust. Do you want to put that in your lungs?"

"I guess not."

The two men sat and were amazed at how dense the dust was. Neither had ever experienced anything like it. They decided, as soon as it passed, they would go to the hospital and check on Holiday.

The darkness began to turn to light as the storm passed. Their wait had only been thirty minutes, but seemed like hours. Turner cranked up the GSA car and drove from the parking lot.

Turner was first to enter Holiday's hospital room. "Hey, Chief, how are you feeling today?"

"Hey, guys, it's good to see you. I literally mean 'see'," replied Holiday with a smile.

"Your eyesight is better?" asked John.

"I still feel like I'm looking through a fog. Which is better than it was when I was looking through water."

"Super. We've been pretty busy," stated Turner.

"Tell me all about it."

Turner and John took turns bringing Holiday up to date. Holiday nodded at times and shook his head at other times. He agreed with actions of the two men with the exception of going after the guy instead of staying with Rachael. He had a few words about that.

"They tell me that I'll probably be released tomorrow. It would be nice if you guys sewed this up by then."

"We're close," said Turner.

"Maybe, just maybe, you missed a note or a tell-tale piece of information at Polly's. She's a smart gal. How hard did you look around there?"

"Basically we just looked around enough to know that she was gone. We didn't inspect each room," answered John.

"That might not be a bad idea. We sure don't have anything else to go on," said Turner.

John remembered Holiday's cell phone. "I forgot to give you this last time." He placed it on the table by Holiday's bed.

"Thanks. Now you don't have an excuse for not keeping me up to date." Holiday grinned at them.

"Thanks, John," said a sarcastic Turner.

"If I don't hear from you, I'll call when they release me. You can come and get me."

"You got it. We're going over to Polly's house now. We'll let you know if we find anything," advised John.

———

"Polly, let me help you with lunch. A one-handed cook is too slow." Rachael took over the cooking. They worked together on the sandwiches. However, Rachael's purse always hung from her shoulder.

After finishing her first bite, Polly asked, "Rachael, I know why you got involved in this mess. My question, now, is HOW did you get involved?"

"I met someone at karaoke. He, somehow, found out where I work. He never told me how he found out. I've always wondered how he did it."

"Rachael, are you telling me that someone at our karaoke is behind this? A person at I and J's?"

"Yep." Rachael took another bite of her sandwich and placed it back on the plate. She washed it down with a drink of coffee.

"Who is it? Can you tell me?" Polly looked at her intently as she reached for her coffee cup.

"Polly if I told you or you ever found out, it would mean death for you. Trust me. For you to stay alive, you must never know."

"What is this person going to do with that information you're carrying around?"

"He's somehow connected to the syndicate in New York. They're interested in what the agency I work for is making."

Polly sipped her coffee. "What is the agency you work for making?"

"There again, I can't disclose that. All I can tell you is that both the Mafia and a certain foreign country want it in the worst way. It's worth a ton of money to them."

"What do they plan on doing with it? Are you involved in something that will hurt the United States?"

"Look at it this way. The United States invented it and has it on hand. The foreign country would be foolish to use it on us."

"What will the Mafia use it for?" Polly placed her cup back on the saucer and reached for her napkin.

"I would think to rob banks. Hell, maybe even Fort Knox. It would give them the capability."

"My God, girl, if they did that it would throw this country into chaos. How could you live with yourself?"

"I gave this country a big chunk of my life. I don't owe them a damn thing. As soon as I get the rest of my money, I'm out of here." Rachael rose from the table and retrieved the coffee pot.

"Where will you go?"

"Why do you continue to ask questions for which I'd have to kill you if you knew the answers?" Rachael replenished both of their coffee cups and returned the pot to its heated burner.

"I'm sorry. I'm just curious."

"Just remember that curiosity kills."

"What time are we going to I and J's tonight?"

Rachael started to drink her coffee, but found it too hot. "I don't want to get there too early. The commander is never there early. I certainly can't wait around for him."

"Listen. Hush. The news is on." Polly jumped up and ran to the front room. "I think they're talking about a guard being shot last night."

Rachael followed her to the television set. "Damn it all to hell." She looked at a picture of herself on the screen. She listened:

"Rachael Holmes, a coworker of the victim, is wanted in connection with the guard's murder. She is 45 years of age, six feet tall, weighs 144 pounds. She has brown eyes and brown hair. She was last seen in the vicinity of Sun City West. It's possible she may be driving a 2012 Silver Porsche Cayenne.

If you see this person, do not attempt to approach her. She is considered armed and dangerous. If you have any information pertaining to Holmes please call...."

<end excerpting>

"Wow, Rachael, you're a celebrity. Everybody in the state knows what you look like now."

"Damn it! Damn it! Now everyone at karaoke knows about me. I have to think. What the hell am I going to do?"

"Well, I don't think you're going to walk into I and J's tonight."

"You're right. I can't go in but he can come out."

John saw the car as soon as Turner turned onto Polly's street. "There's the Porsche."

"It looks like Rachael has returned. I wonder why?" questioned Turner.

"Park around the corner and let's go find out why."

"Which door do you want, John?"

"I bet the front door is locked. Maybe the back door isn't. I would like the back door."

They parked the car and began walking back to the house. John cut through the neighbor's yard to the gate in Polly's fence. He was in luck. The gate wasn't locked. He continued down the side of the house. He cautiously looked around the corner of the house and saw that the patio was clear. The drapes were drawn across the back glass, sliding door. He tried the door and felt it slide a few inches. He moved it slowly and as silently as he could.

Turner, as quietly as he could, tried the knob on the front door. John was right. The door was locked. He had two choices; either kick it in and hope he made it on the first kick, or knock. If he knocked it might keep Rachael's attention away from the back door.

The knock on the door startled both of the women. They looked at each other as Rachael pushed her hand down into her purse. She started toward the door with the gun drawn.

"What do you want me to do?" whispered Polly.

"Be quiet. Don't let whoever it is think anyone's home."

"It's obvious someone is here. The car's in the driveway," Polly spoke softly as she followed Rachael to the door.

"Were you expecting anybody?"

"No. It's probably John coming back to check on me."

"All right. Ask who it is," ordered Rachael.

"Who is it?" Polly called out.

"Tom Turner, Polly. Can I come in?"

The women looked at each other again. Both of them were worried. Polly worried for Turner. Rachael worried for herself. Rachael moved over against the wall by the hinged portion of the door.

"Open the door and get rid of him. I will shoot him if I have to," whispered Rachael, putting her back to the wall with her hands down by her side.

Polly unlocked the door and opened it wide. She attempted to smile. She kept her head still but looked to the right, fast, three times. Turner drew his weapon. Polly threw her weight against the door and pushed hard pinning Rachael between the door and wall.

Turner rushed in. Rachael couldn't raise her weapon until she was free of the door. As soon as she was free she came up with the weapon. Polly grabbed Rachael's wrist and pushed it up toward the ceiling.

"It's over, Rachael," said Turner with his weapon pointed at her. "Polly, take her gun."

"Polly, have you got any teabags?" hollered John from the kitchen.

Polly laughed and ran to him. After a warm hug and kiss, they joined the other two in the front room.

"What are you going to do with me?" asked Rachael.

"I bet you could send her to Guantanamo," offered John.

"I'm not a terrorist, damn it," said Rachael.

"No. You just spy for a terrorist country," stated Turner.

"I spied for a man that is affiliated with the Mafia. I didn't do it for no damn terrorist country." Rachael's voice began to rise as she put her hands on her hips. "Why do you say that?"

"You know good and well the information you're providing your buddies was going to wind up in some foreign government's hands," said Turner.

"What in the hell makes you think that? That's just asinine," hollered Rachael, raising her hands up in frustration.

"Knock it off, woman. Tolman told us all about it," informed John.

"You've got Cleduus?"

"We do, and he told us everything. He told us about the Commander, Mafia and who the Mafia was going to sell the information to." Turner pointed his finger at Rachael with a jabbing motion.

"If I turn state's evidence on the Commander, can you get me into a witness protection program?"

"Woman, spying is the least of your problems. You have at least two counts of first degree murder, one of whom is an American soldier." Turner couldn't keep his voice down when he mentioned the soldier.

"What can I do? I don't want to go to jail. I couldn't live like that. I could be in there for life."

"Don't worry about jail. You won't have to live there that long. The executioner will take care of that," said John.

"The executioner! Oh, my God, Tom. Tell me what to do. I damn sure don't want to die."

"Your only chance to beat the grim reaper is to cooperate with us. If you don't, you haven't got a chance."

"What do you want from me?"

"I want the man you were working for. I want those documents you took from the lab."

"If I do help you, will it keep me alive?"

"We will let the judge know that you helped us. That could mean the difference between life and death," advised Turner.

"All right. Let's talk." Rachael let out a sigh and her physical appearance indicated surrender.

Turner had everyone move to the kitchen. John sat beside Turner while Rachael sat across from him at the table. Polly offered everybody drinks. They talked for over two hours and laid out a plan for the evening at I and J's.

"Hey, Chief," Turner said into his cell phone, "we've got Rachael and the documents."

"Excellent. What's your next course of action?" asked Holliday.

"I want to turn her over to the Bureau if you don't have an objection," replied Turner.

"Why?"

"Since the Mafia is involved, I think it should be an FBI case. They can even take the foreign connection part of it."

"So you want to just hand it to them on a silver platter?"

"Why not? It won't be the first time we did their work for them. I'll call and give Rachael to them. I still want to go after the guy she calls the Commander."

"You plan to give him to the suits, too?"

"Yeah. We've gone this far with the case. We might as well finish it."

"Fine. Go ahead if you want. Let me know how it goes."

"Will do." Turner closed his cell phone, reopened it and called the Phoenix FBI office.

Turner turned Rachael over to the two FBI agents who responded to his call. He gave them a brief scenario of the situation. He told them he would have another subject for them in the morning. He refused to tell them what his plans for the evening were. He needed to spend some time with the Commander before he turned him over to the agents.

It was ten minutes after seven when Polly approached the Commander who was sitting at his normal table. She leaned over and whispered in his ear, "There are two men who would like to talk with you at the door." She immediately walked away.

He looked across the dance floor of I and J's at the entrance. He didn't recognize Turner. He stood and started to walk around the table to the door when he recognized John.

He reached under his shirt and pulled out an automatic handgun. He fired one shot at the two men. Jerome instantaneously jumped up from the same table and started for him. The Commander fired one quick shot. Jerome grabbed his stomach and doubled over, falling to the floor. The singers and listeners were screaming and dropping to the floor. Isabel and her helper, Elizabeth, ran for the kitchen.

Turner rushed into the entrance to the kitchen and looked around the corner at the Commander. John saw that the Commander was moving toward the back door and moved out of the entranceway into the lobby. From there he continued out of the building and around to the alley in the rear of the building.

The Commander came out the back door and started toward the street. He stopped when he saw John and the gun he was holding. He hesitated, attempting to decide whether to fire or surrender.

"Freeze, Big Jack. I'm an excellent shot...are you?" hollered John.

It was a good thirty seconds before Big Jack dropped his gun and raised his hands above his head. He walked slowly toward John with his typical swagger. "I should have killed you when I had the chance."

Turner came out the back door behind Big Jack. He was surprised to see him with his hands in the air. Then he noticed John. He shook his head and smiled as he came up to the two men.

They heard the sirens in the distance. Isabel had called 911 and asked for medical assistance for Jerome. The police arrived just seconds before the emergency medical team.

The two officers saw John, drew down on him and ordered him to drop his weapon. John knelt down and placed his gun on the asphalt. Turner produced his credentials and said, "Federal Agent, this man's with me. We're the good guys. This is the bad guy," he indicated Big Jack.

The police wanted to arrest Big Jack for the shooting of Jerome. They argued with Turner when he said, "You'll have to get in line. Homeland Security has him now. Then, the FBI get's him. Sooner or later you guys can have him."

"Damn! I didn't know I was so popular. You people must have heard me sing," said Big Jack.

"Although your singing borders on criminal, that's not what you're being arrested for," said John.

"I haven't heard you sing. However, I'm looking forward to hearing you 'sing'." Turner cuffed him and gave him to John. Then the TACT agent proceeded to argue with the Police. He promised that he and John would give them a written statement tomorrow.

In route back to the laboratory, John couldn't stop the questions running through his mind. *Why did Big Jack betray his country? How did he know there was a secret laboratory? When did he discover Rachael worked there? What means did he use to have Rachael help him?*

chapter

TWENTY-FIVE

Turner led Big Jack up the stairs to the sergeant's office. He refused to take the polygraph that John offered. He had calmed down and his complexion had lost some of its color.

"What the hell would you ask me that you don't already know? You've obviously talked to Rachael."

John pulled his chair over in front of Big Jack. "Come on guy, we have a lot of questions for you. You could really make this easier on yourself," advised John.

"Like how?"

"Like give us the answers we need," said Turner.

"If I do as you ask? What's in it for me? I can't see giving out when there isn't anything coming in." Big Jack ran his fingers through his light-colored hair and gave a fake smile to Turner.

John spoke up, "If you don't cooperate you can expect a full night of interrogation. You can also expect the FBI to continue the interrogation where we leave off. You might get to sleep in a few days."

"Crap. Just what is it you want to know?" Big Jack shrugged and slumped down in his chair. He gave the appearance of a beaten man.

"The first question that comes to mind is, why the hell did you do it?" questioned John as he moved closer to Big Jack. Their knees were only a foot apart.

"Hey, man, if you're going to sit in my lap I ain't saying shit." Big Jack sat up straight and looked wide-eyed at John.

"This is as far as I'm going with this space invasion. I just want to be able to hear you clearly. If you notice I happen to be wearing hearing devices. Thanks to an exciting job with Uncle Sam."

"You're crowding me. I'm not happy about this."

"Relax Jack. Is it all right if I just call you Jack? With your six-foot overweight frame, I can see where you get the prefix of 'Big'."

"Is it all right if I call you John? With your potty mouth, I can tell why they call you John," returned Big Jack.

"Touché, Jack. I think we have established a rapport.

"Now, let's get back to the question." John reached down and got his clipboard and pen.

"Which one was that?" Big Jack nervously pushed his hair back again.

"Why did you get involved in this mess? Why did you betray your country? How could you do this"?

"Hey, I served my country. I helped pay for your freedom. I don't owe the USA a damn thing. This government has gone to hell. I tried to preserve freedom and they're taking it away from us little by little. It's my chance to get even with them as well as pick up enough money to put me on easy street for the rest of my life. I could buy the 'Columbian Proof Set' of stamps and others totaling over $40,000. Life was going to be good."

"How much did it take for you sell out your country?"

"Simply a million dollars."

"I hope they paid you up front."

"Actually, I received half a million to finance the operation. I was to get the million upon completion." Big Jack shook his head slightly.

"I know why you became involved. The question I have now is how did you know there was a secret laboratory?" John made a note on his clipboard.

"I met this guy, Farouk at a stamp meeting. We became friends...."

John interrupted him. "Hold on. Was he an Iranian? By now he would be in his thirties?"

"Yeah. That sounds about right. Why? Do you know him?" Big Jack looked surprised at John.

"If it's who I think it is. I know him all too well."

Big Jack moved to the edge of his seat. "He said he had been involved in that secret laboratory before."

"Yeah we chased him across the country, before he got away." John shook his head in disbelief.

"Holy crap, John. Those two are back. What's it been five years?" Holiday moved over by John and looked down at him.

"Yeah. I have reasons to never forget him or his killer girlfriend Silvi." John turned to Big Jack. "You'll have to excuse us, Jack, as you said, these two were involved in an incident years ago at the same laboratory. We thought they were dead."

"His girlfriend is quite a looker in an exotic kind of way." Big Jack smiled.

"More in a deadly sort of way," corrected John. "So he convinced you to get the information from the laboratory?"

"Yeah. He told me he had been following employees to find one that might help. After a few drinks and a couple of nights with Rachael, she was willing to help. She got the same deal, a million dollars upon completion."

Holiday came over and placed his hand on Big Jack's shoulder. "You should be glad you never completed the operation. You would never have lived to see the money."

"How did you and Rachael get together?" questioned John.

"We have been friends for years. I admit I was surprised when that Farouk fellow invited me to dinner and Rachael was there.

That's when we formulated the plan. I didn't want Rachael to give me the papers directly in case she was ever followed."

"So the two hillbillies were her idea?" John did a quick glance over to Holiday.

"She said she would find a delivery boy for me. I told her how and where I wanted the hand-off to be done."

"They told us she seduced them into working with her. By putting the papers under the dumpster, she never had any contact with them once the operation started." John continued writing.

"I can turn the Iranians in if you can get me in the witness program."

"Don't kid yourself Jack. By now those two are long gone. They have survived two previous attempts to catch them. At least now, we know they are still alive." John finished his notes and rose from his chair.

"I should get some kind of deal for that." Big Jack looked up at Holiday with a pained expression.

"Yeah, maybe I can get you a room with a view." Holiday walked over to the phone to call the FBI for transportation.

———

Jerome, thanks to Isabel's fast call and the EMT's quick response, survived his wound. After a couple weeks' rehabilitation, he was back entertaining the karaoke family with his songs. He was as good as ever.

The singers at I and J's breathed a sigh of relief knowing the killings were over. However they were in shock over the involvement of their two friends. Big Jack and Rachael were the topic of conversations for weeks to come.

I and J's lost the stigma of the karaoke killer. The winter visitors began to show up. The restaurant actually prospered with the attention it got from the press.

Holiday's sight was better when Turner picked him up from the hospital. Turner helped him clear out his motel room. Other than a slight headache, Holiday's mood was upbeat. They drove by Polly's house to pick up John's written statement for the police.

Holiday returned to Georgetown, and home. He needed to finish his recuperation. He also needed to get rid of his embarrassment over his choice of women.

Turner remained in Avondale to clean up the remaining paperwork. The TACT agent worked with Sergeant Steel in establishing a better security program. He enjoyed a couple of meals at I and J's before leaving town. He also slipped in a couple of dances on a few nights with Julie.

John moved out of the motel and stayed with Polly for a couple of days. They had no idea how long it would be before they saw each other again. Since they had matching appetites, they made the most of those days. They didn't have much time for anything other than snacks and wine. They were like teenagers with a new toy.

It was difficult for John to leave. He made up his mind that he would return. Being a winter visitor had suddenly taken on a new meaning for him. He might even practice his singing in anticipation of his return to I and J's and give Jasiu, the clown, some competition.

Made in the USA
Charleston, SC
28 July 2012